TO BELONG

TO BELONG

A Novel

by

Judith Galblum Pex

CLADACH
Publishing

To Belong: A Novel
© 2022 by Judith Galblum Pex

Published by Cladach Publishing
PO Box 336144 Greeley, CO 80633
https://cladach.com

Front Cover Design: Jeff Gerke

ISBN: 978-1-945099-30-4
Library of Congress Control Number: 2022942491

*To refugees everywhere
in admiration for their courage and resiliency*

1

As children surrounded her car, Tamar Goldman slowed her driving to a crawl. The last thing she wanted to do was hit somebody. When she stopped the car and opened the door, a few kids tried to push their way in. But she managed to ease herself out. A group of teenage girls stood a short distance away, with babies in their arms. She walked over to them.

"Do you know where's Rivka?" she asked.

The girls looked at each other. Two of them walked away—perhaps to find Rivka, the kibbutz woman in charge of the refugees.

Hopefully Rivka wasn't taking a nap. She'd looked tired at the clinic. When Tamar had a plan, she didn't like to put it off; but she began to wonder if she wasn't being too spontaneous this time. The idea had made sense: drive ten minutes to the kibbutz, quickly find Rivka, return the vaccination card, and still be home in time to prepare dinner for her family. Steve liked eating on time, and he'd gone diving today, which always gave him an appetite.

Though she hadn't asked where the Sudanese lived on the kibbutz, as soon as she turned into the access road and saw the tall black men standing at the gate, she knew she was in the right place. A left turn at the sign, *Nof Eilot* (the former youth hostel), and she was transported to an African village, the feeling enhanced by the burning sun and parching wind of an Eilat summer day.

She looked around. Had she thought Rivka would be sitting in a nice room labeled *office*? Women clustered in groups on the spotty grass holding and breastfeeding their babies. Children and toddlers raced in circles chasing each other. Men at picnic tables talked, and papers skimmed the ground among discarded, empty plastic bottles. Tamar was used to chocolate-skinned Ethiopian-Jewish immigrants coming to Tipat Halav, her well-baby clinic; but though some didn't speak Hebrew yet, they lived in regular neighborhoods and were in the process of integrating into Israeli society.

This place was another world.

Until three o'clock, she'd had a routine day. But then came the "invasion." Neither Tamar nor her co-workers had ever experienced anything like vaccinating twenty-two Sudanese toddlers in one go.

Under the circumstances, things went pretty well, with the volunteers mostly keeping the kids orderly. Besides being the blackest, they were some of the cutest children she'd ever seen. Tamar prided herself on her neatness, but amid the usual screaming and crying, one of their vaccination cards fell unnoticed to the floor. Organizing the office before going home, Tamar caught sight of the yellow booklet under a chair.

Maybe her mix-up had something to do with that argument with Steve last night. She'd continued to rehearse it in her mind all day, planning how she could answer him better tonight after the children were in bed.

They were taking a long time to find Rivka. One of the girls near Tamar asked, "What is your name?"

"Tamar. And yours? Do you speak English?"

"A little."

"Where's Rivka? Your friends went to find her?"

"I am fine."

So much for communicating in English. Tamar dug in her bag for her phone and looked at the time. She'd better call Steve.

"Hi, motek. Where are you?" Tamar asked.

Steve was panting and the wind carried away his voice. "I'm on my bike. What's going on?"

"I'll be a bit late. You wouldn't believe where I am—Africa."

"Africa?"

"That's what it looks like. I'll tell you more later, but I'm in Kibbutz Eilot. I dropped one of the Sudanese children's vaccination cards so came out to bring it, but it's taking longer than I thought, and I'll make something quick for dinner. Love you." Instead of making that new vegan dish with broccoli and cashew cream, she'd whip up one of her family's simple pasta favorites.

While she was talking, she noticed two small children wandering about, hand in hand, maybe five and six years old. The little boy was crying, but no adult came to him, nor did he run to any of the women. Tamar instinctively bent down and picked him up. As a well-baby clinic nurse, she was used to reassuring crying children.

He hardly weighed anything. His little shorts were wet and wreaked of urine. Tamar's uniform of jeans and colorful shirt worked well here, as it did at the clinic with babies peeing, pooping, and spitting on her.

The boy's sister looked up at Tamar with dark, serious eyes. Tamar pulled a tissue out of her bag and wiped the snot running down into the boy's mouth.

He rested his head on her shoulder and twirled her black curls around his fingers.

"Bubi," she said. "Where's your Imma?"

No answer; just more sobbing. Of course he wouldn't know Hebrew.

"Mama?" she tried again. Wasn't *mother* nearly the same in all languages? What language did they speak in Sudan, anyway?

She glanced around at the women. "Anyone know where these kids' mother is?"

The women seemed to understand but shrugged their shoulders.

Rivka finally appeared. "You're looking for me? Is there a problem with the vaccinations?" she asked, suppressing a yawn.

Tamar shifted the boy on her hip. "Sorry to bother you, and it's kind of embarrassing, but somehow one of the vaccination cards slipped onto the floor, and I only found it when I was locking up. I thought I'd drop it by on my way home."

"No problem." Rivka patted the boy on his head. "Joey, what happened?"

His crying had turned into long sniffs.

She looked at the girl. "Mary, what's wrong with your brother? Why's he crying?"

"Where's their mother?" Tamar said.

"She tends to disappear," Rivka answered matter-of-factly, with a harried frown.

But to disappear and leave her two little children? Tamar checked the time again. "I really have to go now, bubi," she told the little boy. "My children and husband are coming home soon." She tried to put Joey down and pull away from Mary, but they only clung tighter.

"But don't worry, I'll be back." She looked into Mary's eyes. She wasn't sure how, what, or when, but she'd return and check on these kids.

The sun was setting over the jagged mountains of Edom as she drove home, a view that changed according to the hour and season. Now, at sunset, the ridges became defined and the various shades of brown and tan grew vibrant. Aqaba, Eilat's sister city in Jordan, with its low white buildings, stretched out under the mountains, so close yet so far.

She had discovered a different world just a few minutes away from home. *Wait till Steve and the kids hear about this.*

2

"How was your day?" Steve asked as he looked around the table.

Tamar dished out the food while remembering how Joey had clung to her.

Steve spoke to the children in English, a choice he made when Tamar was pregnant with Arava. Although he'd integrated well into Israel and spoke Hebrew fluently now, Steve remained consistent with his original decision. "It's essential today to know English, and this way they'll learn it naturally."

Arava and Gal understood everything Steve said, but answered in Hebrew, the usual practice when one parent spoke a language other than the dominant one.

"I only got eighty on the math test," their daughter, Arava, said. "The teacher goes fast, and it's hard with so many smart kids in the class."

"Eighty's fine." Steve took a bite of the spaghetti then glanced at Tamar. "Delicious." Then to Arava he said, "You'll get used to the teacher's ways. I remember how hard it was for me when I went up to grade seven. But of course you don't have the same system we had in Canada."

Steve and the children were not excited about a vegan diet. Tamar wasn't sure how it would work out, either. But they'd done pretty well as vegetarians, and this seemed like the next step. Steve was happy with whatever food she set before him, as long as he had plenty. One of her colleagues had begun the Paleo diet recently, and she was sure they could never go with that. Growing up on the kibbutz, she hadn't eaten much red meat, just lots of chicken and eggs. She couldn't imagine eating steak three times a day.

Maybe as a vegan she'd lose the extra kilos that had crept on since Gal's birth. In any case, tonight was back to their favorite pasta with cauliflower sauce.

"Gal, motek," Tamar asked, smiling at the way her son was digging into his food. "How was school?"

"We played football. Ben was on my team. He scored a goal. And we won." If Gal had something to report, it was usually about recess.

"Glad Ben's on your team," said Tamar.

"Yeah. He's my friend now."

"Fabulous." They'd encouraged Gal to befriend the new boy in his class. "Why not invite him over after school?" Tamar dished some salad onto each of their plates to make the meal complete.

"He's cool and sits next to me. He used to live in a kibbutz in the north, maybe near where you grew up, and moved down here with his mother and little brother."

Steve brought a melon to the table, and began slicing it. "One of my colleagues brought these in to work. They grow them on his family's farm on a moshav. Really sweet."

Though patience and listening weren't her strongest points, Tamar had tried to listen to the others first. Now she said, "You won't believe my day."

"Another cute little baby?" Arava asked.

Tamar had to admit she liked to gush over newborns, and to describe the developmental tests they gave two-year-olds, like having them stand on one foot, or on tiptoe, or kick and throw a ball. She called it the baby circus because some of them were little performers.

"Not just one, but we had twenty-two little Sudanese children to vaccinate. You should have seen it. Like a production line."

"They came with their mothers?" Steve asked.

"They live on Kibbutz Eilot in the old youth hostel. It's a

Sudanese camp now, and there's a kibbutz member in charge of them, and some volunteers out there too."

"Who're 'them'?" Steve asked.

"Are these those tall black people we see walking around town?" Arava was also getting interested.

"I couldn't converse with them much, between the shots, the crying, and the charts I had to fill out; but I gather they're refugees from South Sudan who jumped over the border from Egypt. We saw something about them on the news last week, right? After they arrived in Israel, the hotel chains invited them to come to Eilat because they need more dishwashers and room cleaners."

"I was reading about their country at war. Muslims killing Christians and enslaving their children. Bombing whole villages. People starving," Steve said.

"So, what'll we do now?" Tamar stood up and began pacing around the room as she did when she got excited.

"What do you mean, 'what will we do?'" Steve asked.

"Somehow, I dropped one of their vaccination cards, so I drove out to the kibbutz to take it to them. That place is like being in an African village. Another world."

"Africa?" Gal leaned forward. He'd recently enjoyed a school trip to the Hai Bar Nature Reserve outside Eilat where animals from biblical times such as ostriches, wild asses, and oryxes roam freely. With its acacia trees, parched ground, and dry scrubby bushes, someone had pointed out the resemblance to an African savanna. Since then, Gal couldn't stop talking about his desire to go to Africa and see lions, elephants, and giraffes.

"There were these two little kids—I found out their names are Mary and Joey—and they were walking around alone, and Joey was crying so I picked him up, and he wouldn't let me go."

"Where was their mother?" asked Arava, who loved playing with little children.

"Rivka, the kibbutz lady, told me their mother leaves them

and disappears. I was thinking we could all visit tomorrow and bring them some of your old toys." Tamar's pace was picking up.

"That could be a possibility," Steve said. "But tomorrow we've planned for Yossi's birthday party. The next day is your folk dancing class, and Arava has ballet."

She loved Steve; but sometimes he was so rational, it drove her nuts. Of course she wouldn't neglect having the party for Yossi, her sister Michal's new friend who had shaken off his orthodox religious background. And yes, Steve knew how she valued folk dancing—a way of life on the kibbutz growing up and an aerobic exercise for her as well. But what was folk dancing compared to Mary and Joey right now?

"They won't be moving anywhere soon," Steve added. "I don't mind going there, but let's wait till next week, plan something, and not rush."

Arava and Gal left the table and headed toward their rooms. They didn't like hearing their parents argue.

"Wait, who's turn is it to load the dishwasher?" Steve asked.

Gal slunk over to the sink while Arava grinned sheepishly and grabbed a sponge to wipe the table.

"The toys are a good idea," Steve added. "Your rooms need organizing anyway, so you might as well give these African kids things you don't use anymore." Leaving the table, he settled into his favorite chair and picked up his copy of *Hamlet*.

Tamar didn't know what Steve got out of Shakespeare, but for him it was like watching the latest soap opera. He couldn't put it down. And he always had a Shakespeare quote handy.

"Something hot to drink?" Tamar asked, starting to brew herself a cup of coffee.

"Thanks, duck." (Steve had adopted that term of endearment for his wife, claiming it was Shakespeare's word for "dear.") "How about mint tea from the garden?" Then he added, "I don't understand how you can drink coffee at night and still sleep."

"Doesn't affect me. Troubled thoughts keep me awake, not coffee." She didn't need him trying to control her. Growing up in the kibbutz children's house, even her parents hadn't told her what to do. In fact, she barely ever saw them. Anyway, she'd read an article recently that said coffee was healthy, so she felt justified in her four cups a day.

Tamar had hoped her family would share in her desire to do something for Mary and Joey, and the rest of those poor people in the camp. Arava and Gal could find a few toys tonight, and she'd go back tomorrow by herself on her way home from work. It wouldn't have to take long. Hadn't she promised Mary and Joey? She'd prepare Yossi's cake tonight, and Michal could help with the rest of the party preparations.

Maybe this wasn't the best time to bring up their conversation of last night. She needed to learn to keep her mouth shut. She had read over and over those verses from Proverbs about taming the tongue; but putting it into practice was something else. She sighed. What was the point, anyway, of arguing with Steve about having another child? He was afraid they couldn't afford one. On the other hand, she had always wanted lots of children to make up for her childhood experience in the kibbutz where she felt the lack of a real family. But after years of trying, and three miscarriages since giving birth to Gal eleven years ago, it was a stupid quarrel. A while back she'd given up worrying about getting pregnant— too much emotional strain. Now, when she felt ready again before getting too old, Steve said their family was perfect as is.

Arava and Gal's voices drifted in from their bedrooms, where they were discussing which toys to give away. They had such an abundance. And the Sudanese children had nothing. The world wasn't fair.

She'd always fought for justice. In her youth, she'd gone with a group from the kibbutz to demonstrate on behalf of the Soviet Jewish Refuseniks and visited an absorption center for

Ethiopian Jews when they were airlifted from Sudan in 1985.

Now that she'd met these refugees, how could she ignore them?

Tomorrow would be busy. She and Michal had planned this birthday party for a long time, but first she'd stop by the kibbutz to find out more about Mary and Joey. Part of her job as a children's nurse was to report abuse and neglect. A mother couldn't just leave two little kids alone.

3

I'll be a bit late," Tamar said to Michal, her younger sister, through her car's speakerphone. "When you get to the house, can you put the hummus, tehina, and eggplant salads in bowls and cut up the vegetables and put them on platters along with the pita?" Michal wasn't the most competent in the kitchen. And Tamar never knew what mood she'd be in. "You're alone?"

"Me and Kinneret," Michal said.

Of course. That dog was like her shadow. "Can't talk. Tell you later. It's Africa here," said Tamar. She hadn't been in Kibbutz Eilot since that co-worker of hers invited their family to their pool on Shabbat.

As she pulled into the parking lot with the children surrounding her car, this time she was prepared for what to expect and in an odd way, it already seemed familiar. With its peeling paint, and wires and pipes hanging haphazardly on the building's exterior, the two-story ex-hostel had seen better days

When she stepped out of the car, six kids jumped in while others jumped on her back, a few grabbed her knees, and others stroked her hair. Her tight curly locks half resembled theirs. They'd really go crazy to see Michal's blonde hair.

The mothers sat in the shade talking. Even in late afternoon, Eilat's summer heat suffocated. She quickly decided not to take the toys out of the trunk of the car right away. What was she thinking? How could she distribute them among all these needy children?

While trying to figure what to do, her eyes fell on Mary and Joey, all alone again, holding hands, and standing to the side. They couldn't get to her for the swarm. One of the teenage girls brought over a plastic chair, motioned for her to sit, and little Joey squeezed his way to the front and jumped on her lap. He had the same dirty shirt on as yesterday, the same smell, and orange-tinged hair. Undernourishment. She knew what a child this size should weigh. His nose was still snotty, and his eyes were reddened with a yellow discharge, nearly gluing shut the left one.

Rivka walked up. "Did you forget something else?"

Tamar looked around. How could she explain to Rivka the connection she felt to these people and her desire to help them?

"Bubi," Tamar said to Joey, who nestled in closer to her, feeling content to hug a little one again. Then to Rivka she said, "I brought some toys my children don't play with anymore. They're eleven and thirteen and their rooms are too crowded. They don't even play with toys much at this stage." Oh no, here she was talking too much as usual. What did this lady care about how old her children were? "But how can I distribute them among so many here?"

"Perfect," Rivka said. "We're beginning a day care center for the one- to three-year olds and could use any toy donations.

Tamar looked down at Joey. "He has an eye infection, probably conjunctivitis. Is he being treated?"

Rivka shrugged her shoulders. "Just getting them to your clinic was a major project. They don't have insurance. No one cares for him. I don't even know how I got this job..."

"What do you mean?"

"After the refugees moved into the old hostel," the kibbutz was looking for someone to coordinate the work with them. I had back surgery last year and a lengthy rehab and somehow got talked into it."

"You never did anything like this before?"

Rivka snorted. "Are you kidding? I worked in the office. There's nothing to prepare you for this. I was on a safari in Kenya and travelled to India, but I think it's the contrast of seeing these people living in our midst that gets to you. They have nothing—no documentation or extra clothes—and as refugees, even their identity is taken away."

"What if I take Joey and his sister home for a few hours? I can give him a bath, wash his eyes, and feed them," Tamar said. She knew that pink eye was highly contagious, though it usually cleared up by itself. Still, Joey kept on trying to blink and scratching his eyes; at least they had to be washed with clean water. Getting fat on his little bones and a normal color to his hair would take longer.

"Do you think it will be okay with their mother? What time should I get them back?"

"I haven't seen their mother for days," Rivka said. "They have someone they call an aunt who supposedly watches after them, though they seem to call everyone 'aunt.'"

If this was called watching...

"Why not?" Rivka said. "They deserve a little happiness in their lives."

∾

Yossi's birthday party was important to Michal. When Tamar had heard that Yossi had never celebrated his birthday, she offered to bake him a cake and organize a party. For Yossi it would be another milestone in breaking from his ultra-orthodox background, and it gave her a chance to do something for Michal. Their relationship needed any help it could get.

But after her spontaneous offer to Rivka, Tamar now wondered whether bringing Mary and Joey home would take the focus off Yossi and his event.

With Michal, she never knew what her reaction would be. Why couldn't she act more normal? Not only didn't they look like sisters, but their personalities couldn't be more different. When they were little, Michal got all the attention with her straight blonde hair. It was from Abba's British genes. In those days before the Russian immigration brought thousands of pale Slavic-looking people to Israel, Michal stood out like a lightbulb. She had Abba's British reserve too; some people called her introverted. No one would say that about Tamar, who had Imma's Yemenite looks and fiery nature.

Standing up, she took the hands of Mary and Joey. "Come on. We're going home. You'll find a new family, and they'll like you too." She knew she was trying to convince herself as much as anyone.

But the children didn't need persuading.

4

Michal sighed as she set the table. She was used to Tamar's unpredictability. But on this birthday, when she wanted to spoil Yossi and give him a feeling of family, how could she be late?

Having a sister and her family nearby was convenient, it gave her a place to do her laundry, eat Tamar's home-cooked meals, and hang out with Arava and Gal. They were always inviting her over; but sometimes after work, she loaded Kinneret on the back of her scooter and they'd hang out and chill in a lean-to on the South Beach.

Tamar never stopped being the bossy big sister. Why couldn't she just leave a person alone instead of pushing her faith down their throat every chance she got? What about live and let live, each to their own?

She'd met Yossi for the first time at the Lighthouse Beach where he was staying with the homeless and hippies, sitting on the side and letting the joint pass by. She didn't mind taking a puff or two but always made sure not to get so stoned that she couldn't walk away on her own. Smoking marijuana was not proven to be any worse than drinking alcohol. With medical marijuana coming into use in Israel in a big way, there was talk of legalizing personal use. The establishment was finally coming around.

On first glance, she had no idea about Yossi's background. From his short russet hair and stubbly beard, she guessed he'd recently been discharged from the army, but she never imagined what a long journey he had traveled from his childhood in B'nai Brak to the beach in Eilat.

The second time Michal met Yossi, he began opening up.

"My father is a well-known rabbi," he said. "I'm the oldest of ten brothers and sisters. When I was in the yeshiva high school, things started to fall apart at our house. I'd been thinking about it for a while, and one day I walked out. After a few months I managed to join the army."

"Crazy s**t. What'd your parents say?"

"No contact."

"Your brothers and sisters?"

"Not allowed to call me, but my oldest sister sometimes texts."

They began meeting, not just on the beach. At a certain point Yossi mentioned he'd never celebrated his birthday.

"They tell us it's unnecessary." He shrugged.

"Unnecessary? Your birthday? What's that mean? I even celebrate the day I found Kinneret." She patted Kinneret, who lay at her side.

"They say that about lots of things."

"When is your birthday? This year we'll have a real celebration, for all the ones you've missed. We can do it at my sister's house. She and her husband are pretty chill, and they like to have people over." Tamar could be bossy and pushy, but they were definitely hospitable. And Tamar baked great cakes.

Yossi lived on the beach when he first came to Eilat for lack of a place to sleep; but those people weren't really his friends. Now that he was working on the Mermaid, a yacht for tourists, he could sleep there; but the people living on the other boats weren't his type either. Who was his type? Her? They had an easy way of speaking, and Kinneret liked him. Kinneret was a good judge of character, and she'd never seen her dog take to another person so quickly.

She told Tamar about Yossi, but left out the part about them beginning to like each other. When she said he came from an ultra-orthodox background and had never celebrated his birth-day, Tamar jumped on the idea of having a party. She probably thought she could tell him about Yeshua. But Michal had warned her often about preaching to her friends, and thankfully it usu-ally worked. Steve was different, though. Michal actually liked the way he so naturally shared his faith with people like Shai.

Shai. He'd been like part of the family. He'd sit for hours phi-losophizing with Steve. The night before Shai died, after their Friday dinner, the two men had stayed up late talking. After the terrorist attack the next day, when Shai was in the wrong place at the wrong time, Steve had told her about his conversation with Shai.

"Everyone believes in something—God, a person, them-selves, a system, or whatever," Steve had said.

"I'm not religious and never will be. I'm not orthodox Jewish or Messianic Jews like you, or anything else. That's not me."

"You don't have to be religious. You believe in making the world a better place and the goodness inside every man, right?"

Yes, he did, Michal thought now to herself. She had loved Shai's idealism, his firm principles of justice and service to others. ...

Steve had gone on to tell how he and Shai had eaten the last crumbs of Tamar's poppy seed cake as they talked. Steve had said to Shai, "When hard things happen, your kind of faith doesn't give you real hope. Do you ever read the Scriptures, just for your-self?"

"Actually, I've recently been getting into them and finding helpful things. ... But look, it's late, and I'd better be off. Early class at university tomorrow."

"Take care," Steve had said. "I read there's a terror cell plan-ning an attack in the area of Beersheva."

Since that day, Michal couldn't stomach poppy seed cake, even though Tamar was the world's best baker.

The cake she made for Arava's sixth grade graduation was nearly as big as their dining room table and looked like a whole coral reef to go along with the theme of "preserving Eilat's natural beauty." She even had a little business of cake decorating. Once people saw and tasted her cakes, they were sure to order one for their next event. She said that using the best ingredients was one of her secrets, first-rate chocolate and top-quality butter.

For Yossi's birthday, Tamar had skipped all the edible roses, borders, and fondant accents and made a multi-layered cream and chocolate tart. Michal knew that even that would take Tamar a couple hours because of her perfectionism. And beside the cake she'd made tabbouleh, two kinds of eggplant salads, home-made hummus and tehina, and her healthy version of potato salad. Michal picked up bourekas on her way over, so altogether they'd have a feast. She'd asked Yossi if he wanted to invite other friends, but he said her family was enough. He had met them once when Michal was driving him home on her scooter and stopped to pick up her laundry.

But now Tamar was late, and Michal was left to organize things herself before Steve came home from work and the kids from their clubs. Tamar kept those kids busy. On the one hand, she maintained a close rein on them and wouldn't even let them sleep over at Michal's house, but on the other hand, every day they seemed to be in some kind of after-school activity. But don't try to mention anything to Tamar about her parenting skills or you'd have a major blow-out.

So here she was doing everything herself. At least she didn't have Tamar looking over her shoulder. She could listen to the music she liked on their stereo, alone except for Kinneret who rarely left her side since Michal found her as a scruffy ball of wet fur when she was camping in the Galilee. She'd thought to call her "Moses" having found her among the bull rushes but liked the sound of Kinneret and anyway, she was a female. Who would have known that smelly, matted thing would grow up into a gorgeous German Shepherd mix and with the best personality?

Then the house filled up. First Steve came in with his quiet, deliberate stride and still catching his breath from his bike ride. He smiled, stared at the table, and looked around. "What's happening? Where's Tamar?"

Steve was brilliant in his field, but Tamar made all their social arrangements, and he didn't even try to keep track of them.

"You forgot Yossi's birthday?"

"Yossi?"

"My new friend. ... Tamar called to say she'll be late."

"I'll take a quick shower before everyone comes."

Nothing seemed to get that guy ruffled. Not even Tamar's crazy moods. Steve was the best thing that happened to Tamar, and he, strangely enough, seemed to think the same about her.

Next, Arava burst into the house, her dark curls flying behind her. She threw her tennis racket on the sofa and was opening the fridge before Michal could tell her to wait for the party. Gal was the sweet one, more like his dad. He was everyone's friend, and a thinker like his dad, too.

The door swung open, hitting the wall behind it. A backpack over her shoulder, Tamar was clutched the hands of two little African children. She glanced at the table with the cake on one side and the salads on the other. "Sorry." Then she glanced at the children. "Too complicated to tell you on the phone. But don't worry, we're here, and it'll be a great party."

Michal glared at Tamar. "Yossi's party. I told you he didn't want anyone but our family. He's shy."

"I know." Tamar slipped off her bag and sat on the sofa. The children snuggled close to her.

The children looked like they were trying to make themselves as small as possible, unnecessary, because a gentle wind could have blown them away. Michal had never seen anyone so dark and with such black eyes. "Maybe you want to explain?"

Steve peeked around the corner, wrapped with a towel. "Calm down. All's okay." But even his eyes widened when he saw his wife sitting with Mary and Joey. "Give me a sec to dress. I'm looking for my shirt with buttons."

For Michal, Steve's uniform of shorts, old t-shirts and sandals would've been fine, but Tamar must have spoken to him.

She looked at the clock on the wall. "S**t. Yossi will be here any minute. Tell me later." Uh oh. She'd promised not to use that word in their house. Those kids didn't look like they'd be any trouble, their mouths were glued shut, and they barely seemed to breathe.

"Quick. Arava! Turn off the lights! I hear the front gate opening." Tamar jumped up and assumed her bossy-mother mode. "Michal, light the candles!"

"Happy birthday to you!" They sang as Yossi stepped through the door.

Michal had never seen such a broad smile on his face nor seen him in a white shirt before. Must be one left over from his yeshiva days. Kinneret ran to him and licked his hand.

"Now you blow out the candles, one for each year and for the coming year too." Arava explained happily.

"Wait a minute!" Gal said. "What about a wish?" He liked everything done in the right order.

"A wish?" Yossi's eyes narrowed.

"Like what you want to happen in the next year."

"You mean a prayer?" Yossi said.

"That's a better way of putting it," Steve said. "A prayer."

"Shall I say it aloud or to myself?" Yossi looked around.

"Whatever you want. In your heart is okay too."

Yossi's pursed lips turned into a little smile as he closed his eyes and bowed his head.

"Here's some plates. Help yourselves to the salads, and we'll have the cake afterward."

Michal noticed the two children get up from the sofa and wiggle their way to the front of the table, eyes wide. She bent on one knee to talk to them. "Do you know what a birthday is?"

They nodded their heads.

~

They'd finished scooping up the salads with the fresh pita and were enjoying Tamar's latest cake creation. Steve leaned back in his armchair, hands folded on his stomach. "Great food. You outdid yourself again. Now sit down, relax, and tell us what's going on?"

The children were again curled up to Tamar on the sofa. "This is Mary and her brother, Joey. They're Sudanese refugees I met when I went to Kibbutz Eilot with the vaccination card. They know a little Hebrew from going to a daycare center."

"But why are they here?" Arava asked. "Did they also want to come to Yossi's party?"

"I stopped by today on my way home from work to bring your old toys, and they were sitting alone, looking sad. When they saw me, they jumped in my lap like I was their mother." Tamar gazed down at the two children.

"But what about their mother?" Gal asked. "She let you take them home?"

"She wasn't around. She must have been busy with something else." Tamar didn't like telling her innocent children about mothers who abandoned their children. "But there's a kibbutz woman who watches over the refugees, and she said I could invite them to our house for a couple of hours. I want to treat Joey's eyes and give them baths."

Gal nodded, his dark eyes staring at Joey. "Maybe some of my clothes that are too small would fit him." He looked down at Joey's worn out flipflops. "And my shoes."

"Wait a minute." Steve scratched his temple as he tilted

his head to one side. "Let's consider the consequences. What authority did this woman have to say you could take them home? Couldn't this be considered kidnapping?"

Tamar raised her voice. "First of all, Rivka knows what she's doing, and secondly, look at them. Do they look like children whose mother would miss them? Come out there with me and you'll understand."

Michal hated their bickering. She and Shai hadn't argued like this. On the other hand, things had turned out okay this evening. When she glanced around the room, Yossi, leaning back and petting Kinneret who lay at his feet, seemed to be enjoying his first birthday party. Tamar hadn't preached at him. Steve was his usual calm self, and Joey had moved from Tamar's side and fallen asleep on Steve's lap. He looked like a little black angel, and Steve looked content too. They looked natural together, like she and Kinneret.

5

Tamar loved the quiet at the end of the day and the feeling of seeing everything in order as she cleaned up the clinic. After looking over the day's record to make sure she hadn't forgotten anything, she organized the toys in the waiting room.

"How was your day?" Leah asked.

"Fabulous. I registered four newborns, weighed and vaccinated two older babies, and tested a five-year-old's development. I'm referring him for further testing. Looks like he's on the autism spectrum." She dropped the last crayon in the box.

"How did things go with that little Ethiopian baby?" Leah wiped her hand over her pink hair and tugged her flowered shirt over her hips. "I'll overlook it this time, but you know you're not allowed to take patients in your car."

"You saw him. ..." Tamar could feel the color rising in her cheeks. "He looks like skin over bones."

"African babies are often small. Why didn't you just question the mother about her feeding methods and then set her on the right track?"

"She didn't speak Hebrew or even understand when I took out my cell phone and showed her pictures." Tamar loved her job, especially seeing the mothers interacting with their babies and the intimacy she developed with many of them. But she couldn't stand the patronizing attitude of many older nurses.

"All I could understand was that she wasn't breastfeeding." Tamar knew this was rare among Ethiopians, so she concluded that maybe the mother had AIDS. But she needed the mother to show her how she made the formula.

"Taking them home seemed to be my only option."

"I hope you didn't ask her about AIDS."

Why was Leah always so critical? Tamar tried not to become defensive. "Of course, I know we're not allowed to mention AIDS, though it crossed my mind that if he did have it, I should tell the rabbi who would be doing the circumcision."

"That's also getting into a tricky area." Leah lowered herself into the chair behind her desk.

"It's good I went, because when I came to her house, she showed me how she put one scoop of formula into her baby's bottle instead of the required six."

"Typical. Always trying to cut corners. And you spoke to the rabbi?"

"He thanked me for calling him. And don't worry, he understood my hint."

Since Tamar was a little girl on the kibbutz, she'd always run over to the baby house to hold and play with the little ones. Deciding to study nursing was a natural choice. Some of her colleagues, on the other hand, seemed to do it as a job, to pass the time and pay the bills. Or maybe the older nurses had been idealistic when they started out and through the years had lost their enthusiasm and didn't know how to change with the times. Today the trend was to listen to the mothers; they know their child best. You don't have to boss them around all the time.

"Sit down for a minute," Leah said and paused. "My neighbor's daughter was at Kibbutz Eilot bringing toys to the Sudanese day care center—she'd asked me if I had any—and I told her I wouldn't have any part in helping those Africans. She saw you sitting around with some of the women and children."

Tamar thought a moment before replying. As much as she enjoyed Eilat with its snorkeling and diving in the coral reefs— which felt like entering a new dimension of weightlessness and freedom—she also loved hiking in the surrounding mountains.

And this is where she met Steve and where he found a job. But sometimes she couldn't stand that everyone seemed to know everyone and watch what you were doing. It was much worse in the kibbutz where she grew up, but she always knew she'd never choose to live there.

What business of Leah's is it that I visited the refugees? I was following up on patients.

Tamar decided to lay things clearly on the table.

"I've been out there a couple of times. The first time I made a mistake when the group of Sudanese children came to be vaccinated and one of their cards fell on the floor. I went to return it and—"

"Ah, a mistake—"

"There I discovered a different world, and those people are so needy that I began asking myself what could be done." Tamar visualized the children with their raggedy and ill-fitting clothes and the women sitting on the ground with their babies.

"Our mayor doesn't want Eilat being overrun with infiltrators." Leah put her feet up on the extra chair. "We already have hotel workers from Africa, India, and Nepal. And all those Thai workers on the kibbutzim! In the old days, volunteers from Europe did the farm work."

"I grew up on a kibbutz," Tamar said. "But then the volunteers stopped coming. Israel isn't popular anymore. And people don't want to work without pay. Besides, I hear the Thais are exceptional workers."

"A small country like Israel doesn't have room for more foreigners, especially poor ones who come with nothing. And they're not even Jewish."

Tamar's face turned red, and her body tensed. *He who holds his tongue is wise.* She could barely contain herself. While her parents had made the mistake of putting her as a baby in the children's house and letting her grow up there, at least they taught her to be color-blind and treat all human beings with dignity.

Leah stood up to leave. "Don't get involved. We have enough poor people of our own in Israel. And don't even think about aiding them to the harm of your work here."

Tamar wanted to tell Leah about Joey's red-tinted hair, his eye infection, and how she'd taken him and Mary home for a few hours to feed, bathe, treat, and hug them. But she let it go for now.

6

Tamar stared at her four-tiered creation, a YouTube video on her laptop screen next to her on the table along with a tall cup of coffee. (She was still trying to figure out which kind of milk to use that wouldn't cause her coffee to curdle—soy, almond, or rice.) She had the bride and groom, with their dog next to them, encircled by roses. When alone, Tamar became absorbed in her projects, like a kind of meditation. This time Steve was there, and Tamar said, "I've never put a dog on top of a wedding cake, but this couple doesn't go anywhere without their dog."

"Sort of like Michal and Kinneret." Steve had settled into his favorite recliner. He glanced up from his thick book. "Funny. It's written in *The Merchant of Venice*, 'One half of me is yours, the other half yours mine own.' How does a dog fit into the equation?"

"I don't ask," she said. "I'm not their marriage counselor," she replied. "Arava says the dog I drew as a model looks more like a rabbit. What d'you think?"

Steve stared at her drawing. "Hmm. Maybe a longer tail and ears would help?"

Tamar didn't understand Shakespeare, but she could feel the bond between her sister and Kinneret. For a while, that dog was the only thing keeping Michal going.

"Now that I've made the dog and the centers of the flowers, I'll leave it to dry and continue tomorrow. The wedding is on Thursday." Tamar wiped her hands on her apron and began clearing the table. She loosened her hair which she'd tied in a ponytail to keep out of her eyes and off the cake. If she had a second kitchen like that of her religious neighbor, she could keep her ingredients and tools out till she finished. But was thankful they could buy this old house and slowly fix it up.

After washing the dishes, Tamar allowed herself to sit down and lean back on the pillows in her favorite chair She'd been going the whole day. Since Arava and Gal were little, this was one of her favorite times of the day, when the children were in bed and she and Steve could talk, but now—for a change—she was at a loss for words. How to get started?

"I had a dream last night."

"Okay." Steve didn't look up from his Shakespeare.

"I usually don't remember dreams, but this was different." Tamar put her hand on Steve's book. "I dreamed about Mary and Joey."

Steve finally looked up. "Mary and Joey?"

"Oh, come on! They were at Yossi's birthday party."

"Okay, Mary and Joey," Steve said. "What'd you dream?"

"I dreamed they were living with us. They were eating dinner at our table, and then you took them to bed."

"You're so preoccupied with them, no wonder you had a dream like that." Steve closed his book. At least she had his attention. "Give yourself a break. Relax. Do you really think this dream means something?"

"I didn't say it, you did," she said. "I see their sweet little faces before me looking around for their mother who never comes." Tamar blinked back tears.

"But what can you, or we, do? They have a mother and it's not you. You had a mother too, even if she let you down."

"I'm not sure." She sighed and looked up at the ceiling. "But you saw them."

Steve sat up straight. "Listen. I'm thankful for what God gave us. Most of all for you and the children, but also for our jobs and house. It's more than I ever deserved. But we're just getting by. Our car seems to be gasping its last breath. I didn't tell you the garage said they have to change the gears. I don't know how we'll manage. My father—"

"The car is serious, but come on," Tamar began raising her voice but stopped herself, not wanting to wake up the children. She tried to be a good daughter-in-law and respect Steve's parents, but why did he always bring up his father when they began talking about finances?

"What's your father have to do with Mary and Joey?"

Even as Tamar asked, she knew the answer. Steve's father had wanted him to be a doctor like himself and Steve's younger brother, a successful, and rich, plastic surgeon. Steve had chosen a different path.

"You know as well as I do." Steve shook his head. "As if my coming to belief in Yeshua wasn't enough of a shock for them, then I moved to Israel."

Tamar couldn't understand the North American Jewish mindset. Steve's parents had sent him to the Jewish day school in Toronto and to Jewish camps in the summer, so what was wrong with immigrating? What bothered her was Steve trying to prove to his parents that he could make it while they were expecting him to fail.

"You're setting yourself up to get hurt," he said. "Take them more toys. Bring them home for another meal. But we don't have the resources to do more than that. Our plates are full." He looked at the clock on the wall. "I have to get some sleep. I'm meeting some students at three in the morning for a dive, to look at the underwater coral nursery. But I'll be home early."

He rose from his chair and yawned. "Don't get too involved. Take my advice."

Tamar also stood up. "I know what it's like not to have a mother nearby."

7

Squeezing herself out of the car between the children who'd piled in, Tamar spotted Steve at a picnic table, engaged in a conversation with a group of Sudanese men. After a few days of unspoken agreement not to bring up the subject of Mary and Joey again, Steve himself suggested they come out here together.

Thankfully, with Arava and Gal both coming home late from their tennis and sailing clubs, things worked out today for her to meet Steve at the kibbutz after work. Steve, who bicycled from work, arrived first.

Steve greeted her. "You have to see this place to believe it," he said. "So close to Eilat but feels like a different continent. A few of these guys speak some English, but I wish my Arabic were better."

Now he'll understand my pull toward the refugees. With his heart for people and God, he'll want to help. Does he have to spend so much time mulling over decisions?!

"I'm trying to figure out what's going on with them, how they got here, and why Israel?" he said.

She sighed. That was Steve. Always interested in back story, in current events and history. "I've been trying to understand that myself," Tamar said. "But the women I meet don't speak English. ... You got here fast."

"Ten and a half Ks in twenty minutes. Sat at my desk the whole day, so it's good to move. They're telling me about civil war, Egypt, the Sinai, and crossing the border."

"You can feel they've been through trauma." Tamar shook her head. "All these children! It's crazy."

36

Rivka was walking toward them. Tamar greeted her. "This is my husband, Steve."

"I'm trying to learn what's happening with them," Steve said. "How did people from Sudan end up in Eilat of all places?

"I could try to explain, but why don't you ask Michael over there? He was an English teacher in Cairo, before being forced to flee, and is a sort of spokesman for the others." She pointed to a man participating in an animated discussion.

As they approached, Michael turned and reached out his hand with a big smile. "The women are complaining that they have to provide diapers for their children in the daycare," he said. "They think diapers should be included."

"Glad to meet you." Steve shook his hand. "Sounds like you have a lot on your plate. This is my first time here, though I hope not the last. Rivka said you could tell us what brought you here."

"It is a long story," Michael said.

"We'd love to hear all about it," Tamar said. "But unfortunately we don't have much time because our children are coming home soon."

"Can you maybe tell us the short version?" Steve asked as the three of them moved to the available plastic chairs.

"We are all from South Sudan, mostly from the Dinka and Nuer tribes, and we are Christians. The people in the north of Sudan are Arab Muslims, and since Sudan gained independence from England in 1955, we have been having a civil war off and on between the north and the south. After bombings and massacres, many of our people fled down the Nile River to Egypt hoping to find a better, peaceful life."

Tamar saw Steve's mind spinning, processing the information.

"Did you ever hear of the Lost Boys?" Michael asked.

Steve scratched his head. "I know them from the story of Peter Pan and the vampire movie."

"I do not know who is the Peter Pan or what is a vampire, but in Sudan many children become orphans, so we run away on foot in groups to Kenya and Ethiopia. Lost Boys is the name the aid workers give us. I was eight when I leave my family and never see them again."

Michael spoke in a flat voice as if he were telling someone else's story.

"My mother sent me away. She could not protect me anymore."

Tamar had heard many stories of Jewish mothers in Europe who handed their children over to strangers to save their lives from the Nazis, and always felt her heart torn as she thought of their self sacrifice.

"In the year it took me to reach the refugee camp, many friends died from lion attacks, crocodiles, enemy soldiers, and no food."

"Everyone here is a Lost Boy?"

"Not all."

"Did you find help in Egypt?" Steve asked.

Michael shook his head. "Egypt is a poor country with too many people, not wanting refugees. They also did not accept us because we are black and Christian. Every day we struggle, until one day, the end of 2005, we hold a peaceful demonstration in front of the United Nations office in Cairo, and Egyptian soldiers begin shooting us. Soon after, I left, one of the first."

Mary and Joey suddenly appeared out of nowhere. Mary ran to snuggle onto Tamar's lap, and Joey jumped on Steve and burying his face in Steve's chest.

"Bubi, where've you been?" Tamar kissed the top of Mary's head.

"We thought we heard our mother's voice and went to look for her, but it was another mother who came here today with her children," Mary said.

"I still don't understand why Israel." Steve scratched his head.

"Where you can go from Egypt?" Michael said. "No country wants refugees. Yes, we only heard bad about Israel in Sudan and Egypt. But we think nothing to lose, and Israel looked best."

"Like the ancient proverb: 'The enemy of my enemy is my friend'," Steve said.

"We just had to pay Bedouins to drive us through the Sinai to the Israeli border and climb over fence."

"Just?"

"We move in the dark because, though Egypt does not want us, they shoot as we run away. One man here has big sore on his leg where bullet went through."

Sounds crazy. Tamar made a mental note to track down the man with the bullet wound.

"But big surprise when we make it across, Israel soldiers welcome with food and drinks."

Tamar couldn't imagine herself in his place, running in the dark while being shot at. How did they manage with the children and babies? She'd love to stay and hear more, but the shadows were getting longer.

A ball made from tightly wound plastic bags hit Steve's leg, and he kicked it back to a group of boys.

"Reminds me of the balls they had in Kenya when I was there building an orphanage," he said. "What can we do to help you? First, I'll bring a regular football next time."

"This brother with sore leg, can you help?" Michael said. "And crutches for Joseph? His leg blown off by bomb that killed his father."

"I'll talk it over with brothers in our fellowship." Steve stood up. "If we come out in the evening for Bible studies, would you translate from English to Arabic? We'll bring the man with the wound to a doctor, and get crutches for Joseph."

Tamar gently unwound Mary's arms from around her neck while Steve did the same with Joey, and they began walking to their car.

"Couldn't we take them home with us again for a couple of hours?" Tamar said. "You've seen the conditions here."

"Mouse, remember what I told you last time about not getting too involved?" When Steve called her 'mouse,' another of Shakespeare's pet names, he was getting serious.

"Here's what we'll do—I'll talk to the guys. With your connections, you can find a way to help the man with the wound. And we'll announce in the congregation about a collection of toys and clothes. Some of our young people can come out to play with them." After a pause, he added, "But give yourself space from Mary and Joey. This fixation could ruin your life and mind and the rest of the family's too."

Easy for Steve to say. He obviously didn't understand.

8

Steve meant well, but didn't she know what was best for Mary and Joey? Tamar couldn't get mental pictures of them out of her mind. If she gave up on gardening today, she'd have a few free minutes. And she found herself driving to the kibbutz again.

On the way, she thought of her husband. The kindest and most thoughtful man she knew. From the day they had met fifteen years ago when she took a break from her nursing studies and came down with her girlfriend to do a scuba diving course in Eilat, she knew he was amazing. He was an exchange student from Canada working on his MA at the Marine Science Institute and doing a project about divers' influences on Eilat's coral reefs. She'd been impressed not only by his passion for his work, and that he'd left his family and comfortable home to come to Israel, but also by his steadfast faith.

"Why Eilat?" she had asked him over an iced coffee at the Aroma coffee shop, where he'd asked her and her friend to join him at the end of the day. "Can't you study marine biology in Canada?"

"My grandparents were Holocaust survivors. I was raised in a home where Judaism and Israel were central to my identity," Steve spoke slowly and thoughtfully, his green eyes meeting hers.

"They must be happy you're here." She was tired from three dives, but also refreshed. Her studies weren't leaving time for dating, and she was happy for conversation with an intelligent man. Her skin tingled as the sun sank over the Mountains of Edom opposite them. The Red Sea, living up to its name, turned a purple red. The juxtaposition of a mountainous desert dropping into the sea mesmerized her.

"You might think so," Steve said. "But we had a kind of falling out a few years ago. They're afraid I'm over here as a missionary."

"A missionary?" Tamar's curiosity was aroused.

"My roommate at college was a Jewish guy who believed in Jesus, and we had long discussions, arguments really. I decided I had to read the New Testament to better answer him, and to my surprise—to make a long story short—I also started to believe in Yeshua."

"You're kidding! My parents started to believe in Yeshua when we lived on the kibbutz, and they raised us also to believe in Him. But lately I'm not sure anymore what I believe."

"I've been going to a Messianic Jewish congregation here in Eilat." Steve took out his wallet to pay. "Why don't you come with me on Shabbat? You'll love it. And tomorrow let's meet again after your course, okay?"

She never had a minute's regret that they had married, but they were so different. Now she knew that Steve was trying to protect her emotionally when he told her not to get involved. But he couldn't understand Mary and Joey's pain as she could. Besides, she needed to stop by again to see how Joey's eyes were responding to the treatment. Or was this her excuse? She couldn't get that dream out of her mind.

As she turned into the driveway, Mary and Joey were waiting at the gate, sitting on a rock, holding hands. Recognizing her car, wide smiles spread over their faces. She pulled them into the car with her and drove into the parking lot.

"Ta-mar! Ta-mar!" children yelled as she stepped out with Mary and Joey, closing the door quickly so they wouldn't get in. A dozen children grabbed, hugged, and jumped on her. When Tamar sat down on the ground, Mary and Joey snuggled against her. Joey's eyes were still red. Was no one taking care of him? Besides the ointment, proper hygiene would help. But Joey's dirt-smeared face and odor of fried food and urine told her that wasn't happening.

She found Rivka standing in the midst of a group of refugees. Several of the men had questions about their hotel jobs, Michael interpreting. A woman urgently needed clothes for her baby. Another wasn't satisfied with the room she'd been given.

"No one's treating Joey's eyes?" Tamar asked. "Something has to be done."

Rivka shrugged. "Same story. Haven't seen their mother in days."

"As a nurse in Tipat Halav, if we become aware of a situation where parents have abandoned their children, we're required to report to the authorities."

"A different world out here." Rivka looked around. Electric wires were strung between old buildings. Water puddles had collected from leaking pipes.

"If the Welfare Department determines there's child abuse, the children are moved to a foster home." Tamar tried not to raise her voice, children's rights being one of her passions.

"As a matter of fact, the kibbutz social worker has been here." Rivka looked down at Mary and Joey and paused. "We were wondering," she said looking straight at Tamar. "Would you be willing to take them home to live with you?"

Goosebumps rose on Tamar's arms. She'd dreamed about Mary and Joey, but to hear Rivka express these words and realize it might become a reality, Tamar became mute.

"If you can't take them, we'll send them to the children's home in Beer Sheva. If you take them, afterwards you can contact the social services in Eilat to arrange things officially. I know our mayor isn't sympathetic to refugees. I just hope …"

She'd only known Mary and Joey for a couple of weeks, but it felt longer. They'd met her family: Steve, Arava, Gal, and Michal. But what would those family members say? Maybe she really was being impulsive. Could Steve be right? She'd always wanted more children, but was this the way? Was it fair to Arava and Gal to take some needy children into their home? Could she share her love for them with two more?

"Don't move them to Beer Sheva yet," Tamar said, her head exploding and heart pounding. "I'll speak with my husband and children and pick them up after the weekend." She tried to sound more confident than she felt.

That gave her three days to convince Steve and to prepare the house for them; and with Imma and Abba coming, they had a busy weekend planned.

9

Michal, with Kinneret, walked the gangplank onto the Mermaid.

"Up here!" Yossi called. "The ladder's on the right."

She joined him on the top deck, where he lay back on large pillows. "Welcome to my simple home and workplace. Thanks for coming."

From the pier Michal had easily recognized Yossi's boat with its turquoise hull and the blonde, bikinied mermaid on the bow. She'd seen the yacht anchored off the Dolphin Reef to allow tourists a chance to see dolphins jumping from close by. A friend from work had a bachelorette party on a different craft. But Michal had never seen the marina as a neighborhood, where someone she knew actually lived.

"What d'you mean?" She settled down into a stack of pillows. "Thank you for asking me. What an awesome way to live." She wondered whether his inviting her had a deeper meaning, or did he just see it as another way for them to get together?

Michal looked around. "People live on other boats too?"

"People like me, folks who work here. But see that small one over there?" Yossi pointed to a square barge with an outboard engine. "A guy bought it just to live on. He doesn't even have a skipper's license."

"So why would he want to live here?"

"A different and cheap alternative to a normal neighborhood, and generally quiet."

"So, what's that loud disco music?"

"Must be one of the boats leaving the marina now for a night sail, a bar mitzva or engagement party or something. Sorry."

"It's not your fault. ... Do the boats have toilets and showers? Sorry for all my questions." In a crowd, she preferred to listen rather than talk, but with Yossi the words came tumbling out.

"Once they're sailing, it'll be quiet again, and sometimes I use earplugs. Some have showers or just a hose, or we can use the outdoor shower in the marina. The toilet downstairs has a tank we empty."

Yossi rose to his feet. "Wait a minute, I invited you for dinner. I'll start the grill. We took a group out fishing today, and they didn't want to take their catch home."

As he was placing the fish on the grill, Michal asked, "Do you have friends here? Do you get together sometimes?"

"How shall I say it?" Yossi sat on the pillows again. "The folks here are kind of special, not really my type. But that's okay. I liked visiting your family. You're lucky."

"Ever been to Aqaba?" She pointed with her chin toward the twinkling lights of Eilat's twin city.

"Growing up, we didn't take vacations." Yossi leaned back on his elbows. "When we had our three-week break from yeshiva every year after Tisha Be'Av, they organized hikes for us because of what God told Abraham, 'Arise, walk in the land, for I give it to you.' We believed that every place we set our foot down was ours. We often traveled to Judah, Samaria, and the Galilee. But Eilat isn't part of the Promised Land. What about you?"

"We didn't have a lot of money in our family. After we left the kibbutz, we started from nothing. But we came to Eilat every Pessach with a few other families and set up a tent camp on the beach. We all love the water. You must like it too, to live on a boat. Do you jump off sometimes?"

"Can't swim. Sports were considered a waste for us, taking time away from studying. One guy from our yeshiva drowned jumping into a stream near Safed."

Between living in the kibbutz and then Arad, Michal knew

nothing about the religious lifestyle except that they had lots of kids, their own schools, didn't go to the army, and dressed differently. They lived in their own bubble, and in Eilat you never saw men in black coats or women in long skirts and assorted head coverings.

"Crazy, I'll teach you. I can't remember ever not swimming, entering water brings me to a peaceful space." Michal breathed in the aroma of grilled fish mixed with garlic. "What a smell."

Steve talked about meditation, not like the gurus taught, sitting still and emptying your mind. He said it was focusing on God and the Bible. For Michal, swimming was a moving meditation with its rhythmic breathing and being immersed in another element.

Yossi got up again and poked the fish gently. "It needs another five minutes. Our rabbis told us that praying and reading the Talmud was the gateway to a higher plane. But it never worked for me."

Michal reached out instinctively to scratch Kinneret between her ears.

Yossi continued, "Can you believe the first time I came to Eilat was on a vacation from the army, and I didn't know that Aqaba was in Jordan? Or that Egypt was south of here and that this is the Red Sea? I only knew those names from the Torah."

"No way!"

He carefully removed the fish from the grill. "I'll bring the rest of the food up here."

"Awesome," Michal jumped up to help and followed Yossi down the ladder, ducking her head as they descended the steps into the kitchen on the lowest level.

"On a boat this is called 'the galley.'"

"And that's your bedroom?" She peered past the galley toward the bow.

"Look if you want. It's small but compact."

A glance revealed Yossi's bed made and everything in place. Was it because he knew she was coming? Her eyes fell on the open Bible next to his bunk that Steve had given him for a birthday present.

"Didn't know you cooked," Michal said.

"On a boat you learn to do everything." A grin stole across his face. "I told my boss a friend was coming for dinner, so he left us the snapper, and I threw a couple of potatoes in the fire and added some salads. I've never invited anyone before. My boss knows a bit of my background, so he was happy for me, even though I told him you weren't my girlfriend or anything."

"Yeah, sure." While nothing was clear about their relationship, she would have liked to hear that he gave his boss a different answer. Though she had to admit she probably would have said the same if asked. But things could change.

They ate their meal in a comfortable silence while enjoying the gentle swaying of the waves. As they picked the last pieces of meat off the fish bones and mopped up the remainder of the hummus and salad with the fresh pita, Yossi spoke again.

"I don't even know what it's like to have a girlfriend."

The topic must have gotten stuck in his head.

Michal reached over and opened her backpack. "I stopped at the bakery and picked up apple pastries for dessert. Here you go."

As darkness fell, it was easy to talk while they lay back against the pillows. "Is it true your families arrange marriages?" she asked.

"We usually meet the girl once before the wedding."

"No way! And that leads to marital happiness?"

Yossi paused and thought before he answered. "Sometimes it works. Coffee?"

"Tea, if you don't mind."

Yossi poured a cup of hot water from a thermos into a mug. "What do you think about arranged marriages now?"

"Not for me. I can tell you, I've never met a couple so happy like Tamar and Steve."

"Them? So happy?" Michal sipped her tea. "You haven't heard them arguing."

"I haven't, but I can see their love and respect for each other. I'd like a marriage like that. Their children are great too. Steve told me a little about what they believe. Maybe that helps them?"

"I'm crazy about those kids. That's my only problem with going to Berlin—leaving Arava and Gal ... and Kinneret, of course. And who knows what will happen with Mary and Joey? Seems like Tamar will be needing my help more than ever ... though she always only wants it on her own terms." Since they'd been little, Tamar always set the rules—deciding who would play who in games of make-believe, not letting Michal play together with Tamar's friends. And being such a good student, too. No wonder Michal had gone off in the opposite direction from perfect Tamar who did everything to please their parents—studying, marrying at the right age, and gifting Imma and Abba with two grandchildren—a boy and a girl.

"What *will* you do with Kinneret? I've never seen you without her." Yossi patted Kinneret on the head, who was stretched out between them on the deck.

"Not sure." Her hand touched his as they were both stroking the dog. She pulled it away quickly.

"The problem with not having your parents find a bride is that in the army I was in a combat unit and too busy or tired to have a girlfriend, and now I don't go to bars or pubs where people seem to meet," Yossi said. "I don't have time for a girlfriend anyway. I want to go to university and have started to study for my matriculation exams. I've been thinking about being a marine biologist like Steve. How *do* you meet someone?"

How did we get into this subject? "I don't know either. I knew Shai for years. We were both Scout leaders in the same troop.

But when he went into the army, that's when we realized we liked each other, and he became my boyfriend."

Yossi's voice took on a different tone. "You have a boyfriend?"

"No, well, Shai …" she paused. "Do you remember the terror attack at the bus station in Beer Sheva in 2005, two years ago?"

"Sure, I was in the army then in the south, and we were put on high alert," Yossi answered.

I never speak to anyone about this. But… "Shai was a student at Ben Gurion University. He'd been home for the weekend and was on his way back to school. Wrong place at the wrong time."

"I'm sorry."

"Yeah s**t, that's when my life ended. So now I just want to get out of here. Go to Berlin. Begin a new life. I'm fed up with this place."

"But why Berlin? Most of my family died in the Holocaust. Our rabbi barely escaped with his life, together with a few of his students."

"It's a place you can be free, and things are cheap. When my girlfriend's work contract finishes in three months, we're planning to fly there together. I've been looking on the internet for a place to live and have some leads."

"We have an early sailing tomorrow," Yossi lifted himself off the pillows. "I better get some sleep."

Did he suddenly want to get rid of her? Not surprising. Why would he want to get involved with someone who was leaving soon?

"Yeah, me too. Thanks for the special time and good food."

Kinneret stood up too and shook herself. Michal had looked forward to meeting Yossi on the Mermaid but was more confused than ever. But she admired Yossi's sincerity and his bravery in leaving family and community. And she could understand the emptiness that came from not really believing in anything.

10

"Gal! Arava!" Shoshana pushed open the door and hugged Arava while Peter wrapped his arms around Gal and lifted him off the floor.

Imma took a step back and exclaimed, "Let me look at you. It seems ages since we saw you and haven't you grown!"

"Savta, it's only been a month since we visited you during summer vacation," Gal said.

"Well, it seems long to me. Arava, you began junior high? And Gal, I think you're as tall as me now. You're going to be tall like your Saba and father."

Gal beamed. "But it's not hard to be taller than you, Savta."

Tamar stepped out of the kitchen and embraced her parents.

"How was your drive down?" Steve asked, putting down his Shakespeare and hugging his parents-in-law. "Much traffic on this Friday afternoon?"

"Not bad. Less than three hours," Abba said. He glanced around the house he'd helped remodel. "You're working on your office now, I see."

"We didn't need that extra porch, so I've enclosed it and put a desk in. It gives me a place to work quietly from home. Sometimes that's better than going to the Institute where there's lots of socializing, and I don't get much done."

Imma opened the shopping bag she was carrying and took out two pans. "I brought your favorite vegetarian soup and the semolina cake, especially for Arava and Gal—"

"With the recipes you got from your mother!" Arava said.

Imma laughed. "And from my mother's mother. But we didn't

51

have recipes in Yemen. They didn't even know how to read."

"I hope they don't have eggs or milk in them," Tamar said.

Imma's smile faded. "No meat, of course. I don't bring that oxtail soup anymore that Steve liked so much, but what's wrong with eggs and milk?"

"We're vegans now. It's healthier and I've already lost a kilo."

Imma scrutinized her. Her parents had just arrived, and the tension was rising already.

"Steve agreed? He doesn't need to lose weight. And what about Arava and Gal? Where do they get their protein?" This visit with her parents wasn't starting off in the best way.

"Don't you think I've researched this?" Her mother was always finding ways to criticize. "We eat a lot of beans and whole grains, and when you eat them together, you get all the protein you need. Once I get the equipment, I'll start making sauerkraut, one of the best sources for probiotics which is a key for good digestion."

"You aren't busy enough already? Pity you didn't tell me before. Can the children and Steve at least eat the food I cooked for you, one last time?" Imma walked out of the kitchen.

Tamar was thankful to hear Michal's scooter stopping outside and to see her sister coming through the door. Michal didn't have the same issues with their mother; but then, she didn't grow up in the children's house. Described often as "willowy," Michal never paid attention to her weight, either.

"Darling! You look wonderful!" Imma smiled as she hugged Michal. "Life seems good to you. But you haven't been up to Arad to see us for ages."

"I know, Imma, and I really want to come soon, but the Dolphin Reef was crazy busy all summer and during the holidays."

Imma bent down to pet the dog. "Kinneret looks good too, her coat is shiny, and she's gained weight."

Apparently dogs gaining weight is acceptable, thought Tamar.

Her mother always commented negatively if she gained even a few grams. Michal stayed the perfect weight in Imma's eyes, and she didn't hesitate to say so.

"Yeah, Kinneret's come a long way." Michal turned to Arava and Gal. "Now that things are becoming more normal, you'll come to the Reef with me, and I'll give you a lesson in dolphin training, like I promised."

The kids had been waiting for that, but Tamar had told them not to bug their aunt.

"Will we see the new baby dolphin you told us about?" asked Arava. "Mitzi?"

"Sure, you'll see her," Michal said. "She's stays close to her mother, and she already knows me."

"Dinner's nearly ready," Tamar announced. "You can put your bags in Gal's room and wash up." She scanned their Shabbat table one last time—white tablecloth, the silver candlesticks she'd inherited from her grandmother whose own grandmother had brought them from Yemen, and her braided hallah bread, now made without eggs and milk.

"Smells delicious!" Abba exclaimed.

Tamar knew grilled chicken was the aroma they usually associated with Shabbat dinner, but the quantities of garlic she used, as well as the cilantro, also radiated a homey atmosphere.

"Peter, we're so happy to have you here with us. Will you pray for the food?" Steve asked.

After the prayer Tamar said, "Imma, can you dish out the tofu and veggies, Abba the lasagna, and Steve the quiche? I'll pass the salad and tehina around." She'd found interesting blogs with vegan recipes and was proud of herself for putting together a festive meal.

"How's the work going, Steve?" Abba asked.

"We have several new master's students this year and a couple of PhDs I'm advising. There's interesting research going on, like growing corals with different genotypes." Steve became animated when he spoke about his work. "Basically, everything dies, and it takes a hundred tries to succeed in keeping something alive; but if you're persistent, it's worthwhile. Come out, and I'll show you."

Tamar liked how the conversation passed easily between her husband and father. Abba was one of the few people outside of Steve's work who could follow what he was talking about.

"And your jeep tours?" Steve put down his fork and looked across the table at his father-in-law. "Mostly individual tourists or do you have groups lately?"

"Tamar, this is all delicious," Abba said. Then to Steve, "Work's not bad. I had a group from Liverpool. Did you know that your parents gave my name to a couple from their synagogue?"

"You still have connections with people from home?" Steve asked and turned to Tamar. "I love the lasagna, and everything."

"A friend I grew up with, and recently we got in touch again through Facebook," Abba said. "And there's lots of potential in the Christian market. You'll find plenty of history around Arad and old synagogues like the one in Susiya with both Jewish and Christian symbols. Tamar, maybe you can give Imma the recipe for the quiche." Abba leaned back.

Tamar looked at Imma. Abba wasn't being tactful to suggest Imma could learn about cooking from her.

"And how are your babies?" Abba was unaware of his blunder.

Okay, here we go. She'd waited for this moment, but when it came, she didn't know how to begin. She'd blurted out to Rivka that they'd pick up Mary and Joey after the weekend but hadn't even found time to talk it over with Steve. Was she crazy?

Michal pushed back her chair. "Let's move to the living room and talk more over a game of Rummikub. I told Arava and Gal we'd play again this week, though I'm afraid I'll lose again. They're both getting so good!"

Thanks to Michal's suggestion Tamar had another few minutes to formulate her answer.

Gal who'd been concentrating on finishing his food, suddenly leaned forward and flashed one of his cute grins. He used his daily computer time to play Rummikub online and loved beating his aunt.

"Who dares take on Arava and Gal and be the fourth player?" Michal stood up and began clearing the table.

"Savta and I will be a team," Abba smiled, helping take the dishes into the kitchen.

"'Two are better than one, because they have a good reward for their toil. For if they fall, one will lift up his fellow.'" Steve said. "Tammileh, you sit down and let me do the dishes. You rest tonight, remember?"

"Oof, Daddy. Shakespeare again?" Gal looked up at the ceiling. In line with Steve's speaking English with the children, they called Steve and Tamar, Daddy and Mommy.

"No, Gal," Steve said. "This time it's from the Bible, the book of Ecclesiastes. Worth remembering. And by the way, did you know that Rummikub was invented by Ephraim Hertzano, a Romanian Jew who immigrated to Israel in the 1930's. He began by making the first sets by hand in his backyard. At one point he published a rulebook with three different versions of the game: the Sabra, the American, and the International, but the Sabra took over. Like you two, your mother and aunt, prickly on the outside like the sabra fruit but sweet inside."

"What's that have to do with Rummikub?" Arava said.

"Nothing," Steve said. "Thought it was interesting."

They divided up the tiles, shuffled them around on the table, and each set up their rack in front of them.

"Everyone choose a tile," Michal said, "and we'll see who goes first."

"Me!" Gal thrust his fist in the air. He was in his element.

It had been a long day, but finally Tamar settled into her place on the sofa. This was how it was supposed to be, the family sitting around and having fun together. Even the sound of Steve humming and the water running in the kitchen was soothing. But she still had Abba's question to answer and her bombshell to drop. Their concentration on the game gave her a longer reprieve.

"Rummikub." Abba laid out a blue and red "seven" tile and a joker. "I guess Savta and I didn't lose our touch completely. We used to play this on the kibbutz once upon a time before we had televisions and computers."

Gal's face fell but then he shrugged his shoulders. They'd been trying to teach him to be a good sport.

"Mommy, Saba asked about your babies." Arava was good at getting people back on track in their conversations. "Tell Saba and Savta about Mary and Joey."

"Who are Mary and Joey?" Shoshana asked.

"They came to Yossi's birthday party," Arava said. "And—"

"Yossi?" Abba asked.

"You really haven't been here for a long time." An amused expression appeared on Gal's face. "It was his first birthday. Yossi is Michal's friend."

"Michal has a baby friend who just turned one?" Tamar could see Imma's puzzlement.

"Ga-al, let me explain." Arava said. "Yossi isn't a baby, he turned twenty-five but never celebrated his birthday because—"

"Because his family are super religious, and they told him birthdays weren't necessary," Gal said.

"Gal, Arava, one at a time." They always seemed to vie for attention.

"So, Mommy made a cake like she always does—"

"Chocolate with layers," Arava said.

"And we sang 'Happy Birthday' and had a party."

"But you still didn't tell us who are Mary and Joey." Tamar

could see her father trying to absorb it all, but not ask too many questions.

"They're from Africa." Gal answered.

"Gal stop! I'm talking," Arava said. "Saba, Mary and Joey are from Sudan and came to Mommy's clinic for shots, and she went to bring them toys where they live at the kibbutz, and they were crying and needed a bath, and their mother wasn't around so Mommy brought them to Yossi's party, and Joey fell asleep in Abba's lap, and that's all." Arava paused and looked at her grandparents.

"You've certainly been having an interesting time around here, and we missed it all."

It's now or never. Might as well throw it out. "You haven't really missed it all, Abba, because the last time I was there, Rivka, the head of the Sudanese camp, asked me if we'd be willing to have Mary and Joey move in with us." She turned her attention to Steve. "Sorry motek, I didn't get a chance to tell you this yet."

"Didn't get a chance?" Steve sat up straight and pursed his lips.

She knew this wasn't the right way to break the news to Steve, in front of her parents who were judging her all the time anyway, but what could she do? And Steve, rightly so, didn't appreciate when she took matters in her own hands and made the decisions in the family. *Please, God, turn this around for the good*, she prayed silently.

"I know it all happened quickly and I'm glad that even with all your new students you came out there with me, so you know what I'm talking about." She tried to speak in a calm voice. "Joey's eye infection isn't getting better—it's getting worse, and their mother's never around. Rikva told me that if we don't take Mary and Joey, the kibbutz's social worker said they'd have to send them to a children's home. I told her I'd talk with you and the children and give her an answer after the weekend."

She recognized that troubled look on her parents' faces: 'Here she goes again with her impulsiveness.'

But this time she really did know what was best for Mary and Joey. The only problem was convincing Steve.

"I wouldn't rush into anything," Abba said, always the diplomat. "You're finally getting your feet on the ground after fixing the house. Surely their mother will turn up or some other relative."

"Adding two more children to your family, just like that?" Imma said. "Does this woman understand what she's asking?"

"Rivka spoke of us being a foster family."

She knew what her heart was telling her but didn't want to argue. Thankfully, Steve also understood that things were getting out of hand and that this topic was better discussed when they were alone.

"I found Kinneret when Shai and I were camping in the Galilee, and she needed a home ... and look at her now. Awesome." Michal put her arm around her dog's neck, as Kinneret rested her head on Michal's lap.

"Excuse me," Imma said. "We all love Kinneret, but a dog is different from children."

"Yeah, I'm crazy about her, but she's been tons of work and expensive with all the shots and dog food."

"You know what?" Steve said as he stood up and began walking to their bedroom. "I'm tired. We'll pray about this, and I'm sure God will make things clear."

Tamar raised herself out of the chair too. "Imma, Abba, your bed is made up. See you in the morning."

"Gali, I've pulled out the bed for you in Arava's room." Gal grimaced, he didn't like her calling him by her pet name anymore, and not Gali or Gal-Gal either.

11

"Hey, duck!" Sitting in his armchair, Steve glanced up from his well-worn Bible. "What're you doing up so early? I thought you'd sleep in and let me make breakfast."

Tamar didn't know how Steve did it. A storm, physical or emotional, could be going on around him, and when his head hit the pillow, he was asleep. He was already snoring last night when she lay down next to him after kissing Arava and Gal good night. She, on the other hand, had barely slept, planning in her mind her arguments in favor of taking the children. But what was she thinking? How could she expect him to agree to foster Mary and Joey after meeting them twice, at Yossi's birthday party and at the camp? She set her alarm to wake up early so she and Steve would have some quiet minutes before her parents and the children appeared.

Steve always woke up with the birds and spent time reading the Bible. He read through the Bible in a year, his habit since college, but she never could have orchestrated his reading today.

"I didn't sleep so well." She sat down at her place on the sofa.

"Too much coffee," Steve said.

"I've told you that coffee doesn't keep me awake but now, I need a cup. I thought we should talk before everyone wakes up."

"It would've been nice if you'd told me about your new plan before throwing it out in front of your parents and the kids."

"I meant to, sorry it happened like that."

"As a matter of fact, you wouldn't believe the verse I read this morning." Steve sat up straight and his eyes widened. "I'm reading through Deuteronomy and came to chapter ten, verses eighteen and nineteen."

"Okay...."

He read slowly. "'The Lord defends the cause of the fatherless and the widow and loves the alien, giving him food and clothing. And you are to love those who are aliens, for you yourselves were aliens in Egypt.'"

Tamar's heart beat faster. "So ..."

"I guess Mary and Joey come under the category of fatherless because you told me there's no father in the picture and their mother disappeared, and they're also what's called 'aliens' in the Bible, or 'strangers.' As you know, when you first told me your idea, I told you not to get too involved. All I could think of, I'm ashamed to say, was the burden for us."

"I heard you. But something kept pulling me back to them."

Steve scratched his head. "I'm trying to stop thinking all the time about my parents' reactions to my plans and making decisions mainly from financial considerations. If it's the right thing to do, God will provide. I think we should go out to the kibbutz this afternoon as a family and be open to taking Mary and Joey home."

Thank you, God. Tamar knew that for Steve to talk about being open was as good as giving his okay.

~

When cooking yesterday's dinner, Tamar had prepared enough for today as well, and a cauliflower quiche made with soy cheese just for today, to add to the leftovers. She didn't like spending time in the kitchen on Shabbat.

Steve placed a portion of quiche on his plate next to the lasagna and fresh salad. "The lasagna's delicious, what was good yesterday is better today."

In their congregation this morning she'd noticed Steve leaning forward and taking notes during the message. Now at lunch, as usual he asked the children what they learned in their classes and had something positive to say about the teaching.

When Steve was asked to speak, he used Power Point presentations. "Takes time," he'd say. "But I've learned from my students at the Institute that people retain information when they not only hear but have visual stimulation." Tamar loved Steve's passion for sharing God's Word when speaking to a group or an individual and how he spoke from his heart with illustrations using fish, his birdwatching hobby, and the desert.

"Did anyone hear what I did this morning?" Steve stood up, took a Bible from the shelf, sat down again, and opened the Scriptures. "Speaks right to our family."

They were doing a series from Matthew, and today's portion was from chapter twenty-five. Tamar had been distracted this morning, not unusual for her, but today she had an even harder time keeping her mind on the words of the speaker.

"Listen," Steve read. "And he will place the sheep on his right, but the goats on the left. Then the King will say to those on his right, 'Come, you who are blessed by my Father, inherit the kingdom prepared for you from the foundation of the world. For I was hungry, and you gave Me food. I was thirsty and you gave Me drink. I was a stranger and you welcomed Me. I was naked and you clothed Me. I was sick and you visited Me. I was in prison and you came to Me... And the King will answer them, 'Truly I say to you, as you did it to one of the least of these my brothers you did it to Me.'"

"Why is that for our family?" Gal said as he slurped down Savta's soup.

"What do you think, Gali?" Steve said. "Why is Yeshua talking about sheep and goats? Are they real animals?"

Arava looked up from her plate. "He's talking about two kinds of people—the sheep are those who help others in need and the goats don't help."

Steve put his fork down. "Well said. What's his conclusion?"

"If we help the ones he talked about, it's like helping Yeshua."

A satisfied smile raced across her face.

"I wonder if there's anyone like that around here?" Steve asked.

"I know!" Gal jumped up. "The Sudanese."

"Mommy and I have decided to go out there this afternoon," Steve said. "Who wants to come?"

After cleaning up from lunch, the children searched for more toys to bring to the kibbutz, including Gal's prized remote-control car he didn't play with anymore and Arava's old dollhouse.

Tamar hadn't been sure her parents would want to visit the kibbutz with them, so she was pleasantly surprised when they insisted on coming and foregoing their Shabbat afternoon nap. Still, she hoped they were joining the family's excursion because they wanted to meet Mary and Joey and not to persuade her against taking the children. They'd always considered her headstrong and maybe as a teenager she did some stupid things, but their obvious disapproval of many of her decisions was painful.

When she was younger, they taught her to fight for justice, and as a family they went to the absorption center for Ethiopians; but when she asked why Ethiopian families couldn't come to live on their kibbutz, they couldn't answer. And though they'd brought her up with a belief in co-existence with the Israeli Arabs and used to go to Nazareth on Shabbat afternoons to eat hummus and became friendly with the restaurant owner, when she wanted to go with her class to spend a weekend with an Arab family, they didn't allow her. So now when it came to helping refugees, Abba and Imma were fine with bringing them clothes and toys but couldn't understand why she wanted to foster children whose mother abandoned them.

Finally all the family, including Abba and Imma, were coming to see the camp and meet Mary and Joey in their own environment in preparation for taking them home tomorrow. Why was she so surprised when her prayers were answered?

"I recognize this place," Abba said as they turned into the driveway. "Some of my groups used to stay here when they traveled to Eilat."

Arava's and Gal's eyes opened wide as they grabbed the bags of toys and stepped out of the car. Before they knew what was happening, Mary, coming from behind, grabbed Tamar's neck, while Joey threw himself on a surprised Steve and they both tumbled to the ground.

All the children broke into smiles and began jumping up and down as Gal demonstrated his remote-control car and showed its tricks. While standing around the picnic table, the girls watched Arava move the little dolls from one room of the dollhouse to another, pretending they were talking to each other. Tamar's only frustration was seeing Abba and Imma sitting on the side, seemingly indifferent. Knowing them, they would have enjoyed playing with the refugee children in other circumstances. Thinking that two of these children would soon be added to their family, changed their whole attitude.

Never mind. They hadn't been there for her either when she needed them. Most importantly, Steve had changed. Nothing could stop her plan now.

12

I'll be right there." Tamar nodded in Steve's direction as she headed toward Arava's room. She hoped he wouldn't fall asleep quickly because they needed to talk about plans for tomorrow. "I'll pray with Arava and Gal and give them their kisses."

Abba and Imma had excused themselves to go to sleep early. They'd missed their naps and needed to get going early tomorrow for Abba's jeep tour and the ceramic class Imma was teaching.

Tamar glanced around Arava's room, her daughter, on the brink of womanhood. Half the time she seemed grownup, and Tamar could speak to her like a friend; other times she was still the little girl who fought with her brother and forgot to tie her shoes. On one wall was a poster of a dolphin mother and baby, a gift from Michal, the aunt she was crazy about; on the other wall hung a picture of two grinning babies in a bathtub splashing water at each other. A few of her old Barbie dolls were still in the corner gathering dust, and on her desk a framed picture from her bat-mitzva trip to Croatia with the family, standing in front of a castle.

Tamar sat on the end of the trundle bed pulled out for Gal. "Thanks for giving your room to Saba and Savta."

"When can we go up and stay with them ourselves, without you and Daddy?" Gal propped himself up, resting his head on his hand. "We're big now. Saba wants to take us on a jeep trip."

"And Savta is going to teach us how to make ceramic bowls on the wheel in her workshop." Arava's eyes sparkled. She'd inherited her grandmother's creativity.

"Don't worry. It will happen one of these days." How could

she tell her children how hard it was for her to let go of them? Even for their overnight school trips she found reasons not to send them, as much as they protested. Steve thought her unreasonable; but even after so many years, her memories of separation and abandonment were still too strong.

"Anyway, where will they sleep?" Gal sat up now.

"What do you mean?" Tamar asked. Of course the children would have questions about the new family situation.

"Mary and Joey." Arava suddenly wasn't tired anymore and sat up too. "Will Gal have to sleep in my room?"

"No. We'll make Daddy's office into a room for them. They're little and don't need much space."

"But doesn't Daddy need an office at home too?" Gal said.

"Someday we'll build another room on the back, but in the meantime the corner in the living room is a good office too."

After agreeing to take in Mary and Joey, giving up his office wasn't a problem for Steve. Once he became convinced of something, he went all the way, like how he left his family and friends in Toronto and moved to Eilat. She'd never want to live anywhere other than Israel, even though some of her friends thought that marrying a Canadian was her ticket to live in a more peaceful and prosperous country.

"They'll live with us forever?" Gal asked.

Tamar wondered if she was asking too much from them.

"A friend in my class was adopted," Arava said. "Her real parents couldn't take care of her."

"We'll just wait and see." Tamar tried to sound natural. The situation was complicated. Had she thought it through enough?

"Saba said that it will be hard for us because we won't have much money." Since when was Arava worried about money? But she always hung on her grandfather's words.

"Bubi, we have all we need and more." Arava had moved around to lay her head on Tamar's lap like in the old days. "You

65

and Gal are everything to Daddy and me, the answers to our prayers. But I think we have enough love to share."

"Tell me again how you named me." Gal rolled over to be closer to his mother.

"Daddy and I met the first time scuba diving, so we decided on Gal, 'a wave in the sea.'"

"And you called me Arava also to connect with Eilat, right?" Arava gave a wispy smile. "Because the Arava Valley ends here."

"In the Bible the Arava was mentioned in the wanderings of the children of Israel," Tamar said. "It means a dry and desolate place. It's mostly barren, but water runs deep underground and when pumped up for irrigation, the desert blooms and turns into a garden. Bubi, I see you as a beautiful garden, growing and sending out green shoots and flowers."

"Can we still go visit Savta and Saba and go camping on the Kinneret in the summer?" Gal yawned.

"Sure, we'll go to Arad and camping." Tamar stood up and pulled the sheets around them. "I'm glad you're asking questions, but it's late, we'll talk more tomorrow." She gave them both kisses.

She and Steve tried to create an atmosphere where the children could be honest and express their fears and hesitations. They'd soon need to pull together as a family, and the children would have an important role.

That discussion went well. After all her years of wanting more children, God was doing it differently than she ever imagined, and it was happening tomorrow.

Would Steve be still awake? She doubted it.

13

"Arava, Gal, we're home!" Tamar and Steve walked through their front door, she with little Joey in her arms while Steve carried Mary. Each one held a plastic bag containing the children's clothes.

"You must be hungry." Tamar put Mary down and hugged Arava and Gal. She kept talking to hide her nervousness. "Look, Michal's put dinner on the table."

"I'll put their bags in my office, I mean in their room." Steve settled Joey on the sofa. "Hey kids, come to the table."

"Hope you like spaghetti." Tamar looked at Mary and Joey still cuddled together on the sofa like two rag dolls, in the position she and Steve had placed them. "It's Arava and Gal's favorite with tomato sauce and now we have tofu cheese instead of the usual cheese made with milk."

Who was she talking to? What did these undernourished kids care about health food?

"Arava, Gal, can you sit down please?" Steve said.

"These are Arava and Gal's places so you can sit on the end." Tamar pointed out their chairs.

Unlike most of their family meals, no one seemed to have anything to say. Tamar kept trying to fill the gaps.

"Shall I help you?" she said to Mary. "Look how Arava twirls the spaghetti around on her fork but maybe I should cut yours."

With her fingers Mary grabbed a strand of spaghetti.

"Joey, see how Gal likes spaghetti?" Tamar tried to sound positive. "Do you want Steve to help you?" She raised her eyebrows at Steve who got the message and began feeding Joey with a teaspoon.

"Yum, yum," Steve said as he used to when feeding their babies.

She'd forgotten how much work little children were but when Arava and Gal were these ages, they could eat by themselves.

Gal scraped the last bits of food off his plate. "Maybe they don't like the sauce. I didn't use to like it. Maybe not the soy cheese either. Takes getting used to."

"Right," Tamar said. "Why didn't I think of that? Here's some plain spaghetti." She dumped the first helping into the compost and began again.

This time it went better, especially when they let the children feed themselves with their hands.

"Do you have forks in Africa?" Arava looked at Mary. "In China they use chopsticks." Mary kept bringing the strands of spaghetti into her mouth.

"What school will they go to?" Gal said. "The one near our house?"

"Rivka and the social worker from the kibbutz think they should continue at the Sudanese school there," she answered. "They're already going through enough changes."

"They have their own school on the kibbutz?" Arava asked.

"The local authorities don't want to mix refugee children with the locals."

"I made a special dessert tonight," Tamar said. "Granola bars, a family favorite. And have some grapes."

Gal smiled impishly at Arava. "Your turn for the dishes." He grabbed a couple of bars and a bunch of grapes. "Mommy, I finished my homework. Can I play Rummikub on the computer?"

"Half hour computer and half hour library book," Steve said. "You too, Arava, when you've finished the dishes and your homework. Mommy and I will bring Mary and Joey to bed."

Tamar turned on the light in Steve's converted office, recently renovated from the enclosed porch. They had laid two mattresses on the floor, found an old cabinet for clothes, and put a picture on the wall of giraffes on an African savanna. Tamar had seen how an entire Sudanese family had crammed into one room, which included a tiny kitchenette and bathroom.

"Bath time." Tamar tried to sound casual and cheerful. "Steve, you undress Joey, and I'll take care of Mary, and we'll put them in the bathtub together."

When she had bathed the children the first time she brought them home, Mary eagerly sat down in the shallow water and began playing with the cups and plastic containers she'd put there for them, fascinated by the colorful bottles of shampoo, cream rinse, and shower gel. But Joey was another story. She decided he just wasn't used to her, their house, or even taking a bath. He protested so violently that she let him stand in the tub and tried to rub soap on him before dousing him with water. Seeing the panic in his eyes, she didn't force him.

This time should go better. "Joey, bubi." Tamar touched his arm. Naked he looked even smaller and skinnier. "Don't you want to sit in the warm water with Mary? You'll feel nice and clean afterward, and you'll be sleeping in clean sheets in your new bed." Joey didn't budge.

"Joey no likes water," Mary said.

Tamar looked at Steve. How had she expected things to go smoothly the first day? "Never mind, it's fine. I'm sure you'll get used to it and begin to like baths like Mary."

"I guess you've never been swimming either." She tried to sound lighthearted. "Where would you have? In the Nile? Don't worry. We'll teach you. When it's warm, our family goes to the beach every Shabbat."

Steve shot her a look. "Will you calm down and not talk so much? And if he doesn't like a bath, do you think he would want to swim?" Tension was rising in his voice.

After Steve had bathed Joey the best he could and got

pajamas on him, Joey snuggled into the Snoopy sheets on the mattress on the floor.

Mary clearly was used to dressing herself, and she seemed happy to get into the bed with the Snow White sheets.

"Now let's close our eyes and thank God," Steve said.

Sitting on the floor between the beds, Tamar rested a hand on each head but while her eyes were closed, Joey crawled over her legs. When she opened her eyes, the children lay together in Mary's bed with their foreheads touching.

"Oh, you want to sleep together. But it's crowded in one bed." She raised her eyebrows and looked at Steve. But Tamar understood what it was to sleep alone far from your parents. ...

"Imma, Abba!" She remembered sobbing and climbing out of the window in the children's house. The darkness and strange noises frightened her, but she needed to escape the monsters under her bed. ...

Everything looked different in the night. She soon became lost and gave up. A man on the way to work in the cowshed early in the morning found her curled up under a bush, shivering and wet from the dew. Pluto, the family dog, nestled next to her. She hadn't got far from her home, but the caregivers warned her not to do that again. She couldn't help it. When she heard the monsters, she needed Imma.

"Why can't you be like the rest?" Imma would say while hugging her.

"This isn't a healthy way to raise children," Abba had said to Imma more than once. But even when they did finally leave the kibbutz, Tamar's scars remained.

Tamar brought herself back to the moment and stood up. "Now a kiss and I'll turn out the light. We'll leave the door open a crack."

Stepping out of the room, Steve sank into his chair and picked up his book.

Tamar let out a long breath. "Sorry, didn't think it would be so hard."

"You could have figured it out. What'd you think? They'd be like two little angels after all they've been through? But this is what you wanted, and it's good we can't see the future."

"Thanks for reminding me." She'd planned to look online for a flamingo cake for her supervisor's granddaughter's bat mitzvah, but all she could do was collapse.

Gal appeared in the living room. "Mommy, they're not sleeping. I hear Joey crying and Mary talking to him."

"I'm tired from all the excitement today," Tamar said to nobody in particular. "You'd think they would be too."

"I tried to talk to them," Gal said. "They don't want to sleep alone."

"How do you know, Gali?" Steve said.

"Mary said they want to sleep with you."

She could have guessed. "With us?" Tamar pulled herself out of her easy chair. "Sure, we'll move their mattress into our room. Thanks, motek. You're a good brother."

Uh, oh. This had always caused friction with Steve. After Arava and Gal were born, Steve wanted to move them into their own room as quickly as possible. But she understood Mary and Joey. Steve would have to put up with it for a couple of nights till they were used to the new situation.

14

Tamar was trying to grab her first cup of coffee at ten o'clock, two days after Mary and Joey joined their family, when she heard a knock at the door. It could only be Eva.

"Better is a neighbor who is near than a brother who is far away," Steve often quoted when he heard Eva's footsteps outside.

"I'm not bothering?" Eva looked around the house and lowered herself into a kitchen chair.

"Never. Coffee?" Mary and Joey huddled close to Tamar as she poured a cup for Eva.

"I noticed you were home this morning," Eva said.

Tamar wasn't used to missing work, but Steve had insisted she take time off. "If we'd already been accepted as a foster family, you would have received maternity leave," he said.

"I'm not aching like after a birth."

"It's an adjustment," Steve said. "Maybe even harder because it was unexpected."

"Who are these two beautiful children I've seen in your garden?" Eva took plastic wrap off the plate she'd laid on the table. "Come to Bubbe. That's what all the grandchildren call me. I'm sure you like Hungarian blintzes? Everyone does."

Count on Eva to keep an eye on what was going on at their home. With the houses sharing a common wall and their kitchen windows not far apart, as well as plenty of time on her hands since she retired, Eva had become like family.

The children clung closer to Tamar.

"Mary and Joey are from Sudan but they're living with us now."

Mary and Joey stared at the plate of rolled crepes filled with sweet cream cheese. Tamar cut a blintz in half and handed a piece to each child. After watching Mary take a nibble, Joey did the same.

"Nu? Bubbe knows how to cook. Next time I'll bring you my apple strudel. And not to forget goulash. We'll get some fat on those bones in no time." She turned to Tamar. "Tammy bubileh, you're not eating?"

"We ... I am a vegan now. That means no eggs and cheese."

"Not even a bite?!" They did look delicious, and the sweet smell of fried butter was tempting; but either she was a vegan or she wasn't, and Tamar was determined to go all the way.

"How's Yakov? Haven't seen him for a while," Tamar said.

Mary and Joey wiped their mouths with the backs of their hands and eyed the plate.

"One more and then go play in your room."

Eva leaned back in her chair. "First tell me about Mary and Joey, and then I'll tell you about Yakov."

Tamar tried to make the story short.

"That's wonderful," Eva said. "I'm proud of you. You have a big heart making your home open to Yakov and me and inviting us for holidays. Even our own children..."

Tamar knew that Eva and Yakov's relationship with their children was problematic—typical for Holocaust survivors.

"You give to us too," Tamar said. "Grandparents next door." She could never let her mother hear her say that.

"Sometimes, you'll wonder if you took on too much." Eva laid her hand on Tamar's. "But you can do it, you have a wonderful husband, and we're here to help. Those children need a lot of love. I still remember when I arrived at my new family. ..."

Eva's eyes teared as they did every time she told her story. "My parents did the bravest thing they could by giving me to their Christian neighbors. And that family raised me as their own."

Tamar and Eva sat in silence, letting the memories wash over them, hearing in the background the happy chattering of Mary and Joey at play.

"You know their two daughters came to Israel and planted trees at Yad Vashem on behalf of their parents?"

Tamar had heard this story many times. "Wonderful. You're still in touch with them?"

"Nu, mishpocheh. They wanted us to come to Hungary, but by the time we found them, Yakov couldn't travel."

"Now tell me about Yakov."

Eva sighed. "More forgetful lately. He can't play chess anymore with his friends in the park, because he can't concentrate, and he can't volunteer with the special needs children he loved."

"The children must miss him."

"He's been going to the shop for me to buy groceries, but two days ago I gave him a list with ten items, and he came back with only halva and olives. I didn't say anything."

"Poor guy. And you too."

"I tried to talk to our children about it, but they aren't taking me seriously. They haven't seen their father for six months, so they don't understand."

Tamar felt the heaviness of her friend's problem.

"And we almost don't have friends left in Eilat," Eva continued. "Some moved to the north to be closer to their children." Her voice trailed off. "And others ... sadly ..."

"Why don't you come for dinner on Friday night?" It wouldn't be a problem since Abba and Imma wouldn't be here this weekend. If Imma could get past her jealousy of Tamar's neighbor, surely she and Eva could be friends.

"I'd like Mary and Joey to get to know you, and they'll be good for Yakov."

"I'll bring goulash and make some vegan on the side for you."

74

15

The weekend hadn't gone as quickly or smoothly as Tamar had hoped. She'd tried, though, to get to know Mary and Joey and help them to feel at home. As Steve liked to say, "a journey of a thousand miles begins with one step." At least they'd taken a few steps. Things were bound to get easier ... weren't they? The last thing she wanted was for a wedge to come between her and Steve—or worse, to damage her own children—because of her impulsive idea.

Returning to work at the clinic on Monday, Tamar was back in her familiar environment and routine. She was happy in the morning to see that little Ethiopian baby gaining weight since his mother had begun using the correct amount of formula. The mother was smiling more, too, and hopefully getting treatment for AIDS—though, of course, she couldn't ask about that.

Her first case in the afternoon was a newborn called Noam Shemtov. When she began as a Tipat Halav nurse, Noam was always a boy's name, but these days you never know. The grandmother came in with the mother and baby, a common occurrence.

"What a beautiful baby," Tamar said. She liked to open all visits on a positive note—especially the first time, to establish rapport and reassure the mother she was a good parent.

""Have a seat, please. I'm Tamar. You must be Elisheva. ... And this is your mother?"

"Yes," the grandmother said, looking around. "I'm Dalia. Can you believe I brought Elisheva to this same Tipat Halav?" She glanced around "The clinic looks better these days, more friendly, and I see you've computerized."

Tamar was interested. "If you brought your baby here, you must be one of the founding families of Eilat."

"I came with my husband when we finished the army. He worked in the port and I worked, and still do, in the Ministry of Interior. Eilat has changed since those days, not that I like the changes, but what can you do?"

"I love his name," Tamar said. "Noam, pleasant or beauty. Reminds me of the verse from Psalms, 'Behold the beauty of the Lord.'"

Elisheva nodded, a smile parting her lips. "My husband suggested it."

"I told Elisheva it was confusing," Dalia said. "Many girls are named Noam these days, I told her to call him after my father, Shmuel, blessed be his name. That's a strong boy's name."

Noam began whimpering.

Tamar turned to Elisheva who was trying to put the pacifier in Noam's mouth. "I want to ask you a few questions. Tell me about the birth."

"I was with her all the time," Dalia said. "Twenty-four hours and she nearly needed a vacuum, but finally Noam was born naturally, thanks to God."

"And what about breastfeeding, Elisheva?" She'd seen some pushy grandmothers, but this one broke the records.

"It's something I knew I'd do," Elisheva said. "I'm a lawyer and have taken a leave of absence. My partners are filling in so I can give time to Noam and continue to breastfeed for at least half a year." A lawyer must be a good orator, but when Dalia was around, Elisheva didn't have much to say. Elisheva gazed admiringly at Noam kicking his legs while lying in his stroller.

"Fabulous. It's time to weigh him. Elisheva, can you lay Noam on the table and undress him please?" For Tamar, this visit wasn't only about weight gain, but to get a feeling of how the mother was doing, and how she responded to her child. She paid attention to the naked infant's skin tone, joints, and skeleton.

"Come here, bubi!" Tamar lifted Noam and placed him on the scale. She glanced at his chart and then at the scale. "Fabulous! He's back to his birth weight and even gained six hundred grams." Elisheva looked at her mother, and they both beamed.

"I'll measure his crown and fontanels so we can continue to track his growth," Tamar said. "You can dress him again. Do you feel you need a home visit? We do that sometimes." She recorded everything in the computer and in the mother's Tipat Halav card.

"In our day, the nurse always came to our house, but Elisheva doesn't need help. I'm here for her," Dalia said. "You can give Noam to me."

"Your first grandchild?" Tamar asked. "Wonderful they live in Eilat so you can help your daughter and be involved." *Hopefully not too involved.* She handed Noam to Elisheva.

"I thought I'd be retiring on the first of January and caring for him full-time when Elisheva returns to work, but they're pressuring me to stay on another year," Dalia said. "Hard to find people willing to come to Eilat and who know what they're doing, especially these days when we're swamped with work. In all my years, I've never seen anything like this." She shook her head and frowned.

Tamar nodded absentmindedly, looking at her computer to see who was coming next, but Dalia had grabbed the baton and was off running.

"Those black people, infiltrators!" Dalia raised her voice. "Taking over our town. You see them everywhere, mostly hanging out on the street corners. I'm afraid to walk around alone anymore. Thieves and rapists, the way they look at you, it's awful. I've heard millions are lying in wait at the border to get in."

Elisheva gently laid Noam on his back in the stroller and stood up. "Imma—"

"And these do-gooder, north Tel Aviv types think we should help them." Dalia was unstoppable. "As if we don't have enough needy people in Israel, like those who live near Gaza and have bombs falling on them."

Tamar turned her head and looked at the clock on the wall in an obvious way, hoping Dalia would take the hint. She didn't want to argue, that would be unethical, and she couldn't imagine Leah's reaction if she entered the room and found Tamar facing off with a grandmother about the Sudanese refugees. Better be careful not to let this get out of hand. But on the other hand, was she supposed to sit here and listen to this spouting-off?

"You know what's the worst part?" Dalia said to no one in particular. "In the Ministry of Interior, we're supposed to be registering them. We were busy enough without this tsunami of blacks. I've reached my limit, that's for sure. I say we dump them on the other side of the border where they came from."

"I hear you," Tamar said, trying to say something to end the conversation, or monologue. "You feel overwhelmed with the extra work. I wouldn't want to see our small country overrun by Africans, either, though I doubt millions are trying to get in. The way I see it, we have to treat those already here in a human way. That's how I read the Torah." At least she said something.

"Imma, really..."

As Elisheva opened the door and pushed Noam's stroller into the waiting room, another woman stuck her head in. "I don't have all day," she said. "My older son comes home soon from kindergarten."

Tamar hadn't expected to encounter such hatred at work. She was trying to find the right balance between speaking up for justice while not offending a patient.

16

Tamar rang the buzzer on the bolted outside door at the Welfare Office, was admitted into the waiting room, and walked up to the counter. Though she'd been here before in her capacity as a nurse, this was her first time asking for help.

"I don't have an appointment," she said to the secretary. "But I need to speak to someone. To clarify a few things."

"Please sit down and I'll see if someone has time for you," the secretary said. "Wait, aren't you Tamar from Tipat Halav? I can tell you that the family, where the father had to be put under a restraining order because of violence in the home, is in counseling." Here we go again. Small town. Everyone knows everyone.

Her face heated up. "Actually, that's not the reason I'm here," she said. "It's something personal." Was she imagining the clerk looking at her strangely? *Calm down. No reason to be ashamed. We aren't doing anything illegal or immoral.*

The reactions from Leah and Dalia made it clear that many people in town weren't in favor of the refugees; but surely the social services would understand the importance of arranging a stable living environment for two abandoned and vulnerable children. She knew Steve was right when he told her they had to officially establish their role as a foster family. In fact, that was one of the conditions he laid down before they took the children. She avoided the "A" word with Steve, but that could come in time.

"If their mother ever turns up, or their supposed aunt or anyone, they could accuse us of kidnapping," Steve had said. "And we need health insurance and papers to register them for school."

She hoped to get Mary and Joey in a regular school soon. And concerning a health fund, all children got sick, and Joey looked especially vulnerable, though with her healthy cooking, good hygiene, and most of all, love, he'd soon fatten up and become stronger.

Tamar sat down on the molded plastic chair and gazed around at the other people waiting, envisioning the tragic stories that brought them to this office. And now she was one of them, a client waiting for a social worker. She jumped to her feet when the secretary called her name.

"Tamar, you can step into the second room on the right. Estie has ten minutes before she leaves for a home visit."

The poor social workers were so overworked, so although generally professional and friendly, they often didn't have enough time to devote to each case. She hoped for someone sympathetic.

Tamar entered the room and closed the door. "I'm Tamar Goldman. I live in Eilat, work at Tipat Halav, and have some questions."

"I'm Estie," the young woman with long, dark ponytail said. "I don't have much time, but sit down. How can I help you?"

Give me the right words. "In my work at Tipat Halav, we vaccinated the Sudanese refugee children who live in Kibbutz Eilot. Later, I went there a few times to bring them my children's old toys. I noticed a young brother and sister who were obviously neglected. Rivka, the kibbutznik responsible for the refugees, told me their mother left them with an aunt, and on a later visit she suggested my family take them home or else they'd be sent to an orphanage. Rivka said this after speaking with the social worker from the kibbutz."

Estie nodded, and occasionally wrote notes. "And you took them?" Her sincerity was encouraging.

"I told Rivka I needed to speak to my husband and two

children. I'd already brought them home to a family birthday party."

"Have you ever applied to be a foster family?"

"No. But even my husband realized this was a special case, and we'd quickly become attached to Mary and Joey, so last week we brought them home." Although she'd always wanted a larger family, fostering had never been on her agenda. "Now we need your help for official documentation."

Estie sat up straight and looked straight at Tamar. "What you're asking, as I understand, is for me to grant you custody of two Sudanese refugee children?"

"And it would be useful if we could get the documents quickly, because Joey's eye infection needs treatment." Tamar twirled one of her curls between her fingers.

"You said this is a special case, and it is," Estie said. "We're aware of many social problems among the illegal migrants, but we have yet to deal with children among this group who need foster care. Furthermore, we have our procedures and a number of criteria that must be met in order to become a foster family." She reached into her desk drawer, pulled out a packet, and handed it to Tamar. "Take this home, read it, and you'll understand more." Estie pushed her chair back and fingered the star of David pendant around her neck.

Tamar's eyes blurred as she glanced over the small writing and the eight points on the first page.

"As you can see, you and your husband will need to fill out a rather lengthy form, supply a doctor's confirmation of good health, pay slips to prove you have a suitable income, references from different entities in the community who know you, and have a series of interviews."

"Sounds more complicated than I expected. How long should we expect this process to take?"

"Normally, we're talking about several months. However, we

may be able to speed things up, with God's help, since the children are already with you ... depending, of course, on what my supervisor says about undocumented aliens. Ask the secretary to make an appointment for a home visit, and we'll discuss the next steps, with God's help. I really must be going." She stood up, and as she went out the door, Estie brushed her fingers over the mezuzah on the door post and kissed her fingers.

A special case, several months, undocumented aliens. It didn't sound promising.

17

Gali, motek." Tamar held the phone to her ear while picking through the tomatoes for the reddest ones. "I tried to call a few minutes ago but the number was busy." Surprising, since her son seldom used the phone. "I forgot to check how much milk we have. Can you please look while I hang on?"

"Sure, Mommy, but would you buy something else besides that yucky oat milk?"

Tamar rarely left the children alone, but today she didn't have a choice.

After a few weeks, Mary and Joey were settling in as well as could be expected, although Joey still wouldn't take a bath and their table manners left a lot to be desired. Besides the fact that they ate with their hands, they seemed to be either picking at their food or stuffing it into their mouths. They hadn't yet moved to their own room, not Steve's first choice, but he was trying to be a good sport, and hopefully they'd soon be ready. Most of the time, Arava and Gal were trying their best to make Mary and Joey feel at home by sitting with them and drawing pictures, reading stories, and watching cartoons together.

Still, life with four children was hectic. Especially in the morning, trying to get everyone ready for school. She hadn't been to folk dancing in ages and needed to get back for the sake of her mental as well as physical health, the only activity she did all week for herself. She wasn't losing weight as quickly as she would have liked with the vegan diet, in fact a half kilo in a month couldn't really even count. Hopefully as her body adjusted and she returned to folk dancing, she'd see the kilos fall off.

But to get to her folk dancing class tonight, they had to eat dinner early, and to eat early she had to run to the supermarket. Last week she took Mary and Joey with her, but they were so distracted by all the food on the shelves, it took her twice as long as whipping through alone. Gal was home with his new friend, Ben, and Steve had called that he was on his way home. The children would be home alone for five minutes at the most. More than she liked, but Steve and Michal would be proud of her for loosening up a little. Not that she wanted to make this a habit, but good to know it worked when necessary, like today.

"Only one?" Tamar said. "Thought so. We're drinking a lot with Mary and Joey here. What are they doing now? Still watching the cartoon I put on?" She moved to the cucumbers.

"What do you mean, you don't see them?" Her breath caught in her throat. She put down the plastic bag of cukes. "I thought you were together. Where's Daddy? Not home yet?" Did something happen to him, an accident on his bicycle?

Her body tensed, and she tried not to raise her voice. "You were talking to Savta on the phone in the other room and when you came back, they were gone? Gali, I thought I could trust you. Maybe they're in the bathroom." Her worst nightmare. Gal was usually responsible. "Look around some more and call me back. I'll call Daddy and come home right away."

She held onto the cart as her head spun. Should she first call Steve or rush straight home, leaving the shopping behind? With a shaking hand she pressed the speed dial on her phone.

"Where are you?" She couldn't help herself, even if people turned their heads as she yelled in the phone. "Getting off your bike at home? A grad student cornered you and needed advice as you left work? Don't your children need you? Gal just informed me that Mary and Joey are missing. Yes, missing as in gone, disappeared from the house." She couldn't trust anyone, not Steve, not Gal, not even herself.

"I'm on my way and in the meantime, you, Gal, and Ben begin searching the neighborhood. They're little." At least children weren't snatched off the streets like in America, and when she and Steve drove them from the kibbutz to their house the second time, she noticed their remarkable sense of direction.

Trembling, she threw her phone in her purse and fumbled for her car keys while rushing to the supermarket's entrance. Suddenly she stopped short. It couldn't be. Two skinny black children holding hands and peering inside. Seeing her, they ran and grabbed her waist, wide smiles spreading across their faces. "Mommy!"

Her heart was beating as if she'd run a sprint. "Mary, Joey! What are you doing here? How did you find me? Didn't I tell you to wait for me at home?" *Don't be upset. This isn't the time to be angry with them.* Tamar squatted down and hugged them.

"Gal was talking on the phone," Mary said.

"He wasn't playing with us," Joey said. "We like buying food with you. Can you buy chocolate milk again?"

"Bubi, of course, we'll get chocolate milk. But let me call Daddy." Tamar held their hands and walked back to where she left her shopping cart.

"They're here," she told Steve. "Somehow, they walked all the way to the supermarket and waited for me at the entrance. We'll be home soon."

She had to be careful not to be angry with Steve. He was known as a teacher who always had time for his students, and now she was asking him to change. He wasn't complaining, but she sensed an undercurrent of annoyance and tension. Sometimes it seemed like he went through the motions of bathing, feeding, and reading stories but his heart was someplace else. Gal could lose patience with Mary and Joey's whining, and she didn't want to see a repeat of that blowout fight that happened after they took apart the Lego fighter jet he had received for his birthday. He'd spent hours building it with Ben.

How could she be angry with them when it was her fault? Bad judgement to think she could leave them to go folk dancing. Better cross that off the list for the next few years. Who said life with two foster children would be easy?

18

Exactly at the appointed time, Tamar heard a knock at the door, which had been left open so they didn't have to get up when neighbor children came over.

Tamar got up to greet Estie. "Shalom! Welcome and thanks for coming." *I hope I sound calmer than I feel.*

She tried to look at her house objectively—toys straightened in the children's rooms, beds made so they'd pass inspection in the army. The furniture was dusted, and there were no dishes in the sink. But what about their old sofa bequeathed by Imma and Abba after they bought a new living room set? It had smeared chocolate cake stains and the red splotch from the l'chaim for Steve's birthday party when Gal accidentally bumped into him?

She was afraid from the document Estie gave her about how many square meters the foster children's bedroom had to be, that their porch, turned office, turned mini bedroom, wouldn't pass. The pictures on one wall, the mural with a sun, flowers, and birds she'd painted on the other, and the Disney duvet covers at least gave it a cheerful touch. Never mind that Mary and Joey weren't sleeping there yet. Would Estie see that as positive or negative?

Steve was sure they were ready to move to their own room, but Tamar kept giving in to their pleading. Steve said he missed their special time together at the end of the day, and it wasn't the same with two little children sleeping next to them, but she found herself flopping into bed and asleep in an instant.

Adoption was still a sensitive subject, but she was certain the topic would come up today and could already visualize Mary and Joey joining her family for good. Their mother was gone, her family loved them, what could make more sense?

Tamar made sure to be home early and found a time when Arava and Gal were at their clubs. This would keep down the noise level in the beginning until they came home, and then she'd introduce them to the social worker.

"My pleasure." Estie touched the mezuzah and kissed her fingers as she stepped inside. "It's part of my job, but I do enjoy getting out of the office and seeing how people live."

"Have a seat. Coffee, tea, water?" Without waiting for an answer, Tamar poured a glass of cold water and set a fruit bowl on the table, making coffee for herself.

"Water's fine."

Steve rose from working at his computer in the corner and sat down next to Tamar. Estie said it was important that Steve be there, and he'd even agreed to put on a shirt without holes and a pair of shorts instead of his usual bathing suit.

"This is my husband, Steve." Tamar hoped her voice sounded natural. She turned to where the children were playing.

"Mary and Joey, can you say shalom to Estie?" They were slowly learning to play with toys and liked building houses with blocks. Tamar had positioned them in the corner of the living room and, for a few minutes at least, they were playing peacefully.

Mary frowned, shrugged her shoulders, and looked at the floor while Joey jumped up and threw himself on Estie who tried to regain her composure and fell back against the sofa pillows. Tamar knew you couldn't dictate children's behavior, especially when they had been with you a short time, but she wondered which appeared more troubling, Mary's refusal to cooperate or Joey's over exuberance? They both looked expectantly at the fruit bowl.

"Take some grapes, and when you're finished, you can draw pictures in your room." Tamar tried to give the impression of a capable mother.

Estie opened her briefcase and took out a folder, as well as her laptop. "Nice house. I'm only three years in Eilat, coming from Sderot, and it's fun to find gems like yours hidden in old neighborhoods."

Gems? Nice house? Sounded positive. Coming from Sderot and with her mezuzah kissing, Estie was obviously from a traditional family and must have been through a lot with the shelling of her town and days spent in bomb shelters. Tamar tried to free her thoughts from wandering and analyzing too much and to concentrate on Estie sitting in front of them.

Estie flipped through the papers Tamar had submitted. "You've done a good job with your documentation. Confirmation of good health, pay slips, references from work colleagues and friends, police certificate of good conduct, and the form with your signatures acknowledging you accept our conditions."

Arava and Gal suddenly bounded into the house, heading toward the fruit bowl before stopping and remembering they were supposed to greet guests.

"Our two children, Arava and Gal." Tamar said. "This is Estie, the social worker who came to talk to us about Mary and Joey. How was Scouts today?"

"Fun! We're planning our Hanukkah party and inviting the people from the old age home," Arava said. "I'm playing a game with them, charades because many don't speak Hebrew, only Russian."

"And our group is making crowns for their heads." Gal picked up an apple and took a bite.

"I'm sure you both have homework so can you try to get it done before dinner?"

"Did you tell Estie my birthday's next week?" Gal said.

"Wonderful. How old will you be?"

"Eleven. We're going to eat a shawarma with all the family, and my friends are coming over for pizza and a movie."

"Sounds like fun. Happy birthday already."

Estie put down the papers and fingered the star of David around her neck. "I see you have your hands full, so in summary, we were able to grant you custody of the two children for three months. I'll begin visiting the children regularly, God willing. I'm sure you'll have questions as things progress, so don't hesitate to contact us. We have psychologists available for you and the children, school expenses will be covered, and your monthly grant will come to your bank account, with God's help."

When Tamar and Steve decided to foster Mary and Joey, they weren't thinking about receiving a payment, but she couldn't object.

"And one more thing," Estie said, smoothing out her skirt before preparing to stand up, "In case you'd thought about adopting them at a future time, I wouldn't count on it, according to the guidelines we received from the Ministry of Interior. Even to register you as a foster family, we had to proceed under the radar—that is, not to publicize it in any way. As you probably understand, our mayor doesn't want refugees in Eilat and certainly doesn't want refugee children in the foster system."

19

"What will it be?" Steve asked as the children jostled for chairs, Joey making sure to sit as close as possible to Steve. "Shawarma or falafel? Everyone can choose what they want and a drink too." Steve was feeling generous. Normally he ordered water for everyone.

They didn't eat out often. Who could afford it? Even fast food in Israel wasn't cheap like in Canada, as Tamar noticed the couple of times they'd visited Steve's family. She could cook a good, healthy meal for a fraction of what it cost in a restaurant. But once in a while, they liked to splurge and because it was rare, Arava and Gal enjoyed it even more.

Tamar wanted to do something special with the family for Gal's birthday. After a month having Mary and Joey with them, it would be a good time for bonding at their favorite falafel and shawarma joint.

"Felafel for me," Tamar said. "And water."

"I'll have a shawarma," Steve said. "Wouldn't mind meat for a change, and cider. What about you kids?"

"Shawarma!" Gal piped up, his eyes widening. "And coke!" Two foods they never ate at home.

Arava looked at Tamar. "I'll have a shawarma too, if you don't mind, and lemonade."

"Whatever you want," Tamar said. She could change the diet at home but not their tastes. "Now Mary and Joey can choose."

They both looked expectantly at Steve. They probably didn't even know what either a falafel or a shawarma was.

"This place does halves," he said. "I'll get them each half a shawarma and an orange juice to share. Arava can come with me to fill the pitas with salads. Everyone wants a bit of everything? Tehina but no hot sauce?"

While Steve and Arava stood in line for the five shawarmas and one felafel, people were streaming to the parking lot opposite them and milling around in front of a podium that had been set up. By the time Steve and Arava returned to the table with the food and drinks, a noticeable crowd had gathered, some carrying banners and others lifting placards in the air.

"Let's pray," said Steve, closing his eyes and bowing his head. "Thank you God that we can come eat shawarma and felafel for Gal's birthday and that Mary and Joey are with us."

When they opened their eyes, the mass of people was becoming noisy and agitated, and police had appeared.

Tamar pursed her lips together in a faint smile. "Good appetite." She looked at Steve, raising her eyebrows slightly. "Enjoy your shawarmas and drinks. Steve, can you help Joey hold his and I'll help Mary?"

"Mommy," Gal picked up pieces of cucumbers and tomatoes that had fallen on the table. "What's going on over there? Why are people shouting, and why did the police come?"

"Don't you see what's written on the signs?" Arava squinted and read aloud: "'Sudanese go home.' 'No infiltrators.' 'Eilat for Eilati's.' 'Protect our families.'"

"Why do they say that?" Gal wiped his mouth with the back of his hand. "What's wrong with Sudanese? Where do they want the refugees to go?" Gal had heard enough discussions in their house to understand they had no place to return to.

"Of course, there's nothing wrong with Sudanese." Steve held Joey's hands in his and helped him bring the pita to his mouth. "Good?"

Tamar scanned the crowd to see if she recognized anyone—a certainty in small-town Eilat—all the while trying to help Mary not to spill the contents of her shawarma. "Another bite, bubi? You like it, don't you?"

Arava must have had the same idea. "There's a girl from my class, with her mother. And Leah, your boss from work."

Bad news, but not surprising. Tamar could only hope Leah didn't see her with Mary and Joey, dreading the conclusions she might draw and the implications for her job.

A smaller group of people stationed themselves opposite the first group, also carrying signboards. This group was quieter, and their placards said, 'Love your neighbor as yourself' and 'Love the stranger.'

Bad luck that they chose this day and place to eat out. Why hadn't she heard about a demonstration against the Sudanese? Even the mayor was here—in fact, he was the leader and the first speaker.

She wiped tehina from Mary's mouth. "Well done, you finished your shawarma. One more gulp and you've finished your orange juice too. Let's get going and have dessert at home." Looking at Mary's innocent face, tears came to her eyes. What had this sweet girl done to bother anyone? Or, for that matter, the rest of the Sudanese—people like us who only wanted to escape from war and persecution and raise their children in peace. Thankfully, Mary and Joey seemed oblivious to the protest across the street and the people walking by their table and staring.

Rising to leave, Tamar and Steve gripped Mary and Joey's hands. A middle-aged man approached them.

"Who are these children?" he asked.

Tamar flinched at his belligerent tone of voice. Steve's face muscles tightened. Even after fifteen years in Israel, he wasn't used to the in-your-face style of Israelis who said whatever was on their mind. Tamar actually preferred it to the overly nice, saccharine talk of North Americans.

Rather than ignore him, she wanted to give a message to her

family, and gave him her most polite smile while gazing in his eyes. "Our four children."

"Also these two?" He pointed his finger at Mary and Joey, who tightened their grips on her and Steve's hands.

Gal put his hands on his hips. "Didn't you ever hear of foster children? They live with our family, today's my birthday, and we're here to celebrate."

Wow, that's our boy.

A woman passing by stopped next to them. "Here, young man." She reached into her purse and pulled out her wallet. "I'd like to treat you and your family to ice cream. My birthday present. You've got a great family." She looked at Tamar. "Keep it up."

~

Soon after they arrived home, Eva came over. "Yakov and I were at the post office and saw the demonstration. Disgusting. They should be ashamed of themselves, and our mayor too. Reminds me of my town in Hungary when Nazis told people we Jews had no rights." She shook her head. "This isn't the Israel I knew."

"Did everyone finish their homework?" Steve was, thankfully, taking responsibility this evening to get the children to bed.

"You and Yakov still go out together?" Tamar motioned for Eva to sit down.

"I try to take him with me on errands." Eva bit her lip. "He'd rather stay home and watch television, but it's important that he leave the house."

Tamar sat down next to Eva, exhausted.

"Eilat's a hard place to grow old." Eva shook her head. "We're far from our children and there's no retirement facility except for in Maccabi which is for people who—"

"Not folks like you."

"We don't see any good options." She stared down at her fingers.

"A live-in caregiver?"

"Yakov couldn't accept a stranger living with us, and we turned the children's bedrooms into a rental unit."

"Moving to a retirement home near your children?"

"We'd love to be closer to our grandchildren, but when I try to talk to our children, they don't react." Eva nearly began to cry, and Tamar along with her.

"Besides television, he sits in the garden under his trees. He says it gives him peace and connects him to his family. I can't argue."

Tamar knew about those trees. When Eva and Yakov moved here forty years ago, they planted two trees in memory of their families who were murdered in the Holocaust. Yakov planted flowers under the trees and every year added a rock to the circle around them.

"He sits for hours in his chair staring into space and dozing off, says he couldn't leave his trees, but I don't see how we can go on like this."

Tamar gave Eva a long hug. Life was complicated and filled with hypocrisy. The hatred in those peoples' eyes. They didn't want the refugees here, but they gave them the jobs they wouldn't do themselves—without benefits, of course.

And poor Eva and Yakov, after all they'd been through. She wished she had a solution for them. Why didn't their children take more responsibility? But who was she to talk? Her relationship with Imma also left a lot to be desired. She hoped their visit next week would go well this time.

20

Tamar was taking a chance by having her parents join them for Steve's birthday celebration, but what could she do when they invited themselves? Imma didn't understand hints and subtleties.

"We thought to have a quiet party this year, just with the family," she had told Imma on the phone a few weeks ago. "The last months have been intense." She hoped Imma wouldn't interpret that negatively.

"Wonderful. Abba bought the special saw Steve wanted, so we'll bring it with us."

No, Tamar couldn't exclude her parents. And hopefully, after two months of having Mary and Joey with them, Imma would see how well the children were doing and the rest of the family was coping. Why did it seem they were going from crisis to crisis and that she collapsed in bed dead tired every night? She hadn't made a cake for ages, though people still called wanting to place orders; and reading her favorite food blogs was a distant memory.

"I guess Steve will want a picnic in the desert," Imma said. "I'll bring jachnun. Goes with everything."

That part Imma understood—the desert, Steve's favorite place except for under the sea. The desert and the sea were the two things that drew and held them in Eilat. Where else in the world could you find this combination?

"We'll meet you there," Imma said. "We have something already planned here on Friday evening."

"Nahal Mangan," Tamar said. "The children love sliding down the big sand dune."

≈

Steve pulled the car to a stop on the ridge, surveying the wadi below for an acacia tree to sit under.

"Oof, Saba and Savta beat us." Gal jumped out of the car and began running down the hill. "I wanted to be first, so I could help Saba start the fire."

"Wait a minute," Steve said. "Everyone carries something."

Imma stood up from her folding chair and hugged Steve, as the four children crowded around her. "Mazal tov!"

"Which psalm are you reading for us today?" Abba wrapped his arms around Steve.

"Psalm 41. I like the beginning."

"Thanks for inviting us," Imma beamed. "I wouldn't want to miss spending time with my favorite children."

"On our birthdays we read the psalm of how old we are," Arava turned to Mary who'd moved away and was sitting on a rock by herself.

"Come here, bubi," Tamar walked over and put her arm around Mary. What in her past might have caused this sulking and neediness?

"I'll make the pita dough." Abba dumped flour and water into his big bowl. "And while it's resting, you kids can run down the dune, and then come and help me."

Mary and Joey looked puzzled. Making fires, climbing sand dunes, these were new experiences for them.

Abba glanced up. "Nice place here next to Timna Park. I come here with hiking groups, and they always comment on the shapes and colors of the rocks. Americans say it reminds them of places in Utah."

Steve grasped Mary and Joey's hands while Arava and Gal charged ahead. "Let's go!"

With Abba sitting next to the fire pit, Tamar found herself

sitting next to her mother, wondering what she'd find to criticize this time.

"You and Steve look tired," Imma said. "Are you sure all this isn't too much?"

"I'm fine and Steve had early dives this week," Tamar said, "Desert trips wouldn't be the same without Abba's pitas. I even brought chicken wings to grill—Steve's favorite."

"Hope you don't mind I brought jachnun. I know we'll have pita, but what's Shabbat without jachnun?" Imma said. "And my zhug that Steve likes, goes with the hummus and labaneh. Where's Michal? Something between you two?"

"Special event at the Reef. Haven't seen her much lately, but no problems, don't worry." Tamar wondered if Michal's absence had to do with Yossi.

"Why was Mary pouting?" Imma asked. "And she looks awfully skinny."

"She does that a lot. She's been through a lot in her short life and seems to have an ongoing competition with Gal. Maybe this time he hugged you first." Tamar was trying to ignore Imma's usual negativity.

"The dough's ready." Abba took the towel off the balls he'd formed. "You can call the kids."

Tamar jumped up and, waving her hands, walked towards the dune, glad for an excuse to get away from Imma.

The children somersaulted down the dune and crowded around Abba, who began patting and rolling out one of the dough balls.

"Saba makes the best pitas," Gal said. Everything Saba did was the best.

"When I go out with groups around Arad," Abba explained, "we often stop at my friend Mohammed's house. His mother's amazing and took me through the pita-making process step-by-step from mixing the ingredients, getting them nice and flat, and baking them. Go ahead, kids, take one." Then he added, "I'm an amateur compared to Umm Mohammed. That's how they call a married woman, by the name of her oldest son.'"

Arava and Gal immediately got to work stretching and flattening their pitas while Mary and Joey stared, arms at their sides. Abba enjoyed inviting others to join him, even if their creations were lumpy and with holes. "Holey pitas," he called them.

"Sit on my lap." Tamar pulled Mary towards her. "We'll do it together. It's okay to get your hands dirty."

The smell of the grilled chicken brought back memories of Independence Day barbeques.

"Food's done," Steve said. "And everyone's hungry, so let's pray and eat, and I'll read the first verses from my psalm. 'Blessed is he who considers the helpless, he shall be called blessed upon the earth.' I have a lot to be thankful for."

Tamar admired how well Steve read Hebrew. God used his parents' sending him to the Toronto Jewish school to prepare him to move to Israel.

"Who noticed the red flowers on the acacia?" Abba looked up at the tree shading them.

"They're pretty but strange," Arava said. "They grow on a plant with bigger and shinier leaves than the acacia's small flat ones."

"Good observation," Abba said. "They're a parasite. Who knows what that is?"

"Like ticks on dogs," Gal said. "Ben's dog gets lots of ticks, and when they're full of blood they drop off. Yuck!"

"It's called the acacia strap flower," said Steve, knowledgeable in many other fields besides fish.

"It attaches itself on the acacia, lives off it as parasites do, and then kills its host tree," Abba said. "If we let bad thoughts or actions come into our life, they can also take over and maybe not kill us, but lead to bad results."

Tamar noticed the children listening attentively to Abba's explanations. Her relationship with her parents left room for improvement, but the children adored their grandparents and hung on every word.

Mary lay her head in Tamar's lap. She slept enough, so why was she always tired? Tamar had been trying not to think about it, together with Mary's constant thirst. And instead of filling out, Mary was losing weight. When she mentioned her concerns to Steve, who didn't notice appearances anyway, he told her not to worry. She tried, but at the same time wanted to act responsibly.

Imma pulled a colorful package from her shopping bag. "Look what else I brought! Marshmallows anyone?"

"Yay!" Gal stuck one on a stick.

"The coals are just right," said Abba. "Have Mary and Joey ever roasted marshmallows?"

Arava, who had a sweet way with the children, offered to show them how.

Steve flashed a grin at his mother-in-law Shoshana. "I never ate zhug till I came to your house. You told me it was Yemenite hot sauce you learned from your mother. Now it's mainstream, but I've never tasted any as good as yours."

A wide smile spread across Imma's face.

Abba lifted his little pot from the fire. "Turkish coffee anyone?"

"Too late for me," Steve said, "though I like the smell."

Mary was snoring quietly, and Tamar could feel the weight of a sleeping child. This tiredness and thirst …

Tamar loved being a nurse, helping mothers and babies, answering health questions for friends, and knowing first aid. On a trip with one of Abba's groups, a child fell off a camel and she bound up his arm and recommended he see a doctor. Or on the beach when tourists stepped on sea urchins and wanted to go to the hospital, and she assured them that soon the pain would subside, and the embedded spikes would dissolve.

But nursing had disadvantages, and sometimes she knew too much. Being pregnant as a nurse added stress, knowing what could go wrong. She had to force herself not to think of the difficult cases who came to her clinic and the rare ones she'd learned about in her studies. Could Mary really have childhood diabetes or was she imagining it?

"I asked you something." Steve touched Tamar's shoulder. "Were you dreaming? Do we have time for a little walk on the Israel Trail or are we in a hurry to get home?"

"I know you love to walk on parts of the Trail." Tamar noticed the sun low on the horizon. "But Mary fell asleep, and the kids have school tomorrow. Next time."

Tamar kissed Mary on her forehead. "Wake up." She resolved to call the pediatrician tomorrow for an appointment. Thankfully, health insurance had soon been arranged, but if this was diabetes, she didn't want to think about where this might lead.

21

I don't have to go to gan today," Mary announced at breakfast. "Mommy and I are going out together."

To hear the children call her Mommy still made Tamar swallow.

"Tomorrow, we're going to the doctor," Tamar had told Mary as she tucked her in bed the night before. "And then we'll go to Aroma for something to drink."

"What's Aroma?" Mary asked.

"You remember when we sat with the family at that café near the beach and you and Joey had smoothies?"

Mary nodded. She was a bottomless pit for attention—no matter how much they gave, she needed more. If Mary wasn't the first to be served food, she felt ignored. Arava was usually patient, but Gal shot furious glances when she whined and cried. Refusing to be alone in a room with the door closed, last night Mary shrieked when Gal walked by the bathroom while she was on the toilet and absentmindedly shut the door. *Irritability is another sign of diabetes. Could it be—?*

"What happens at a doctor?" Mary said.

"We'll go to an office, wait for our turn, and a nice lady will talk to us." Poor Mary, she had no idea what was in store for her, but soon they'd have answers.

Tamar could have tried to remind Mary of the visit to the well-baby clinic for the vaccinations where all this began a lifetime ago. But reminding her of getting a shot wouldn't bring back the happiest associations.

The next day, as hand in hand they entered the health clinic, the thought flashed through Tamar's mind that for years she had visualized and planned ways to enlarge their family. But who would have thought the first chaotic, screaming encounter with Sudanese children would lead to Mary and Joey joining their family?!

"You can sit on this chair at the table and draw a picture while we wait for the lady to call your name," Tamar said to Mary.

"What shall I draw?"

"Whatever you like. Yesterday you made a nice flower at daycare. Maybe you want to make another one and give it to the doctor."

Mary chose bright crayons and focused on her picture.

As much as Tamar dreaded a diagnosis, it would be better to know.

"Mary Thon please," the secretary said and indicated the open door.

"Our turn," Tamar said to Mary. "The doctor will ask us a few questions, and then we'll go to Aroma,"

An older woman with dyed-black hair and a red dress smiled as they entered her office. "Shalom. I'm Dr. Marina. How are you today, and how can I help?"

"I'm Tamar and this is Mary."

"Aren't you a nurse at the well-baby clinic? I remember you from when I filled in there."

As usual, no incognito for her in Eilat.

Mary sat on Tamar's lap. "What about your picture of the sun and flowers, Mary?"

"It's for you," Mary pushed it towards the doctor while looking at the plate of chocolate wafers on her desk.

"Would you like one, Mary?"

Mary reached for one.

"What do you say?"

"Thank you."

Tamar didn't have the heart to tell Mary that soon she'd probably need to stop eating sugar. Why not give her a few more days?

"I'm concerned with symptoms I see," Tamar said. "When Mary and her brother came to live with us a few months ago, they were both skinny and we hoped they'd gain weight with healthy and plentiful food. Joey's filled out, but Mary is losing weight no matter what she eats. She's thirsty all the time, urinates a lot, and wets her bed.

Mary held the half-eaten cookie in her hand while she dozed off with her head on Tamar's shoulder.

"And she falls asleep at strange times."

"What about irritability? And does her breath smell fruity?"

"Mary is a moody and emotionally needy child, but we don't know if this is from trauma, her personality, or something else. And yes, I did notice a fruity smell on her breath."

Dr. Marina looked with kind eyes at Mary and then at Tamar. "I'm sorry but, as you probably know, all these signs are indications. And according to recent studies, a traumatic event during childhood can triple the risk of developing Type 1 diabetes. From what I've read about the Sudanese refugees, she has undoubtedly been through multiple traumas."

Tamar nodded. In the beginning, Joey was the sickly one; but now he was thriving physically and Mary probably has an autoimmune disease. *You never know the effect of different risk factors.*

"As a nurse, you must know the next step."

"I know she needs blood tests but can't remember which ones after all my years since finishing nursing school."

"On your way out, you'll make an appointment with our secretary for the A1C test, a simple blood test done without fasting, but which gives an accurate diagnosis. The outcome is reported as a percentage which I'm sure you'll be able to interpret. Afterward we'll do regular follow-ups to monitor the levels. At the same time, you can make another appointment with me to discuss the results, further steps, and treatment if necessary."

Tamar drew a deep breath and closed her eyes for an instant. *All things work together for good for those who love God.* What good could come from an innocent little girl, who already suffered so much, having to receive daily insulin shots and follow a strict diet? And the extra work as the mother of a diabetic child? Or was that selfish thinking?

Tamar's mind flashed back to when Gal fell out of the treehouse in their backyard head first onto the tiles below. With blood streaming from his head, she lifted him and drove to the hospital.

He screamed all the way in the car. "Mommy! I'm sorry!" But she was the one who should be sorry. *I failed to protect my son.*

"Hold him tightly so he doesn't move," the doctor had said, as he prepared to stitch the gash on Gal's forehead. Tamar had practiced this procedure in nursing school but not with her own child.

"Mommy!"

She looked away and tried to close her ears. She learned that day that she couldn't nurse her own children.

Tamar kissed the top of Mary's head, waking her up gently. "Bubi, you didn't finish your cookie. Remember our date at Aroma? I could use a coffee. What will you drink? A smoothie?"

"Be strong," the doctor said. "And see you next week."

Between the blood test and their next doctor's visit, at least their planned visit to the Dolphin Reef on Shabbat gave something to look forward to.

22

Her blonde hair pulled back in a ponytail, and wearing a purple swim shirt, Michal looked up from the raft where she was feeding the dolphins and saw a bunch of waving arms at the top of the steps. You could spot those two little, black cuties a kilometer away.

"Michaaaal!"

She motioned to Arava and Gal who had begun running toward her, to find a spot in the shade. Finishing the third feeding today, she was due a break and could hang out with the family.

When she came to them, all four children jumped on her with hugs.

Tamar gave a hug too. "Thanks for inviting us. It's been a while. Life's busy, but the kids've been looking forward to this. At least Arava and Gal have. Mary and Joey don't really know what to expect."

Michal smiled to hear Arava and Gal trying to get Mary and Joey excited. "You sit on the pier, splash your feet in the water, and—" said Arava.

"And the dolphins come up to you," added Gal. Sitting on a chair, he demonstrated by kicking his feet in the air, while Mary laughed and imitated him. But at the mention of water Joey looked down.

"The dolphins smile," Arava said, "and jump and twist in the air. Michal knows their names and says they're her friends."

The children had picked up her love for dolphins and for this special place that was like a second home to Michal, at times even her first home. Some people found it strange when she said the dolphins were part of the closest circle in her life so she didn't say it to everyone. But Yossi understood. Maybe all he'd been through helped him understand.

∼

The Dolphin Reef had been packed with people all summer, and Tamar also seemed to be running at more than full speed lately. Always high energy, but usually in a happy way, now she often looked tense and tired. Sometimes Michal wondered if Tamar and Steve hadn't taken on more than they could handle, though she could see the determination and satisfaction in Tamar as she rose to her role as a mother of four children. Taking Kinneret home, a dirty little puppy with no training, had been a big change in Michal's life and kept her busy in the beginning, but it gave her purpose and filled a void. Perhaps fostering these children did the same for Tamar.

Today should be relaxing, but with Mary's sulking and Joey's fear of water, you never knew how things would turn out. And she hoped Mary's recent doctor's appointment, that Tamar had told her about, wasn't anything serious. Kids and dogs easily come down with things.

But what a privilege to work here, unlike any other beach in Eilat. The Dolphin Reef was an exotic oasis with lush vegetation, peacocks, amazing views of the mountains, and with no strict routine—her perfect job. And, of course, there were the dolphins. If a dolphin was sick, she gladly came in after working hours to care for him.

"Look!" Gal grabbed Mary's arm, turned her around and pointed to a dolphin leaping out of the water in the distance. "Did you see it?"

"I did. What's that one's name?" Arava asked Michal.

"Gal pushed me," Mary said, moving away and beginning to cry.

"Bubi, that doesn't make you feel good, does it?" Tamar put her arm around Mary. "But I think he was trying to show you the jumping dolphin."

Tamar turned to Gal, "Don't push Mary next time, okay?"

"That was Coco," Michal said.

"How can you tell them apart?" Joey asked.

"By their appearance and personalities. Each one has a different character, like people, and even mood swings."

"You told us once they talk to each other," Gal said.

"They have voices, a language, and even names for each other."

"They talk to you, too?" Mary began to become interested.

"We also say a lot of things to each other without words, using our bodies."

"It's called body language," Arava said. "Our counselor was telling us about it in Scouts. She's studying psychology."

"This is how we communicate with people closest to us. Because it's body language and not words, sometimes I know the dolphins better than people," Michal said.

Tamar plopped into one of the beach chairs. "I could use an iced coffee."

"I'll go pick it up," Steve said.

"Soy milk and no sugar."

"Cool, go for it. Use my employee discount," Michal said. "Okay kids, let's go swimming!"

She wanted to give Tamar a break for a few minutes and wondered how Yossi's mother managed with ten children, keeping them from fighting and giving each one attention. People said that with large families, the older ones took care of the younger ones, but she didn't see that happening here, yet. Anyway, Yossi's family wasn't an example, with his parents divorced and the children scattered. But as Steve said, it worked for the good, because Yossi left the religious sect he grew up in, moved to Eilat, and here they were.

Gal dumped out the contents of the beach bag. "I need my mask,"

Arava grabbed hers, too, and the two of them went charging to the water and threw themselves in.

Michal took Mary and Joey's hands. "Let's go!" But neither child budged, instead moving closer to Tamar.

"Swimming's fun!" said Michal. "You don't have to be scared. Dolphins are big but friendly and they like children. And there's a net between where they swim and where we do."

Mary took a shovel and bucket from the spilled contents of the beach bag and began moving sand around. Joey settled into Tamar's lap.

Steve came back with the iced coffee and handed it to Tamar. "Fabulous, thanks!" she said.

Steve looked at Mary and Joey and shook his head. "Joey still won't sit in the bathtub. We can only wonder what gave him such a fear of water. ... Arava, Gal! Popsicles!"

"Did you use my discount?" Michal said.

"Popsicles for them all?" Tamar looked up at Steve. "Have you forgotten the tests we're doing for Mary's diabetes?"

"As a matter of fact, I did forget but wanted to spoil the kids," Steve said. "She's not diagnosed yet, so let's cross that bridge when we come to it."

With this gang, even a fun day at the beach could turn into arguments and tension, and if Mary did have diabetes, things would get worse.

"Come, let's make a gigantic sand castle near the water," Steve said. "Everyone take a shovel."

Michal sat down next to Tamar. "It's not easy, is it?"

"I don't know what I was thinking," Tamar exhaled loudly. "I love them, and I'm not sorry we took Mary and Joey. But they've been through a lot, and it shows in their behavior. However, I won't let the diabetes be a tipping point."

"What about Arava and Gal?" Michal asked.

"It's challenging for them when the kids have temper tantrums and start screaming for no apparent reason."

"I've told you—right?—about the program we have, dolphin therapy?"

"I guess you told me, and that dolphins are sensitive animals … but I don't remember the details. Can it really help?"

"We deal with autism, post-trauma, behavioral problems, depression, and more. The number's limited because we invest a lot in each participant, but I'll try to get Mary and Joey accepted."

"Is it so obvious they qualify?" Tamar took off her beach dress. "I'm getting warm and need a swim."

"As children interact with dolphins, we see them experiencing what we call positive moments, opening up to the dolphins, to us, and gaining self-confidence," Michal said.

"The social worker said they pay for counseling and for clubs, wonder if this is included," Tamar said. "More driving …"

"There's an awesome movie about a teenage Arab boy who stopped speaking after being attacked by fellow students. His parents took him to a psychologist who recommended the Reef, and he began speaking again. The kids will love it—and you too."

Tamar and Steve needed serious prayers. If only she were a praying type … but maybe she could do something to help before she left for Berlin. Hopefully, she'd get Mary and Joey into dolphin therapy.

23

L et's pray," Steve said as they sat around the table. "And thank you for the delicious food Mommy prepared."

Tamar didn't close her eyes but kept scanning the food, thinking about what she could give to Mary and in what amounts. Since the official report in Dr. Marina's office last week, every meal was a challenge.

"Wait a minute!" Gal said. "No one checked Mary's blood sugar before eating."

"Thanks, Gali." Tamar took a deep breath. "Good thing we have you around. Can you reach for the pouch on the counter with the monitor in it?" *What has happened to my concentration?*

"Who shall I give it to?" Gal said. "You or Daddy?" He'd learned that Tamar couldn't bear to prick Mary's tiny finger and see her grimace four times a day. Everyone assumed that because she was a nurse, Tamar would take on the diabetes regimen, but although it probably looked strange, she couldn't bear treating her own family. She forced herself to do it when Steve was at work, but if he was home, because they were in this together, he should take his share.

Tamar had insisted that Steve come with her to Mary's appointment. She already knew what Dr. Marina would tell her and wanted Steve to hear it too, along with the instructions.

Dr. Marina spoke in a caring voice. "You have a lovely little girl. I'm sure you'll do fine."

Easy for her to say. Type 1 diabetes is for life.

"How are you today, Mary? You've been tired lately, thirsty, and going to the bathroom a lot, right?"

Mary's dark eyes stared up at the doctor. "How do you know? … Do you have another cookie for me?" She gazed over the doctor's desk.

"This time I have a piece of apple, even better. You like apples, don't you? We have some ways to help you feel better."

She turned to Tamar and Steve. "We see from the blood test that Mary has Type 1 diabetes. I know this is difficult to hear, but many other families manage with it, and we have a support group for parents with diabetic children and a twenty-four hour helpline."

Tamar gripped the arm of the chair and blew out a series of short breaths to gain control. She saw Steve close his eyes for a second and knew he was saying a brief prayer.

"It should go smoothly for you because you're a nurse and know the treatment process. And you can make an appointment with our diabetes specialist."

"I studied diabetes in nursing school, but I don't see it in my work with babies."

"Do you remember that you'll be checking her blood sugar at least four times a day and giving an insulin injection?"

Tamar looked at Steve. He knew the difficulties she faced nursing her own children.

"You'll also make an appointment with our dietitian. Food is a big component of the diabetes treatment plan, but that doesn't mean Mary has to follow a strict 'diabetes diet.' You'll want her to eat healthy food, low in fat and calories, which is good for the rest of the family too."

She turned to Mary, "You're a special girl and lucky to have an Imma and Abba who take good care of you."

Tamar sat in silence all the way home in the car. When she agreed to take Mary and Joey home, she hadn't considered this. It was irrational, but she couldn't stop feeling guilty and asking herself what she could have done better for Mary. She was even angry with Steve, though she didn't know what he had to do with it. Maybe it was his calmness and continuing to quote, "All things work together for good." She couldn't bear to hear that anymore.

"Delicious. Your mother's done it again." Steve pushed his chair away from the table. "Take your dishes to the sink, and I believe Mommy's prepared dessert."

Tamar smiled faintly at Steve's compliment. Tofu and vegetable curry with coconut cream, served with brown rice and garbanzo beans wasn't much different from any other meal she made, and Mary was allowed to eat it all.

Gal jumped up to bring the baking tray to the table. "I helped! They're low-carb peanut butter cookies especially for Mary, but we can all eat them."

"Next time you can make them yourself," Tamar said. "Cooking and baking's easy. Just read the recipe and do what it says."

Arava reached for a cookie. "Once you said that Savta's mother didn't know how to read, and she still made yummy food."

"Who knows what's a carb?" asked Steve.

"We've been learning about it in our health class," Arava said. "Yummy."

"I know," Gal said.

"I'm glad you both know, but one at a time," Steve said. "These are great. I love the taste and smell of nutmeg."

"Carbs are lots of things," Arava said. "Like sugar, rice, bread, pasta—"

"Things we like," Mary's eyes sparkled.

"What about fruit?" Steve asked. "Is that a carb?"

No one answered. "Fruit's sweet but it's not like bread," Gal finally said.

"Are carbs good for you?" Steve could turn any discussion into a science lesson and get the children thinking.

"I like sweets!" Mary said.

"I'll answer," said Steve. "It depends on what kind. They can be simple or complex. Food can be processed or unprocessed. And, of course, how much you eat is important. For instance—"

"Sorry," Tamar rose from the table. "This is interesting and worth knowing, but it's nearly bedtime, and Arava's turn to wash the dishes. Let's continue another time."

～

"It's been a long day." Tamar sighed, sinking into her favorite chair with a mug of coffee. "Bedtime takes a while these days. ... And your day?"

Steve leaned back and stretched his long legs on the coffee table. "We've got a new group of students for an intensive two-week course. I like teaching these kids, some are really sharp. Reminds me of my enthusiasm when I began studying.... Are you okay?"

"I guess." Tamar picked up her phone and then laid it down. She and Steve had agreed to put their phones aside when they were talking to each other or anyone else.

"What d'you think about Mary?"

"Ups and downs. You can never take a break. The doctor thinks it was a hypoglycemia attack at school when she began sweating and acting confused, probably because of the sports day."

"Something we could do to prevent it from happening again?"

"Just be aware. But on the other hand, she likes the attention. You should have seen her at the birthday party this afternoon. I told Liam's mother about Mary's diabetes, and she had special diabetic candies and cakes for her."

"Mary was happy?"

"Thrilled, she almost got more attention than Liam."

"And you? You're biting your nails again. You managed to stop for a long time. ... Is that a new shirt?"

114

"You noticed? One of the nurses gave it to me. Didn't fit her, and she thought it looked like something I'd wear." Tamar looked at her nails. "I'm only tired. I shouldn't pay attention, but I can't stand the reactions I'm seeing in town. In the beginning, people were positive about the refugees, but the tide is turning. Don't worry about me. I'll be okay."

"I know you will." Steve leaned back in his chair, clasping his hands behind his head. "You're strong. Keep trusting God."

Strong? Trust? Sometimes she felt like Daniel in the lion's den with sharp-toothed beasts surrounding her or a juggler in a circus trying to keep all the plates spinning. In her head she understood ... but living it was another story.

24

Number 86 to the third position." Estie double checked the slip in her hand and stepped into the cubicle. Not bad, less than an hour. In most cities, you waited longer at the Ministry of Interior.

"Why travel so far?" Estie's father had asked when she told him she was going to Greece with friends from work. "Aren't there enough places in Israel? We have a beautiful country. Do you know how we longed to come here when we were in Morocco?"

"Abba, the world's changed. It's bigger now."

She had to promise him they wouldn't get into trouble and wouldn't talk to any of the local men who were certainly on the prey for pretty, innocent Israeli girls.

Estie saw the nameplate on the desk, Dalia Moshe. Wasn't she the legendary clerk who called them at the Welfare Office when they had identity and other issues?

"How can I help you today?" Dalia's dyed-red hair and the gold adorning her neck, ears, and fingers shined, even in the dull office light.

"I'd like to apply for a passport."

"First time?"

Did she look old to be receiving her first one? "Yes, I'm going to Greece next month. It will be ready by then?"

"You'll receive it in the mail in three weeks. You will have to fill out this form." Dalia slid a paper over the desk to Estie. "And I'll take a picture of you."

Simple, she could already see herself walking around the Acropolis and dining at one of those cozy Greek tavernas her friend had told her about.

Estie looked into the camera, the light flashed, and she turned to her application.

"Now your credit card, and that's it. Where are you going in Greece? I just came back and loved every minute." Dalia took a deep breath, a look of satisfaction on her face. "I especially liked the food! Moussaka and stuffed grape leaves, ouzo—"

"Ouzo?" Estie asked absentmindedly. *Name in Hebrew and English, date of birth, address … hard to concentrate with Dalia's chattering.*

"The liquor they drink, like our arak. And the music—you should have seen us dancing." Dalia jiggled in her chair. "My husband took a video of me with a sharp-looking young Greek. When I showed it to my co-workers," Dalia looked around the office, "they said they couldn't believe my moves."

When Estie was with Jens, he kept remarking how quickly Israelis got into conversations with each other—on buses, in the supermarket, on the beach, anywhere. He said in Denmark people avoided talking to strangers. Soon, she'd also be experiencing a different culture, but she had a feeling that Greeks were more like Israelis than the Danish were. They also cooked with olive oil and had dark hair.

"My friend found an Airbnb on an island not far from Athens, so God willing, we're going with a group of girls from the Welfare Office," Estie explained.

Dalia sat up straight. "Welfare Office? I was on the phone with them a few days ago. You have some difficult cases."

"We do have a lot of work, unfortunately. Many people need help." Estie fingered her star of David pendant. "But I love it."

"I spoke with your supervisor. It came to my attention that infiltrators are trying to worm their way in and make use of our welfare services." She pursed her lips. "I had to warn her."

Warn her? About what?

"You see what's happening in our city. Anyone with eyes

realizes these blacks are taking over and pushing the peace-loving citizens off their own streets and sidewalks. We aren't safe here anymore."

She came here for a passport, so how did they get to this subject? "I have noticed them. But honestly, I'm not threatened." Estie pushed a strand of hair behind her ear.

"Not threatened *yet*. I made it clear to your supervisor—what's her name?—that we won't have you enabling these Africans."

"Enabling?" Estie glanced behind her shoulder. The other people waiting must be getting annoyed that she was taking so long.

"Yes, enabling. Here at the Ministry of Interior, we have connections, and I understand two dark children are being fostered by a local family. Have you heard about the case?"

Wasn't this Dalia Moshe overstepping her boundaries? A knot tightened in Estie's stomach. How should she answer? She'd learned that honesty was the best policy.

"In fact," she said in the calmest voice she could muster. "I was assigned to facilitate the paperwork for two Sudanese children living in Kibbutz Eilot who had already moved in with a local family after being abandoned by their mother."

"And you agreed!? I read that you social workers are protesting for being overworked and underpaid?"

Estie tried to be careful with her words. Dalia didn't have any control over her ... did she? Estie had worked hard to reach her position, the first family member who had gone to college and moved away from Sderot.

And she might be needing Dalia's help soon after what Jens said to her on their chat last night.

"Talking on Skype isn't enough," he said. "It's time I come to Eilat for longer. And this time, I'd like to meet your family."

How could she explain to Jens that in her community, being

Jewish was the number one requirement for a spouse. Maybe, with God's help, he'd convert—but did he want to? Jens seemed happy with his own secular, Danish identity.

"I know tourist visas are for three months," Jens said, "but my friend has an Israeli girlfriend, and she arranged a partner visa for him. I'll take leave from the bank and find work or volunteer as a kite-sailing instructor."

Estie had to stay on the good side of Dalia if it ever came to this.

"Did you hear what I said?" Dalia raised her voice. "Enabling infiltrators."

Take a deep breath. She didn't have to answer.

"I'll get to my point," Dalia continued. "The goal of our prime minister and our mayor is to get every Sudanese out of the country. Some people call them refugees, but it's obvious they're only here to work."

"I'm not making policy decisions," Estie said. "I understood these children, Mary and Joey, have no parents and needed a home. That's my job as a social worker."

"Ha! No parents maybe, but did you know they have a relative?" Dalia nearly raised herself out of her chair. "Who's the social worker, me or you?"

"When I was given the case, they were already living with the foster family. I only needed to arrange for their official acceptance." Estie took care not to violate confidentiality agreements by mentioning names.

Estie heard the loudspeaker. "Number 92 to position four." Were people noticing position three wasn't vacating?

"They seem to be a serious family, doing their best, and—"

"The point is not how well the family is doing," Dalia said. "In the Ministry of Interior, we have connections and influence. I hope this is clear. Israel was never meant to be a refuge for Africans looking for a comfortable life."

Estie touched her star of David and brushed the hair back from her face. She'd loved studying Torah in school and passed the first stage of the National Bible Quiz. A verse from Deuteronomy suddenly came back to her: *Love the aliens, for you were aliens in Egypt.* Or did that not apply to the Sudanese? She needed time to process.

Who was Dalia threatening—her, the Goldmans, Mary and Joey, all the Sudanese? And did she really have power or was it bluster? Estie chose to be a social worker to help people, focusing on needy children, but she never anticipated her work would involve taking a political stand.

25

"Can you come to my office when you finish?" Leah asked Tamar.

Although Tamar was more than ready to go home, she understood Leah wasn't asking but rather telling her. She'd sensed something in Leah's manner the whole day, the way she wouldn't look Tamar in the eye, and turned her head as Tamar walked by.

It began after the long phone call she had this morning, and then Leah drank her coffee alone in her office rather than sitting with the other nurses, as usual. Since that first talk with her about the refugees whom Leah called "infiltrators," things weren't the same between them. It didn't help that while participating in that anti-refugee demonstration, Leah had seen her eating felafel with the family; but that was Leah's problem, not hers. *I wasn't breaking any laws. And in my work, anyone can see I go above and beyond.*

"How was your day?" Leah motioned to the seat on the other side of her desk. "I see that little Ethiopian baby who was so underweight is doing better." Her office smelled like cigarettes mixed with lemony air freshener. When the nurses were meant to advise pregnant women and mothers not to smoke, how could Leah not realize that even the odor of cigarettes on clothes affected babies' lung development?

Tamar sat up straight in her chair and tried not to think about how Leah's pink hair reminded her of the corals she'd seen while snorkeling yesterday. She was sure Leah didn't invite her to talk about that baby.

"My day? I wouldn't trade this job for anything," Tamar

answered. "Solving problems, seeing babies thriving, and experiencing the interactions between mothers and their children ..."

"It's obvious you love your work." Leah cleared her throat and gazed over Tamar's shoulder towards the door. "I wanted to talk to you because I had a call from Dalia at the Ministry of Interior about your involvement with African children. I'm sure you're aware of the issues."

Tamar took a couple of deep breaths. *Calm down. Hold your tongue.* "Actually, I'm not sure I understand."

"Are you blind to what's going on in Eilat?" Leah leaned forward and rested her hands on the desk. "It's an invasion and it has to stop, the sooner the better. Thankfully, we have a mayor—and a vigilant Minister of Interior—who understand the problem."

Tamar, Steve, and most of their friends thought the country would be a lot saner if they could get rid of their ultra-orthodox Minister of Interior. Till now their frustrations were with the religious sector's monopoly over all aspects of life from birth to death. Even her parents couldn't marry in Israel because Abba wasn't Jewish—Jews were only allowed to marry Jews, Christians to marry Christians, and Muslims to marry Muslims. Imma and Abba happily married with his family in England, but it was an insane situation. And now they could add to the Ministry of Interior's craziness, their refusal to accept Sudanese asylum seekers.

"I'm sorry, I don't see how this affects me," Tamar said.

"How it affects you?" Leah enunciated her words. "You're harboring two of them, hiding them in your home."

"I'm not hiding anyone. My husband and I have become a registered foster family for two young children whose parents abandoned them. The kibbutz social worker told us that if we didn't take them, they'd end up in a children's home in Beer Sheva. I'd gone out a couple of times to the kibbutz, the first time to return the vaccination card I foolishly misplaced, as you may remember. Working here has taught me to be aware of signs of

122

abuse or neglect in children, so I spotted Mary and Joey immediately."

"You spotted them? You're responsible for every little black child?"

"Isn't it our job to report suspicious cases and deal with them as we're able?"

"Not the infiltrators. We don't want them here. If we make it too comfortable for them, they'll tell all their friends, and we'll have a tsunami."

Tamar was the peacemaker at work and got along well with Leah and her fellow nurses. When she went to conferences, they drove and roomed together, and had deep talks and laughs. She never thought that taking Mary and Joey into their family could lead to a work conflict. A tenured nurse couldn't easily get fired, so she tried to understand Leah's and the clerk at the Ministry of Interior's line of thinking.

"I'm telling you what I heard on the phone from Dalia this morning." Leah reached into her bag for her cigarette pack and laid it on the desk. "Be careful. And think about what you're doing. I've seen instances from your work which may have violated regulations. See you tomorrow."

Tamar's hands were shaking as she walked to the car. What would Steve say when she told him about this conversation? He tried to be supportive, but she sometimes wondered if he thought she'd gotten into something over her head.

Tamar remembered the discussion they had last Friday evening. On Steve's visits to the kibbutz to give Bible studies, he befriended some young people who came down with a group to organize children's activities, and he invited them for dinner.

"One thing that gets me angry," a man with a ponytail and a big appetite had said, "is the government ignoring the 1951 International Refugee Convention."

"The International Refugee Convention?" Tamar had asked.

She loved their idealism and passion even if she didn't understand all the policy details.

"Israel was one of the first countries to sign the agreement because at that time, most of the refugees were Jews from the Holocaust."

"Interesting..."

"It states that a refugee can't be deported to his own country where his life or liberty are in danger," the ponytailed man had explained. "And he has the right to work in the country where he's found refuge."

"I was talking to one of the men," added a girl with dreadlocks as she looked up from the Rummikub game with Arava and Gal. "And he told me about his so-called interview as an asylum seeker trying to get recognized as a refugee. The interviewer yelled at him and called him a liar."

26

"I'm still working on the best recipe." Tamar licked her upper lip as she stood at her kitchen counter and tasted her newest creation. "What d'you think?"

"Think about what?" Steve asked without looking up from his computer screen.

"I thought we were going to have a quiet breakfast finally with just the two of us. Would you mind closing your computer for a few minutes?"

"Right, duck. Just a minute. Checking headlines before heading out and noticed something about the Sudanese. I'll look later. What'd you say?"

"Which smoothie did you like the most this week?"

Steve looked up. "Remind me of the choices."

Tamar knew he wasn't crazy about smoothies for breakfast but went along with them for her sake. "Two days ago, we had the purple one, remember? Based on frozen blueberries to remind you of Canada. But with other goodies added. I loved going out to that self-pick blueberry farm with your brother."

"You couldn't stop eating them." Steve cracked a grin. "We picked so many, Mom and Dad gave them away to their friends."

Tamar understood that distinguishing between one smoothie and the other wasn't at the top of Steve's priorities. With corals, he noticed the tiniest differences. "And what about the one yesterday, with oatmeal and watermelon?" She knew Steve would be happy with plain oatmeal every day for breakfast.

"Today it's a special spinach smoothie with banana, chia, and flax seeds. Nu? Which one?"

Steve was eyeing the green color. "I like them all," he said, always the diplomat. "And I'm especially happy to have breakfast alone with you for a change. Perfect timing—on the day I start work later, your meeting was canceled. Cup of coffee?"

Steve had suggested they go out to Aroma for breakfast. "We'll make it an early celebration for your birthday next week. You deserve it."

"I'd prefer to stay home. Save time that way." For her, sitting at their kitchen table with her green smoothie and strong cup of coffee with soy milk was everything she wanted. She began singing along with one of her favorite songs playing on the radio.

"I haven't heard lately what's going on with Mary and Joey's therapy at the Reef," Steve said. "Great they could renew it for another year. He's not tense anymore when I give him a bath, so something seems to be working."

"I know you're busy, but try to go there with them. It's an amazing program. Joey sits on the platform with the trainer petting the dolphins and getting to know them. You should see him laughing."

"And Mary?"

"She already goes into the water with a trainer wearing a wetsuit and mask and interacts with the dolphins. She loves it."

"Progress. Can I have a piece of toast with my smoothie? Need something to fill me up."

"Sometimes it seems like one step forward, two back."

"Do you know who wrote a book with that name?"

"Thought it was just an expression," Tamar said. "What do you want on your toast? The smoothie has plenty of fiber, so it should be filling."

"Vladimir Lenin."

"Michal's great with her. The children receive a popsicle at the end, so Michal bought some sugarless ones for Mary."

Tamar picked up her phone to look at the time and then quickly put it back down.

"Speaking of Michal," said Steve. "We're not seeing her as often lately. She used to come here a couple times a week."

"She has another interest lately."

"Yossi? ... Thanks for buying this cheese. The soy cheese doesn't do it for me."

"I know they're spending time together, but not sure how this fits in with her plan to go to Berlin. She keeps putting it off."

"She seems happy, and he's a special guy. I'd like to have a good talk with him, but I can't push it."

"About faith?"

"And life. He likes talking to me. His father's out of the picture."

"Was probably never in it. I have to get going. Trying extra hard to stay on Leah's good side. She's looking for excuses to find fault with me."

"Time flies when you're having fun. Did you know Shakespeare first said something like that?: 'The swiftest hours, as they flew.'"

Tamar didn't understand the connection but couldn't deny that time went by fast when she and Steve were together. If she could forget their four children, his busy job, her issues at work with Leah, and everything else, she could still feel excited like when they first met and were two young kids falling in love.

"Let's just check what's written about the Sudanese." Steve opened his computer again and began to read the article.

"Nothing's clear, super complicated." Steve's voice trailed off.

"Can you tell me in short?"

Steve scratched his head and frowned. "The refugees will receive a special visa because they are non-deportable asylum seekers. It's for three months and comes with a stamp that they're not allowed to work."

"But they're working."

"Right. On the one side, employers are threatened with fines for employing them; but on the other, the law isn't enforced."

"Does this affect us?"

"There's talk of building a border wall to keep them out."

"But Mary and Joey are safe, aren't they?" Tamar felt blood rush through her head and she blinked back tears.

"I can't see a problem for them or for us for the time being, but we have to be aware they may be less welcome."

"Welcome or not, Mary and Joey aren't going anywhere! I don't care what rulings come through or what the public thinks. With her diabetes, Mary could never go back to South Sudan. Not to mention the love they receive and the love they give us."

Tamar picked up her backpack, smoothed her curls, and straightened her blouse. "By the way, did I tell you that tomorrow afternoon I need the car to take the kids to buy plants, and after that we'll do some gardening?"

27

Steve walked through the house and stepped into the back-yard. "Looks great, you've been gardening more lately, and it shows."

Tamar looked up from crouching next to a flower bed where the children were gathered around her. "Yes. I'm feeling better all the time, and have more energy for things like gardening. ... Can you lift this mango tree and put it in the hole there in the corner? With the weather cooling down, we can eat meals out here. And I'm getting exercise."

"Who wants to plant these petunias?" she asked the children.

"If you have a garden and a library, you have everything you need," Steve said. "That was Cicero."

"I choose the purple ones," Joey said. He loved to help but, like any child, needed a lot of affirmation.

"They're called geraniums and those others are begonias," Tamar said. "I went with the kids to the Botanical Gardens. They had fun at the waterfall, running around in the jungle section, and helped pick out plants. Now we're putting them in the ground together. Do you have a minute?"

Arava picked up a little plant and took it out of its plastic pot. "I'll do the tomatoes."

"Me the cukes," Gal said. "Yum. How long till they're ready?"

"Mary, Joey, what d'you want to plant?"

"I like the one with red hearts." Mary pointed at the pepper plant.

"Let me help you, bubi," Tamar said. "Roll up your sleeves, take one of the trowels, and we'll dig a hole in the dirt."

Tamar looked at Steve and the flicker of a smile passed her lips. Mary didn't mind getting dirty anymore. When she came to them, she had never even walked barefoot before.

"Flowers, mangoes, and our own salad makings," Steve said. "I'm proud of you guys. I'll bring juice and cookies for everyone."

The first year with Mary and Joey, Tamar hadn't found time to plant anything; it was all she could do to keep what plants they had from dying. Renewing the custody agreement every three months was also stressful. Now, after three years, she could breathe, garden, folk dance, and bake. Life was settling into a comfortable rhythm. Mary had fewer bad moods, and Joey enjoyed playing football with the boys in the neighborhood.

She hoped she was giving enough time to Arava and Gal. They were growing up so fast and, in some ways, didn't need her as they used to. But there were so many temptations for the children these days; so, in other ways, they needed her more than ever. But she liked to think that having Mary and Joey in their family developed their compassion and enlarged their hearts.

Steve took each child on a monthly date night to a movie, pizza or whatever they chose, and Estie came to their house every two weeks to play with Mary and Joey. She'd become a kind of friend, yet Tamar couldn't figure her out. Coming from an orthodox religious family, she wouldn't naturally want to help refugees and was influenced by the mood of the street and the government against asylum seekers.

On the other hand, Estie had mentioned a Danish, non-Jewish boyfriend. Tamar hoped to hear more about him because Estie seemed to enjoy hanging out at their house. When they were her last visit for the day, she often stayed past the allotted time. She'd even asked for the recipe for the pistachio shortbread cookies made with almond flour, not a typical Moroccan dessert.

From the garden, Tamar heard Steve open the front door and say "Come in." But she couldn't hear a reply.

Steve came back carrying a tray with glasses, a pitcher of juice, and a plate of diabetic brownies, followed by a tall Sudanese woman wearing a fitted orange dress that emphasized her ebony skin, and her hair braided in an intricate pattern. Tamar, who knew most of the Sudanese in Eilat, didn't recognize this woman.

"Mama!" Mary and Joey both stood still for a second, their stares turned to smiles, then they ran toward her.

Steve shook his head slightly and cleared his throat. "Let's take a break from gardening. ... Tamar, Arava, Gal, this is Catherine, Mary and Joey's mother."

Tamar's heart began to race, and she froze in place. Then, "Sit down, please," she mumbled. "Can I give you some juice and cookies?" She looked Catherine up and down trying not to gape. She was strikingly beautiful. Mary looked just like her mother.

"You want to know how I find you?" Catherine asked as Mary and Joey moved to sit near her. "I live in Tel Aviv, but my friends on kibbutz tell me where you live." She placed the shopping bag she was carrying next to her chair.

Catherine pulled Mary and Joey close, and they responded by snuggling in on either side of her. They looked at the ground, and then their eyes darted from Tamar to Steve.

"I do not have much time," Catherine said. "My bus leave in two hours. Mary and Joey can take their things."

Tamar glanced at Steve and widened her eyes. She wasn't usually at a loss for words, but now she didn't know what to say.

Steve came to her rescue. "Ummm, Catherine, what do you do in Tel Aviv?" he asked.

"I clean houses." She spoke some Hebrew and obviously understood more.

"And you live where?"

"Took time to find, but now I work and have own room near bus station in apartment I share with two friends and their children. Mary and Joey join me."

A room in the worst neighborhood in Israel? After she hasn't even been in touch for three years?

Tamar took a sweeping look around the garden. Some of the flowers and vegetables were in the ground, others still in their boxes, a labor of love in progress. A few minutes ago, they were working together as a family, relaxed, and looking forward to seeing their plants grow and making salad from their own garden. Then a bombshell dropped. *She* walked in and everything changed.

Tamar had to think quickly. They couldn't deal with this alone. They needed help, support. She prayed Estie would answer her phone and that Michael could come over right away. Together, they'd talk sense into Catherine.

She understood a mother longed for her children, but to disappear for three years then think she could just show up and take the children away? *Maybe that's how they do it in Sudan, but this is Israel.*

Michael would be the key. He was sensible and seemed to be more oriented toward the Western mindset than other Sudanese. And the refugees respected him.

"Excuse me," said Tamar. "I have to make a phone call. Steve would you come inside for a minute?"

She began pacing around the living room while dialing Estie's number and at the same time could see Catherine taking clothes out of the shopping bag. Catherine brought out a shiny black three-piece suit with a white shirt for Joey and a pink frilly dress with a picture of Princess Aurora on it for Mary. The kids would love them. Most of the clothes they—as well as Arava and Gal—wore, were hand-me-downs, except for the new outfits from Imma every Pessach.

Catherine helped Mary pull the dress over her head and buttoned up Joey's shirt. "We try them," she said. She had begun speaking to the children in Arabic but when they answered in

Hebrew, she switched to a broken mixture of the two languages.

"Estie, it's an emergency," Tamar said. "Catherine, their mother, is here and wants to take them back to Tel Aviv on the next bus. Steve is calling Michael from Kibbutz Eilot and asking him to come over. Would you speak to him on the phone and explain that we have legal custody? Then he can tell Catherine in Arabic."

Tamar and Steve finished their phone calls at the same time.

"Michael is on his way," Steve said, rubbing his head. Even the unshakable Steve looked tense.

"Estie said she'll talk to him."

"How about a quick prayer? ... God, you know all about this situation, you care about everyone involved, and we trust in you." They walked back outside and sat down.

The resemblance between the children and their mother was unmistakable. Tamar saw a longing in the children's eyes and Catherine's gentle touch as she helped them into their clothes. *This woman gave birth to these children, and she must have nursed them. Whatever traumas they've experienced, there is a bond between them they'll never have with anyone else.*

Tamar's mind raced with a million thoughts. The children had a good life with a family who loved them, healthy food, school, and clubs. Mary's diabetes demanded constant vigilance to watch her blood sugar levels and diet. Yet, could she ever provide for Mary and Joey the deep sense of identity and connection each person seeks?

There was a knock on the door. Steve jumped up. "Michael, good to see you. Catherine's in the garden. Come on out."

"I know her from Cairo, and we crossed the border from Egypt about the same time. She's had a hard life."

"I told you what's happening," Steve said. "Estie, the social worker, will call soon."

"I will try to help. You are good people."

Michael greeted Catherine, and Tamar and Steve sat back while they spoke together in Arabic.

Tamar dialed Estie's number. To Catherine she said, "We don't have much time till your bus leaves. Estie's on the phone. She needs to tell you something. Michael will translate."

Tamar handed Michael her phone. He listened carefully, nodding and slowly repeating Estie's words. "Custody, court order, judge, children's welfare. I understand."

He handed back the phone and pulled up a chair opposite Catherine, who was still sitting between her children. Michael leaned his tall frame forward. As he spoke, Catherine's body sagged and her eyes wandered. Tamar couldn't tell how much she understood. A few minutes later she got to her feet, hugged the children, and walked out the door.

As she turned the corner, Tamar let out a deep breath and sank into the garden swing, her body shaking. Could things have turned out differently? She hoped never to find herself in this awful situation again.

The children had all drifted to their rooms. "Hey, let's finish planting, and then I'll make pizza," Tamar said.

The baby plants in their containers seemed to be calling her to continue where she and the children had stopped, to press the flowers and vegetables into the soil where they could grow and develop. She would give these growing things a future.

She and Steve needed to speak with the children. This visit brought even more confusion to their already mixed-up lives. Today Catherine backed off, but it was unlikely to be their last meeting. Tamar needed more vigilance and patience than ever.

I'll prepare myself.

28

Steve stood up and looked out the window. "Still raining. Who wants to see a flood?"

Michal saw the grin on Steve's face. Usually calm and unflappable, a few things did get Steve excited: success with one of his experiments at work, spotting a rare bird, and talking about the Bible. But seeing the desert floods, "the power of God in nature" as Steve called them, was also near the top of Steve's list of reasons to get excited.

"With all the rain today and last night, I'm sure Wadi Shlomo is flooding." Steve scanned the room. "Problem is, we won't all fit in the car."

"I'll stay home," Tamar offered. "It's been a busy week at work, and then the fellowship meeting this morning. A nap sounds good. ... Yossi should experience a flood."

"The rest of us can scrunch in," Steve said. "I just checked Mary's sugar, so she's set to go."

"Kinneret too," Gal said. Hearing her name, the dog began wagging her tail. "She loves water and running around in the mountains."

"We'll start at the top of the wadi because it's easier to drive downhill than up," Steve said. "Maybe someday I'll have a four-wheel drive—"

"There are dark clouds in the direction of Egypt," Gal said. "That's a good sign we'll see a flood, right?"

"Sometimes it's not even raining here," Arava said. "And we still have a flood going down the main street—"

"Because it's raining in the mountains," Gal said. They liked to share their knowledge with Yossi, Mary, and Joey.

"Take some snacks," said Tamar. "And be careful. Don't do anything foolish."

"People die every year in floods," Arava explained.

"Can I stay with Mommy?" Joey asked.

"But not in Eilat," Gal added.

"Come with me, bubi," Michal said. "You can sit on my lap."

~

The family squeezed into the car, and with the wipers sweeping over the windshield, they headed out of town.

"The fragrance of the rain always reminds me of winters on the kibbutz growing up," said Michal.

"This is the road to Mitzpe Ramon," Steve said. "We're turning left into Nahal Shlomo and will come out near the Dolphin Reef. Hey kids, I know you're excited, but can you calm down and not yell?"

"Do dolphins like rain?" Arava asked Michal.

"Good question. They don't, so they dive deeper. Our problem at the Reef is that with a serious storm, the outside net can tear or get washed away. For a while, we had an opening in the net, and the dolphins could come and go. They came back, though, because this is their home."

"Like Kinneret," Gal said. "Even when she goes out, she always comes home."

"Right. But people in boats often mistreated them by offering them food and coming too close, so we closed the net again. With this storm, I'm afraid the net may be ruined."

Steve glanced at Yossi who sat next to him in the front. "Do you understand what's happening with the floods?"

"My family didn't take trips to nature. And in the army I was stationed in the Golan Heights, so I never saw anything like this." Yossi stared out the window. "Thanks for inviting me."

"It only rains a few times a year in Eilat—only thirty millimeters, which is nothing. The ground is hard and doesn't absorb the water, so what starts as a small trickle in the mountains, grows as each small wadi flows into the larger one. I guess you know *wadi* is Arabic for *nahal*, a dry stream bed."

"That I learned in the army. I picked up a lot there."

Sounds like an understatement, thought Michal, who was listening to this conversation. She couldn't imagine the steep learning curve Yossi faced, coming from the religious ghetto where he grew up, straight to the army. The opposite of hard dry desert ground, Yossi was like a sponge absorbing information and seemed to especially admire Steve. Shai also had often told her what a cool guy Steve was. Besides putting up with Tamar and her craziness, Steve was always ready to answer the children's questions and to give Mary her insulin shots. And he had a convincing way of explaining how his faith in God fit in with the Big Bang Theory, not that she exactly understood what he was talking about.

"If you didn't celebrate birthdays and go on trips, what did you do for fun?" asked Gal, who had also been listening.

"With ten kids, we entertained ourselves, and we went to synagogue."

Michal liked seeing how Yossi interacted with her family. He certainly needed one. But she hoped he wouldn't take Tamar's and Steve's faith too seriously. It seemed to work for them, but she wasn't about to go down that route after Imma and Abba had tried to push it on her growing up. In all their meetings and summer camps, she'd seen too many hypocrites.

The rain tapered off as they drove on the rough track down the still-dry wadi, the brown, red, and black colors of the cliffs on either side accented by the soaking they'd received. A few other families had the same idea and were driving ahead of and behind them. Steve switched the wipers to a lower speed as the rain tapered off.

"I thought we'd see a flood," Gal said.

"You never know with floods," answered Steve. "The rain may stop or it may pick up. It might even be dry where we are while raining further away, and a flood could come right through here."

"It's not dangerous?" Mary asked Steve.

"Don't worry, bubi. Your daddy knows how to drive in floods. He's done this a lot. And look at the other cars."

"But maybe they're four-wheel drive," Arava said.

"Can we get out of the car?" Gal asked. "Maybe from higher up, we can see a flood coming."

"Good idea," Steve said. "I'll park the car to the side of the road on higher ground where it will be safe. Hopefully, a flood will soon pass, and then we'll drive out."

"Joey, Mary," said Michal. "Give us your hands. The rocks are slippery with the rain."

"And if not?" Mary was still thinking about Steve's comment.

"Don't worry," he reassured as they climbed up a low ridge. "We'll make it home. Let's sit down on this flat spot for a few minutes and eat the apples and the granola bars Mommy made."

"This reminds me where one of the prophets wrote that 'waters will break forth in the wilderness and streams in the Arabah,'" said Yossi, leaning back against a rock and munching on his bar. "I was taught that this is speaking of the time when the Messiah comes."

Steve nodded. "Isaiah 35. The chapter also talks about the blind seeing, the lame leaping, and the deaf hearing. When Yeshua comes back, he'll make all things new."

"For you, Yeshua is the Messiah?" Yossi asked.

"He's for everyone, came to earth two thousand years ago, and is coming back—we don't know when—"

Steve's voice was drowned out by a sudden, roaring sound like that of a huge tractor.

"Run to the car!" Steve yelled. "It's coming!"

"That's how the flood starts," yelled Gal, who grabbed Yossi's arm to pull him down the hill. "With a loud noise."

"And here comes the foam." Arava, trying not to trip, pointed to a line of dirty froth moving down the wadi followed by a growing, brown stream of water.

"I'm scared," Joey sobbed. Michal hoisted him onto her back, invigorated by the power of the water.

"Get in the car, fast!" Steve said. "Maybe we can still beat it."

"Don't forget Kinneret." Arava looked around.

"Pray this works." Steve turned on the engine and was relieved to hear the welcome hum.

"Yay!" Gal leaned forward in his seat.

"At least the engine's dry," Steve said.

But soon the wheels began to spin as the car sank into the mud.

"Should we have been on higher ground?" Yossi's gaze darted up the wadi and back to the car.

"Everyone out," Steve said. "Michal, you sit in the driver's seat and when I tell you, give it gas. The rest of us will push."

"Can I stay with Michal?" Joey asked, clinging to her.

"On the count of three, Michal will press the gas pedal, and we'll all lean on the car and shove as hard as we can."

They did.

No movement.

"Let's try again."

Stuck.

"You've done this before?" Concern marred Yossi's features. "Aren't we sinking deeper?"

Steve huffed and bent in again with his shoulder against the rear of the car. "Works sometimes—"

"Daddy, we've tried a hundred times, and it hasn't moved!" Gal stepped back, chest heaving, shaking his arms. "Now we're only deeper in the mud."

"We need another plan," Steve said, unhurried.

Good thing Tamar isn't here. She'd be going to pieces. And as always, she'd use growing up in the children's house as an excuse for her irrational behavior—

"Did we pray?" Arava said.

"Do we have more granola bars?" Mary asked.

Gal screwed up his eyes and jumped up. "Look! A Land Rover driving right toward us. Could they pull us out?"

"Do you think he'll want to help?" Yossi asked.

"That's what these guys like to do," Steve answered. "For them it's a challenge. We're not far from the Camel Ranch where the road is paved. If he can pull us there, we can drive home."

Yossi's eyes widened as the Land Rover stopped next to them. "Looks like a quick answer to our prayer."

Exactly Michal's fear: Yossi falling under Steve's religious influence. It didn't make sense for Yossi to change one religion for another. She wasn't sure why she cared so much … their relationship wasn't clear anyway, and he was free to do as he wanted. Though whatever ended up happening between them, she wished the best for him.

"Wait till Mommy hears about our adventures," Gal said.

"But don't scare her," Arava warned. "Or she won't let us go again."

29

The children were finally all in bed, and after a sweep through the house to put everything in place, Tamar sat down with her feet up and a cup of coffee next to her. Steve often brought work home with him, but he tried to give time in the evening to reading a Bible chapter with the children and afterward a story. Now it was *The Lion, the Witch, and the Wardrobe.* Although Arava and Gal read books on their own, they still enjoyed having Steve read aloud to them.

"How was work?" Tamar asked.

"I'm almost done." Steve looked up from his computer.

Tamar enjoyed the quiet at the end of the day. Tonight her heart and mind were full.... Life had its ups and downs. She'd always wanted a big family, but four children made life busier than two. And suddenly taking in partially grown children was different than bringing new babies into the home, one by one. She didn't have the colic and night feedings, but the challenge was getting to know someone who already had a personality, traumas, and abandonment issues. As part of her work, she often emphasized to parents how important the first three years of a child's life were. Sadly, Mary and Joey had missed much parental love and guidance during that critical time.

Still, Tamar was thankful to be able to give Mary and Joey a new start and opportunities. Steve's parents, whenever they spoke on the phone with them, liked to instill doubt about how Arava and Gal were being negatively affected. Imma was more subtle. When they visited, she brought presents for all the children but always remarked about how tired Tamar appeared. She didn't need someone telling her she looked awful. She knew she was drained at the end of the day, but at least when she finally laid her head on the pillow, she fell asleep immediately.

"Just finishing this report," said Steve.

"No problem." Tamar looked at her phone and brought her empty mug to the sink. "It's late. Tomorrow's another day."

"Do you know who said that?" Steve said.

"Shakespeare?"

"Scarlett O'Hara in *Gone with the Wind*. Is that movie known in Israel?"

"An old classic, right? Romantic." Tamar closed the windows, looked at the children sleeping, and plopped into bed. She didn't even hear when Steve lay down beside her.

～

She was awakened by the sound of an explosion, much louder than the usual airplanes and helicopters. She'd heard this sound before while visiting the kibbutz when it had suffered a barrage of Hezbollah's rockets. But she'd never heard these booms in Eilat.

How long had she been sleeping?

The blast was immediately followed by the ascending and descending tone of the air-raid siren.

"Steve!" They both sat straight up in bed. Soon all four children had come running and jumped on the bed.

"Mommy!" Mary and Joey screamed.

They were shaking, and Tamar hugged them close to her.

"Keep calm," Steve said. "It's too late to reach a bomb shelter."

"And they're locked anyway," Tamar said.

"I heard three booms," Gal said. "Two together and then another."

"The first two booms you heard were from a rocket being intercepted by the Iron Dome—good to know it works," Steve said.

"And then another rocket landed somewhere. Everyone stay here and let's pray," he added.

"Anyway, we're all okay," Arava said. "Pray that no one is hurt—"

"And they won't shoot anymore," Gal said.

"Bubi, bubi." Tamar stroked Mary and Joey's backs. "You're with us. No one is going to hurt you. Mary, you lie on my other side."

What had these two kids gone through? She'd heard stories about the Sudanese army flying over South Sudanese villages and dropping bombs on them.

Steve got out of bed. "It's early in the morning, the time I get up for work. I'll turn on the radio."

"Arava and Gal, do you think you can go back to bed and sleep a little more?" Tamar asked.

As Tamar held Mary and Joey, the two young ones relaxed and dozed off. Knowing she wouldn't be able to fall back to sleep, she went to the kitchen to make a cup of coffee.

"Just listened to the news," Steve told her. "Two rockets over Eilat and one knocked down by the Iron Dome. The other fell in a parking lot, thankfully empty in the middle of the night. Two others landed in Aqaba, one on a house where someone was hurt, and another came down in the sea. They don't have good aim."

"Where'd they come from?"

"The Sinai, just over the border. ISIS claims responsibility."

Tamar knew that ISIS was trying to gain a foothold in the Sinai but till now were operating in the northern Sinai near the Gaza Strip. What were they doing so close to Eilat? Changing their tactics? Getting bolder?

"Do you think this will affect the Sudanese?" Tamar said.

"Could be. For you does everything tie to the refugees?"

"I don't like hearing on the news about a fence to keep refugees out and now it's bound to come up more."

In fact, Tamar didn't know how she felt about a wall. She realized Israel couldn't absorb an unlimited number of asylum seekers but, as she told people, we have a responsibility to take care of those who are here. Discussions about the wall increased hatred. With incidents like this, the project would gain new momentum.

Arava and Gal had moved back to their own rooms. Mary and Joey were still peacefully sleeping in her bed.

"Mary and Joey are family." Tamar got up, splashed water on her face, and began pacing around the living room. *How can he take it so coolly?* Even if Israel builds a fence, no one can kick out those who are already here, right?"

"Hope not. I'll wake up the kids for school."

~

Tamar was sitting down for a few moments of peace and finishing her second cup of coffee before leaving for work when she heard a knock on the door.

"Do you have a few minutes?" Eva didn't usually come over so early. She was still in her housecoat, and Tamar could see she hadn't slept.

"You heard the booms, right? Yakov went crazy."

Poor sweet Yakov. After surviving Auschwitz and enlisting to fight in the War of Independence soon after he arrived in Israel, against all odds Yakov had managed to make a life for himself. Always trying to help others, he didn't speak about his past, so people couldn't guess the horrors he'd been through unless they happened to see the number tattooed on his arm.

"He's been so forgetful lately and last night confused the blasts with the bombing in World War II." Eva sank into a chair opposite Tamar.

"Poor thing." Tamar knew that with dementia, long-term memory was stronger than short-term. "Coffee?"

"Thanks, but I can't stay. ... Then he began talking about

missiles dropped on him by Egyptian planes. Do you know what he did?"

"Screamed?"

"He can't walk anymore without a cane, but he got up and tried to run out of the house. I managed to calm him down, but it's dangerous." Eva wasn't in the best shape herself to handle Yakov when he was like this.

"Where's he now?"

"Sleeping again."

Tamar put her arm around Eva. "I have to go to work now, but come by later. We'll think of something."

She meant it, but what options did they have?

30

Tamar and Steve had decided to stay home and have a quiet Shabbat afternoon. She was drinking her coffee with a vegan brownie and eyeing Mary.

"African mothers do it, so why shouldn't I be able to?" Tamar said to Steve.

"Do what?"

"Braid Mary's hair."

Steve looked up from his book. "After three years, you're just deciding you want to make braids?"

"Susan was always happy to do it. You remember her, the daughter of Michael and Joanne. I paid her, and she likes coming over here with her friends." Tamar used the braiding as a chance to spend time with the teenage girls and have talks with them about puberty, their changing bodies, and relationships with guys. She wasn't sure how much their mothers spoke to them about this subject but growing up as refugees in the permissive Israeli culture, they needed all the help and guidance they could get.

"So, why not Susan today?"

"She's busy, and didn't you notice Mary's frizz getting out of control?"

"Ummm ..." Steve focused his eyes on Mary. "Now that you mention it, you mean that halo around her head? It's cute."

"It takes upkeep. I have to apply extra moisturizer after swimming, and I notice that we can't go longer than two months before re-braiding."

"So, you mean that in the three years Mary's lived with us, she's had her hair braided eighteen times?"

"I guess so ... or more." Tamar took her empty mug to the sink. "I've watched Susan braid, and it looks like one of the main things you need is patience. I made French braids for Arava a couple of times."

"Mostly when you asked her, she didn't want them," Steve reminded Tamar.

Arava had a streak of tomboy in her and couldn't be bothered about her hair.

"Mary's different, she likes pretty dresses and enjoys having her hair done. She's learned to be patient, and she adores Susan."

"Did you consider that you aren't African?"

It was true; they all did one another's hair. She'd heard one of the Sudanese ladies say it was important to have a daughter so she could do your braids.

"Do you have time? Doesn't it take hours?"

"I'll do a simple version to begin with. The kids can meanwhile watch that movie they've been asking for, Toy Story 3."

"That'll make them happy."

Braiding Mary's hair should be part of Tamar's job as a mother, touching and running her fingers over Mary's head would create intimacy, and she'd watched YouTube videos. Cornrows or braids—she'd watched several to know what she wanted.

"Mary, can you come here?" Tamar called.

Mary came skipping out of her room where she was building a zoo with Joey.

"Remember I showed you those colorful rubber bands and beads I bought for your hair? Susan's busy, so I thought I'd braid your hair this time. Shall we do it now while you watch a movie?"

"Yay!" A grin creased Mary's face. "Joey can watch too?"

"Maybe I'll have a go at Joey's hair at the same time." Steve laid down his book. "Shakespeare can wait. Wonder if the clippers I use for my beard and on Gal's hair will work for Joey?"

"Why not?"

"Different texture, different techniques. Wouldn't want to mess it up. He's sensitive about his appearance."

"Maybe do your beard while you're at it, or do you want one like Herzl with hair like Einstein?" Steve's style fit in at the Institute, but she wouldn't mind if he shaped up his appearance.

Tamar sat on the sofa with Mary positioned between her legs. Next to her, she had the equipment—a rattail comb, hair moisturizer, rubber bands, and beads. The children were watching their movie on her laptop, so she opened YouTube on her phone and placed it opposite her. She'd found a cute style, and the African American woman doing it made it look simple. She'd be happy if Mary came out looking half as beautiful as that little girl.

Mary said, "Can we have popcorn with the movie?"

"Good idea. Gal, will you make popcorn?" Tamar asked. "You make the best."

Okay, take a small section of hair, divide it into sections with the rattail, use the comb starting from the ends of the hair to take out the tangles. The woman says it's important to add moisturizer to the braid's base but she's probably advertising her brand. Now for the actual braiding—get it secure at the base of her hair so they'll remain neat. Keep your fingers at the top of the braid while you work and detangle as you go along. Easier said than done. That little girl's hair is shorter than Mary's. Maybe she should have cut Mary's hair first.

"Mommy!" Mary turned around. "You're hurting me. When Susan does it, she doesn't hurt."

"Sorry, bubi." Tamar bit her lower lip. "I'm trying my best but still learning."

"Why couldn't Susan come? You don't even know how to do our hair."

Tamar paused and shot a glance at Steve, who was busy with Joey. He raised his eyebrows at her.

Steve had balls of sweat on his brow. "Joey's got nice thick hair. Got to keep cleaning the blades on the clipper."

"Oof," Joey said. "Why couldn't we just go again to the barber on Kibbutz Eilot. He's got the right cutter and does all my friends."

"Wanted to try it myself," Steve said. "You're gonna be one handsome guy. You already are."

"Will it look like my friends'? … Are you finished yet?"

Steve did everything carefully and deliberately, not in a rush like her, but she should have reminded him to work quickly because Joey couldn't sit still for long. The teacher yesterday had told her something she suspected.

"Joey is a bright and curious boy," his teacher had said to Tamar at the parent's meeting. "He's come a long way, and the transition from the school on the kibbutz to the regular school wasn't easy."

That school was useless, lacking basic equipment, and normal classrooms. Activists from refugee organizations had fought for the Sudanese to be admitted into normal schools. But it was sickening how parents picketed and stopped sending their children to school when they heard the Sudanese were enrolling. Thankfully, justice prevailed.

The teacher paused. "The problem is that he has a hard time concentrating and staying in his chair. I'd recommend a test for ADHD."

"Mommmy, the movie's finished." Mary jerked her head around. "You're taking too long."

"I'll finish three more braids, and it looks fabulous, doesn't it, Arava?"

"You're beautiful, Mary girl," Arava said. "Love the beads."

Tamar finished the final braid and attached a pink bead. "Done, Mary, you're gorgeous. Let's have dinner, and I have home-made chocolate banana ice cream for dessert." She stepped back to gaze on her handiwork.

Sure, foster and adopted children had questions and issues,

but everyone carried baggage around, some more than others. The identity crisis for Sudanese children living with an Israeli family would likely pop up and grow as they became teenagers, but Mary and Joey didn't fit in any other place. And hey, Mary's hair didn't look bad and neither did Joey's.

31

Estie knocked on the Goldman's open door, touched the mezuzah, and kissed her fingers. "Shalom!"

Mary and Joey came running and wrapped their arms around her.

"How are my two special children today? Ready for some games?"

House visits were one of the things Estie enjoyed about her work. Coming into a home every two weeks, seeing the bonds within the family grow, and developing rapport with not only the children themselves but with the parents and siblings too.

Of course, with the children's tough backgrounds, and parents often ensnared in substance abuse and bad relationships, challenges arose. Not to mention issues with foster parents who might have entered the system for the wrong reasons, or their circumstances changed. Thankfully, she wasn't alone and had her backup team of psychologists and therapists.

She tried to give each case her undivided attention but couldn't help having people with whom she had a better chemistry. Tamar and Steve were one of her favorites, though she wouldn't have naturally been sympathetic to their situation. Refugees? Her family and friends called them infiltrators and wanted to get rid of them as fast as possible. As if it were so simple. Dalia made it sound like she was doing something illegal and seemed to be threatening her job security. And yet, she could see Mary and Joey thriving, and Tamar seemed to be someone she might talk to about Jens. Perhaps today after her time with the kids, they would have an opportunity.

Estie had never had a boyfriend, and, on the one hand, Jens was everything she could have wanted—tall, dark hair, deep blue eyes, smart, and generous. She liked how easy it was to talk to him. As he spoke about his job, she could tell he was hard-working. Her Eilat friends thought she'd be crazy to let him go, but her family ...

Tamar stepped out of the kitchen and gave Estie a hug. "Mary, Joey, let Estie sit down and drink something. Water, coffee?"

"Don't want to bother you. Looks like you're preparing another cake."

"For the bar mitzva of the son of the brother of a colleague from work. But I'm ready for coffee myself." Tamar put the kettle on and placed grapes and apricots on a platter.

"I see you're finding time again for cake making."

"Life is a bit calmer now."

Sorry for the bombshell I'm about to drop.

"Can we play Taki again?" Mary said to Estie.

"How many grapes can I have?" she asked Tamar and ran to her room to get the box of cards.

"I like the memory game," Joey said. "Remember how I beat you last time?"

"I don't know how you do it."

"And I won Taki. Can I have an apricot too?"

"You kids are getting really good at both games. We'll start with Taki and then a round of Memory if we have time." Estie slid to the floor. "Mary, you deal the cards, and Joey goes first because he's youngest."

Estie learned a lot playing games with children. When she met them, Mary and Joey had a hard time losing but now were better. Joey couldn't sit still for long, but he liked card games and was into puzzles lately. He was also becoming more talkative. In the beginning they struggled with language skills. Their mother spoke Arabic and her tribal language, but clearly didn't speak much to them at all. Now they only spoke Hebrew.

Time went fast and Estie looked at the time on her phone. "We'll save Memory for next time. I have to talk to your mother."

She pulled herself up onto the sofa and turned to Tamar. "Do you have a few minutes?" This wasn't going to be easy.

"Perfect," Tamar said. "I just put the cake in the oven. Let's go to the garden. Mary, Joey, you can do your homework."

Estie sat in a black plastic chair and looked around. "Looks like you're finding time for gardening lately."

Tamar leaned back in her chair. "You noticed?"

"How could I not? It's amazing—mango tree, flowers, vegetable garden."

"We sit here evenings, enjoy meals in the fresh air, and the kids love making salads from their home-grown tomatoes and cucumbers."

Estie didn't know how to begin so she looked down at her checklist. "The games went great today. Mary was a good loser though she was ahead most of the game."

"We've been working on that," Tamar said.

"Joey's still jumpy and we may have to get him checked for ADHD, but he's not stuttering as he was," Estie said.

"His teacher said the same about the ADHD, and I've made an appointment for an evaluation."

"Their vocabulary's becoming richer. Although they missed the first three crucial years for language development, Mary, with God's help, has caught up. Joey may need specialized help."

"We work on that, too—we read stories and a Bible portion every night with questions and answers."

It was unusual for a secular family to read the Bible regularly. Tamar had said something about their belief in Yeshua. Tamar and Steve were Jewish but believed in Jesus? Well … it seemed to work for them.

"How are Arava and Gal doing?" Working with the whole

family was important. "It isn't always easy for the siblings of foster children."

"Issues do come up," Tamar said, "especially between Gal and Mary. "She can be demanding and needy emotionally which annoys Gal, but Steve and I try to keep our finger on the pulse. Last week he went to the Extreme Park with Gal and next week Arava and I are going to the Dolphin Reef together for her introductory dive that she got for a birthday present from my sister Michal."

"If there's anything I can do or you have questions, just let me know," Estie said.

"Thanks. Appreciated."

"There's one more thing I have to share with you today." Estie touched her star of David pendant and shifted in her chair.

"Nu?"

"Catherine, their mother, called."

Tamar let out a deep breath and began twirling her curls. "She came here a few months ago."

"I know. You called me, remember?"

"I'd hoped it was a one-time thing." She sunk back into her chair.

"We also weren't sure. With Michael interpreting, we tried to make it clear she can't just show up. We told her at the time that if she wants to see Mary and Joey, we can arrange visits."

"So, what'd she say on the phone?"

"She wants to see them."

"How does that work?"

"To begin with, a social worker in Tel Aviv would contact Catherine to determine if she's stable and able to interact with her children. And then, we would begin monthly visits with a social worker present. We have protocols."

"But she'd never get Mary and Joey back to live with her." Tamar's voice fell away. "I guess I really don't know much about her."

Tamar must know that the policy was to reunite children with their parents when possible. But like most foster parents, Tamar had become so immersed in her role as their mother that she couldn't conceive parting from Mary and Joey. Estie thought about whether she would ever foster and wasn't sure she'd have the unconditional love required. Estie saw it all the time: being a foster parent was an emotional roller-coaster ride.

"I'm afraid I can't say." Estie looked down. "I've seen every sort of case, but remember, our ultimate goal is what we call 'for the good of the child.'" This was her usual line, and she hoped Tamar understood.

Mary came bounding out of her room. "I'm hungry, can I have some more grapes?"

"A few, we'll have dinner soon," Tamar said.

"I'm taking eight." Mary counted as she crammed them in her mouth.

"Talk it over with Steve," Estie said. "I'm available if you have questions. If not, see you in two weeks, God willing." She stood up and walked back through the house, to the front door. "Bye kids. Love you."

The talk about Jens would have to wait for another visit. Tamar needed time to process this information and the new stage they were entering.

32

Coming through the entrance of the Dolphin Reef and hearing the peacocks screeching—Tamar smiled now to think she first thought they were cats meowing—smelling the lush vegetation, and seeing dolphins jumping, was like entering an oasis.

"We've been meaning to do this for too long, haven't we?" Tamar turned to Arava next to her. She looked so grown-up in her new bathing suit.

"Never mind," Arava said. "It was hard to find a time that suited the three of us, but now we're here. It's the best birthday present Michal could give me."

"Have any of your friends done a diving course? ... Hey, here comes Michal."

In her pink swim shirt over a black bikini, Michal looked like she belonged on a poster for the Reef, and in fact, they did use a picture of her on their website.

"Here's a wet hug," Michal said. "Cool bathing suit—suits you. Ready for your dive? Where's the rest of the family?"

"They wanted to come," Tamar said. "But I thought it'd be more special if it was just the two of us this time. Steve took the rest of the family to the beach at his work. He had to check something there anyway."

Michal nodded. "Your course starts in an hour. They begin with a half hour explanation by one of our instructors and fitting your equipment. Then you have a half hour under water with your personal instructor. A couple from France and a brother and sister from Tel Aviv are in your group. In the meantime, enjoy yourselves ... and have a swim."

"Thanks," Tamar said. "It'll be fun to do together and have pictures of us underwater. Arava has been counting the days."

"I'll bring an iced coffee and lemonade to your chairs," Michal said.

"With soy milk and no sugar." said Tamar. She hoped she wouldn't see anyone she knew. Whenever she had gone anyplace with her mother in Arad, her mother always met someone and began long conversations with them, forgetting about Tamar. That's not how she wanted to be with her family.

Tamar and Michal found a spot near the water in the shade and plunked down into the white plastic beach chairs. Since meeting Steve while doing a diving course in Eilat, diving had a special place in Tamar's heart. She loved everything connected to water and was excited for her daughter to have this experience. She'd read someplace that of all kinds of exercises, people rate swimming the highest level of enjoyment. And diving took swimming to a new level.

Leaning back in her chair Tamar watched the children play in the sand and splash in the shallow water. Then, as Arava was swimming out to the line of buoys, Tamar nearly dozed off; but suddenly she sat up straight.

"Help! Emergency!" called an older man as he and a young man were dragging an older woman out of the water.

Tamar ran over as the young man managed to blurt out, "My mother."

"Lay her in the shade," Tamar said.

A small crowd gathered around, but no one else seemed to be a health care worker.

In nursing school she'd learned the four steps for artificial resuscitation. *Help me do it correctly.*

Check consciousness. "Can you hear me?" Tamar pressed on the woman's shoulder. No answer. Her breathing was irregular. Cardiac arrest. She needed help quickly.

""Call an ambulance, fast! ... Stand back!"

Tamar checked the woman's airway and tilted her head back.

Out of the corner of her eye she caught Arava coming out of the water and standing in the back of the circle.

"My mother's a good swimmer," said the man, nearly crying. He covered his mother with a towel. "We're on a family vacation in Eilat, from New York. We were all swimming together when I noticed she wasn't moving her arms and legs. She's a strong woman. ... This is my father. ... Will she be okay?"

Tamar hadn't done CPR for years, but every minute of delay could be life threatening. Fortunately, the woman wasn't overweight ... but wasn't young either.

Now the compressions—one hundred a minute, hard and fast on the center of her chest to the beat of the Bee Gee's "Staying Alive," as she remembered it being taught to her. She began humming the song.

In her concentration on the CPR procedure, Tamar was startled by Michal's voice. "Arava, Tamar, ready for your dive?" Then as Michal drew closer, "S**t. What's going on?"

Sixty-five, sixty-six, sixty-seven ... Tamar couldn't answer or look up.

"Come, Arava," Michal said. "I'm sorry but we've gotta go, they're starting now with the briefing."

Was the woman's breath coming back? For a split second, Tamar had a chance to think, Arava's sixteenth birthday. How did she end up here instead of diving with her daughter?

"It's okay, Mommy," Arava said as she walked off with Michal. "Don't worry about me."

Far off, a siren sounded.

The familiar team in their white shirts came running down the steps with a stretcher. "First Aid! Everyone back!"

The medics bent over the woman and lifted her onto the stretcher. "One person can ride with us," they announced.

The husband grabbed his shirt and ran off behind them. In a second, they were gone.

Tamar stood up, blinked her eyes, and drew a deep breath.

The son rounded up the rest of the family and with tears in his eyes, gave Tamar a hug. "You saved my mother's life."

She heard the siren fading in the distance. The scene on the beach returned to its peaceful self. A man wearing a red t-shirt saying "Dolphin Reef" came up to her. "You saved me," he said. I'm the lifeguard, and if you hadn't been here, she would have been my responsibility, so I'm always glad when we have a nurse or doctor present."

Tamar collapsed into her chair. She'd missed Arava's big moment, their chance to do something memorable together. But how could she have handled it differently? Would Arava be disappointed? They'd planned this dive for a long time.

Life was strange and full of surprises. How often was a person able to save a life? The blessing and challenge of being a nurse— she couldn't put her profession aside when people around her needed help.

What she needed now was a swim. She looked at her phone, twenty minutes before Arava was due to finish. Tamar took a quick dive in the sea. Immersing herself in the cool waters and focusing on her breathing helped her relax. While swimming, she became extra aware of her body and experienced a freedom like none other.

Stepping out of the water, she wrapped her towel around her and walked to the pier to watch Arava emerging from the water. She could still take a few pictures. At least Michal had ordered the package for Arava that included an underwater video. If it'd been up to Steve and her, they'd have passed on that expensive addition.

With wide smile and shining eyes, Arava exclaimed, "Mommy, the dolphins came right up to us, and the diving wasn't hard. You would've loved it."

"I'm sure I would've. Sorry I couldn't join you, after we talked about it so long."

"I didn't mean it that way," Arava said. "You saved a life and nothing's more important than that. ... Now I want to do a real diving course. I'm going to start saving babysitting money."

Michal joined them. "Your mother is a hero. The whole Reef is talking about her."

33

Tamar rarely came down to the marina, but she found her way easily based on Yossi's description of the Mermaid. There it was, docked on the left side of the pier, turquoise hull and wooden mermaid extending from its bow.

"Can you come on Wednesday?" Yossi had asked. "We finish our last trip at five and don't have an evening sail. You wouldn't believe how much stuff people leave on our boat."

Tamar was always looking for places to collect old clothes to take to the Sudanese on the kibbutz—from neighbors, their fellowship, and work. Most refugees had found jobs, but the jobs were low-paying and the refugees didn't have the same rights and benefits as Israeli citizens. So they appreciated all contributions.

"I'll gather things from the other yachts too, bag them, and help you carry them to the kibbutz," Yossi had offered.

For Tamar, having seen Yossi's kind heart and his joining their family, this was another good sign. He obviously liked Michal, but she seemed to be the problem. She didn't talk about Berlin anymore but now without warning, decided to join her friend on a trip to Thailand. How did that fit in? She said she needed a break. But poor Yossi. In the beginning, Tamar thought it just as well they weren't rushing things. Michal couldn't handle a new relationship so soon after Shai. And Yossi needed to find himself, though Tamar could see Yossi becoming more open and self confident all the time. He spoke about university and signed up for a course to prepare for matriculation exams. But how long would Michal keep him hanging?

"Tamar!" Yossi waved his hand and called as she approached

the yacht. "I've got a lot of bags, but do you have a few minutes? I could show you our ship."

"Sure. Why not?" Tamar walked across the gangplank. "I've only been on a sail once, an end-of-the-year party from work. The Mermaid is really nice."

"Let me get you a glass of water," Yossi said. "Or coffee?"

"I came straight from work. Coffee sounds good."

She followed Yossi down the stairs.

"Mind your head," he said. "This is the galley, the kitchen of the ship. You'd be surprised at the meals we put together for our guests."

"You're the cook?"

"I do everything. At home I never entered the kitchen. That was the area for my mother and sisters. Everyone had their own tasks. For us, it was studying. Come, let's sit up on deck."

They climbed the stairs and settled into the low pillows. "You just read the Talmud, right? Did you ever read the Prophets?"

"No. I'm reading them now, though, in the Bible you gave me for my birthday. I like Isaiah, the language he uses."

"What a view." Tamar looked over the sea. "Have you opened the New Testament?"

"I started but not sure what to think. You know how we were taught. To believe in Jesus made you a traitor. We couldn't even mention his name. But his words make a lot of sense."

"Steve would be happy to talk more if you want."

"I'm pretty busy with my course. I have a lot of catching up to do and the exam is in four months. In the yeshiva, we studied all day long, but nothing practical. I didn't realize how much I was lacking."

"We can help with that, too. Steve's good with math and can tutor you in English. And I always liked Hebrew."

"You guys are also busy with four kids." A smile creased Yossi's face. "Those two little ones are lively."

"We like having you come around. Even when Michal leaves, you're always welcome."

The sun was now touching the mountains of Edom. "We better get going, still have to drive to the kibbutz and drop off the clothes," Tamar said.

They stood up. She reached for a sack.

"One more thing." Yossi rubbed his hand through his hair. "I'm shy to ask, but does Michal ever say anything about me? I'm confused. It's just been going on for so long. In the community where I grew, we married quickly. I'm still not sure I understand how most people do it."

"No rules. I know she likes you. Can we keep talking as we load the bags? I think she's simply confused with herself. Hopefully, during this time away she can think and get her priorities straight."

"She's a remarkable woman." Yossi's eyes sparkled. "I like her a lot, but maybe I have to let go. I'm not getting clear signals, but you know, I never had a girlfriend."

"And she's beautiful," Tamar said.

Yossi blushed and looked down.

"She's trying to find her way. About you, and about faith issues, too. Life isn't straightforward for most people it seems."

Yossi nodded and picked up a couple of bags.

"Even for us," Tamar added. "I'm still trying to figure things out. I know it was right to take Mary and Joey, but the situation isn't always clear-cut."

"Not even for you? … Where's your car?"

"Not far away. Identity issues, their mother turning up, differences between Steve and me. More children, more conflicts. Last night—"

"I understand that. We're ten children, and my father couldn't take it anymore, so he walked out. What happened last night?"

"Not the first time, but Gal ran out of the house yelling that

163

he was going to sleep at Ben's. Mary was bugging him."

"He stayed there?"

"No, he eventually calmed down and came home, and Mary apologized."

"One thing I've learned—don't doubt yourself and don't look back." Yossi put his bags down and gave Tamar a hand as she stepped off the boat. "I've had lots of reasons to sink into fear, but the main thing is to go forward, and things do work out."

"For me, it's reminding myself of God's goodness."

"No matter how dark it was around me, I've always believed that."

"About Michal … be patient."

They stuffed all the bags in the car and shut the doors.

Before Tamar drove off she said, "Thanks. For the Sudanese, they'll appreciate these clothes. And for me, your friendship means a lot."

34

Tamar spread a mat on the sand in the shade of a palm tree and laid towels and the cool chest on it. "We'll sit here on the beach and swim while Gal and Ben take turns with their windsurfer."

"Ben's going first," Gal said. "Gonna be exciting today with the strong wind."

The two boys picked up the windsurfer and carried it to the edge of the water.

"Will we be able to see him all the time?" Joey asked.

Gal came back to sit with the family while Ben sped off, skimming over the sea.

"You told us that's Jordan and farther on Saudi Arabia." Mary pointed down the Gulf. "Couldn't the wind take him there by accident?"

"Don't worry," Gal said. "That's one thing they teach us. First, we learn how to stand up and balance, then to move with the wind, and afterward how to turn around and go against the wind. In the beginning when you're learning, a boat follows you in case you go too far."

Mary stared at the Surf Center sign and read out loud slowly, "Windsurfing is suitable for all ages, starting at age 6."

"Well done, reading without vowels," Tamar said.

"I'm already nine," Mary said. "Could this be my activity next year? ... I'm hungry."

Tamar opened the cool box. "How about some snacks, and we'll have lunch after Ben and Gal each take a turn. Gal and Ben bought the board with money they earned—"

"And with help from you and his mother," Arava added.

"For my birthday present," Gal said.

"I'll talk to Estie and ask if they'll pay for windsurfing lessons," Tamar said. "Granola bars anyone?"

"You did well in your gymnastics club," Arava said. "It'll help you with windsurfing."

"It's all about balance," Steve said. "And you're a strong girl."

"You also windsurfed, Daddy, right?" Gal asked.

"Just a little on the lakes in Canada when I was young. But did you know that Eilat is one of the best places in the world for windsurfing? We have international competitions here and—"

"Shahar Zubari from Eilat won a bronze medal in the Olympics," Gal said.

"I know his aunt," Tamar said. "An old Eilat family."

"What about you, Joey?" Arava said. "Seven is also old enough."

"Not yet," Joey said. "But I don't mind going in the water with you with my new mask."

Steve looked at Tamar. "Can I get you an iced coffee?"

"Yalla Joey, let's check out the corals," Arava said.

Tamar couldn't think of a better way to spend a warm afternoon in December. She hadn't been swimming for a few weeks now, with the weather getting cooler, and hoped to take a long snorkel into the Nature Reserve. She also didn't want to miss hanging out with the family. As Arava and Gal grew older, it didn't often work out to go places together. Arava volunteered at Magen David Adom and Gal divided his time between basketball, chess club, and hanging out at Ben's house. But she loved these ages, seeing them develop their own personalities and interests.

If life could just go on like this. And why couldn't they get a year's custody agreement like most foster families? Dalia wasn't making life easy for them.

Ben steered the windsurfer back to the beach and leaped off.

"My turn!" Gal jumped up and began squeezing himself into his wetsuit.

"I forgot to tell you," Steve said. "There've been sightings of a whale shark lately. Keep your eyes open."

"A friend of mine saw one while she was swimming at Dekel Beach," Arava said. "Not even in deep water."

"Sharks aren't dangerous?" Joey said and put his mask back on the sand again.

"Not whale sharks," Arava said.

"Even though it's a type of shark and is the largest non-mammal vertebrate," Steve said. "Who knows what's a mammal?"

"It's warm blooded and—," Mary said.

"Drinks milk from its mother," Joey said.

"Well done, so a non-mammal is …?" Steve asked.

"A whale shark?" Mary said.

"Right," Steve said. "But also fish, birds, and reptiles. And vertebrate just means it has bones."

"We learned about whale sharks when we visited the Underwater Observatory with our class," Mary said. "They look scary because they're so big, but they only eat tiny fish."

Mary's curiosity and ability to remember what she learned never ceased to amaze Tamar. How far she'd come, this ragged little Sudanese girl she met at Kibbutz Eilot three years ago. She could end up being a scientist like Steve, a nurse or doctor, or anything she wanted.

Tamar stood up. "Who wants to swim with me? The waves are breaking down the castle you built, and you're full of sand."

Tamar's phone rang. Her friends didn't usually call on Shabbat afternoon, and Imma and Abba would be taking their nap now. The number was unfamiliar.

"Shalom?"

"Can I talk to Mary or Joey?"

"Who's calling, please?" Tamar asked though the voice and

accent were unmistakable. *How did she get my number?*

"Their mother."

"Catherine, I'm sorry. I think you don't understand." Tamar could feel her heart pounding. She took a deep breath and moved away from where the rest were sitting.

"Mary, Joey," the mother said.

"Don't you remember, Catherine, our agreement with the social worker? Where are you?"

"Tel Aviv, but I'm coming to Eilat tomorrow."

"Estie can arrange a visit for you, but you have to talk to her first. You're not allowed to call us directly." She couldn't let Mary and Joey speak to their mother on the phone. They'd be thrown off balance, just like when a gust caught the sail of the windsurfer, and who knew what mental state Catherine was in? The relationship, if there would be one, needed time and small steps to rebuild.

Click. The phone went dead.

Tamar's mind was racing, Steve wasn't swimming yet … he always knew what to do. She returned to their mat.

"Estie probably has her phone off on Shabbat," Steve said after hearing from Tamar. "But leave her a message. She'll call Catherine's social worker in Tel Aviv, who can, hopefully, explain to her the process of contacting the children."

Maybe Catherine called spontaneously. She was unstable and dysfunctional enough to do that, and had no clue about child psychology and planning ahead for what was best for the children. Even common sense seemed to be lacking.

"The Sudanese Referendum is in another month, on January 10," Steve said. They're all talking about it. Maybe the excitement's affecting Catherine."

Tamar opened the cool box, trying to act as if everything was normal. "Who's ready for lunch? You must be all hungry from swimming."

35

W ho else will be here?" Arava asked as they stepped out of the car in Kibbutz Eilot.

"I hope we're not the only ones who aren't Sudanese," Gal said. They were at the age where they needed to be with friends.

Mary and Joey raced off to join Sudanese children chasing each other around the parking lot.

"Don't worry," Tamar said. "Another couple of families from the congregation told me they're coming. I'm sure Rivka, the kibbutznik in charge of the refugees, will be here, and the children's teachers, too."

Tamar could smell the meat grilling—no vegetarians or vegans among the Sudanese. Cattle played a central role in the South Sudanese culture, from measuring wealth to paying the bride price. Often a hundred or more cows were paid to the woman's family; and milk was an important part of their diet.

Coming here gave Tamar an opportunity to immerse herself for a short time in Mary and Joey's background and to try to understand them better. It also left her with mixed feelings— where did they really belong? The Sudanese children were still their best friends.

"They've been planning this party and waiting for this day for months," Steve said. He came here more than Tamar did now, to give Bible studies. It had taken them time to understand that though most South Sudanese called themselves Christians and that religion was one area of conflict with Muslim Sudan, few of the refugees had any Bible knowledge.

Loud African-style music surrounded them as they stepped

inside the hall that was once the clubhouse of the old youth hostel. From her visits to the kibbutz, Tamar recognized some of the songs and rhythms with their strong drumbeat. She'd been in this place before; but no event they'd attended here, including wedding and engagement parties, could compare to the Referendum. Today South Sudan was voting whether their region should remain part of Sudan or become independent.

The new South Sudanese flag—black, red, and green stripes with a yellow star in a blue triangle—flew on strings across the ceiling, while everyone twirled their own flags. The broad smiles said it all, the whites of their eyes and their teeth seemed even brighter than usual.

Tamar had to swallow and blink her eyes when she saw the large star-of-David created with the Sudanese colors in the entrance. Although there must be parties like this today all over the world wherever South Sudanese were scattered, whoever decorated this place took care to emphasize the special connection the South Sudanese felt with Israel.

"The Sudanese sure know how to dress up," Tamar said to Steve. "Aren't you glad you listened when I told you to wear pants, shoes, and a button-up shirt?" Most of the men and boys had on suits and ties, and the women had elaborate braids, high heels, and nice dresses. Where'd they get these clothes in Eilat? Amazing what they accumulated in four years, people who ran over the border with only the shirts on their backs, many without even documents.

Michael greeted them. "We thank you for coming," he said. "We will start soon our program."

Tamar had learned what "soon" meant for the Sudanese. Good thing they'd eaten at home, because she knew it'd be a while before they tasted any food, after all the speeches and singing. Steve and the children would be happy with the grilled meat, and she expected she'd find rice and bean stew.

Tamar walked over to a group of women.

"How are Mary and Joey doing?" one of them asked.

"Fine. Enjoying school. They're growing up so fast." What else could she answer? The call from Catherine, the conflicts, the lack of stability? She surveyed the room for the children. In Eilat, she could spot them from far away in a sea of white skin, but here they blended in. Thankfully, Arava and Gal had found friends; she saw them sitting on the side.

At one time, she had wondered why a Sudanese family hadn't taken in Mary and Joey, though with time she understood that, for them, fostering was done by relatives. And despite all their fancy clothes and latest cell phones, most struggled financially and lived in small apartments. Now that she understood more about refugees, she realized that the upheaval in their lives resulted in many dysfunctional families. At home in Sudan, they lived among their large extended families and their own tribe, and everyone helped and kept an eye on each other. Here, it was each to his own.

In the Israeli society, Mary and Joey would always be outsiders. But wasn't everyone an outsider in some way? She prayed they would use it to their advantage and become stronger people through their experiences and trials.

"They are pleased to play with their friends," Joanne, Michael's wife, said as she watched the children dashing around.

"What do you think about the referendum?" Tamar asked.

"We are happy." Joanne spoke English like her husband.

"Will it change anything for you?" Tamar asked.

"Like all people, we want our country independent, but Sudan has problems. The war destroyed much."

"We have different tribes who do not get along," another added.

"We need good leaders."

"And patience."

"Would you want to go back now?" Tamar said.

"Not yet." Joanne shook her head.

"Do you have a few minutes?" Tamar asked. "Maybe we can move to the back where it's quieter."

Joanne took Tamar by the elbow. "Of course. Can I help you?"

Tamar sat down opposite Joanne and leaned forward. "I've never understood what happened with Mary and Joey's father and why Catherine acts like she does. I know as refugees, all of you have suffered, but you and Michael look happy together and have two nice children."

Joanne was quiet for a minute. "Hard story. Catherine fell in love with a young man from a different tribe. All parents didn't agree, so her parents married her quickly to an older man from their tribe. She was second wife and soon became pregnant."

"In Sudan men take more than one wife?" Catherine was obviously traumatized, but Tamar hadn't imagined her forcefully becoming an older man's second wife. "I thought you were Christians."

"They do that in our culture, who has enough money. When baby was little, she become pregnant again but then bombings begin in her village. Husband runs away with first wife, but Catherine can't run with little baby and pregnant, so stay with husband's mother. On the way, bomb hits husband and first wife and killed."

Tamar took a deep breath. "How awful."

"That not all, very sad." Joanne exhaled loudly. "Husband's mother not nice, no food, so Catherine has to leave with two babies."

"Mary and Joey ..." They wouldn't remember this, but it would be ingrained in their sub-conscious.

"One man said he helps her, and she live with him in Cairo. I see her there, but she and children sad and all very skinny. This man also not nice, so Catherine goes to Israel with small group of refugees, hire jeep to take them together across desert. I see Catherine again after we cross border, and we come here to kibbutz together."

"I understand she had a hard life, but then what happened? Why did she leave her children?" Not only did she abandon Mary and Joey, but there was Joey's undernourishment and eye infection. Mary's diabetes …

"We do not know, not acting normal, very sad."

"And what about Catherine now?" Tamar finally asked the most important question.

"She lives in Tel Aviv. We do not hear from her. Hope she getting better."

"You think she wants her children back?"

"Not now, maybe later. She—"

Mary came zipping by and stopped in front of them, holding a slice of apple in one hand, a sugar cookie in the other, and an expectant smile on her face.

"Guess it won't hurt you," Tamar said. "Where'd you get them?"

"They've set up tables of food in the back, and one of the ladies gave them to me." Mary took a bite of the cookie.

"Good of you to ask me."

Michael walked up to them. "The program will begin, and afterward the women have cooked us a meal."

The men were sitting on one side of the hall and the women on the other. Steve, who'd been talking with some of the men, came over to Tamar.

"Please, sit you two in front," said Michael. He led them to chairs. "We are happy you came. You know how important for us is this day."

"Isn't it expected to be a landslide vote for independence?" Steve asked.

"This is true," Michael said. "Our people suffered terribly, and many lives were lost in the civil war." He sat next to them.

"I've been reading books about Sudan," Steve said, "and see parallels with Israel's independence."

"I never learned about Israel's history, but we all want to separate. Most speeches will be English because we are different tribes. But when they speak Arabic or our tribal languages, I will interpret for you."

Tamar was trying to process what Joanne told her about Catherine. She knew that a date in July was already determined for the creation of the independent state of South Sudan. Would this change anything for the refugees in Israel, for Mary and Joey? A lot might shift, and probably not for their good.

Israel was less welcoming to the Sudanese than when they arrived, and they weren't receiving the status as asylum seekers for which they'd hoped. On the other hand, however, they were becoming more rooted here and uneager to return to a country with few roads or schools but plenty of diseases.

Michael strode to the podium. He looked over the crowd and stood silently for a moment. "Thank you all for coming, Sudanese from different tribes, and our Israeli friends. We are brothers and sisters, and this is a great day for us. We have suffered too much and are ready to begin a new period."

The room burst into applause while the children hopped to their feet waving their flags. High hopes, but what were their chances of success? Israel faced tremendous challenges with independence but had a strong core of educated people. In Sudan, the majority were subsistence farmers, corruption reigned, and infrastructure was totally lacking.

Never mind, whatever happened, Mary and Joey were part of her family now and going to South Sudan wasn't an option.

36

Michal knew she was taking a risk inviting Yossi to their Seder, though he'd spent enough time with Tamar and Steve to understand something about their faith in Jesus, which was a contradiction to everything he experienced at home and learned in the yeshiva. Of course, every family in Israel celebrated the Seder in their own way. All read the Haggadah, used four cups of wine, three matzos, the lamb bone, bitter herbs, lots of singing, and more. With Abba and Imma it was the same, except here, as Abba liked to say, everything pointed to Yeshua.

Steve had borrowed a van from work large enough to take Michal, Yossi, and Kinneret along with the family, so they had driven up to Arad the day before in order to help with the final arrangements—the food and setting the table. Not that Imma allowed anyone else to cook; she had her traditional Yemenite recipes and didn't think anyone could prepare them the right way.

After helping Imma with her painstaking Passover cleaning and even painting the house for her, Abba wisely stayed away on the morning of the Seder. Now, Steve understood that the best help he could give was to get the children out of the way and use up their excess energy.

"Who wants to go for a short jeep trip?" Abba said. "Yossi, there's so much we'd love to show you around this area, while we're all in Arad."

"Can we go to Masada?" Arava asked.

"That's a bit far for today. I was thinking of heading to Tel

Krayot, a great place to scramble around the ruins and caves."
Steve turned to Tamar. "You don't need my help, duck?"

"Enjoy, just be back in time to set up the extra table and chairs," Tamar said.

Michal and Abba had learned to give Imma space and go along with her plans in the Seder preparations. Why not? Who wouldn't like the Yemenite chicken soup, Charoset made with dates instead of the apples that Ashkenazi Jews used, and all the greens that had to be laid just so on the table?

Only Tamar would argue with Imma. She wanted to start at a different time, sit in another order ... and with Tamar's strict diet, neither could understand the other. Michal wished Tamar would drop the diet for this one special evening, for the sake of peace, but apparently that wasn't possible.

"You don't even eat eggs?" Imma asked Tamar. "It doesn't make sense at Pessach, eggs are one of the symbols of the meal, and the desserts all need eggs."

"I've been a vegan for four years, and you still don't get it?"

Imma shook her head.

"So let everyone eat them but me." Tamar sounded like she was trying to be adaptable. But it seemed to Michal her sister was really just being selfish.

Pessach was the highlight of the year for Imma. She spent time planning the menu—even though it was the same every year, shopped like crazy, cleaned the house till it shone, and began cooking days ahead of the Seder. But most important was having her family together around the table.

Even without Pessach, Michal had been ready to come home. Four months traveling around Thailand and Vietnam was enough. Just as she had known she had to get away, see new sights, meet different people, and reflect on her life, she knew it was time to return. She missed Eilat, the dolphins, her nieces and nephews, Kinneret, and especially Yossi, thanking her lucky stars, whatever, or whoever, that their paths had crossed. Even while she was gone, Yossi kept in touch with her family, and this year, for the first time, was joining her family's Seder.

∾

The door flew open, and the four children burst in followed by Steve, Yossi, and Abba.

"Did you think we were Elijah?" Abba laughed.

"Saba," Gal said. "They know it's not time for Elijah yet. We only open the door for him at the end of the Seder."

"Everyone take showers," Tamar said, "and then you can help us set the table."

Michal took Yossi aside. "How was it?"

"The kids, all of us, had so much fun in the caves. Your father made the place come alive. He told us that many people think it's the hometown of Judas Iscariot, the disciple who betrayed Jesus. I read about him last week in the gospel of Matthew."

"I know. For you it's new and interesting … but don't forget, I grew up on those stories."

"And today you don't think they're true?—"

"Michal, I need help." That was her bossy big sister calling.

"Cool," she said to Yossi, and to Tamar she called back, "Coming." But she briefly turned back to Yossi. "One more thing. Our Seder might be different from others you've been to. They compare everything to Jesus."

"Don't worry. I'm old enough to make up my own mind."

∾

Imma gave a contented sigh as she sat down opposite Abba on the chair nearest the kitchen. Her eyes scanned the table to make sure they hadn't forgotten anything—the Haggadah next to each place, candles, wine, matzo, of course, and all the bowls with the other Passover symbols—salt water, bitter herbs, Charoset, and eggs. A smile spread across her face as she looked from one family member to the other.

Imma said, "Peter—"

"Sorry, just a moment," interrupted Tamar. "Steve, did you check Mary's—"

"Done. She was low after all the running around in the caves so gave her extra insulin." Then to his father-in-law Steve said, "Go ahead."

"We want to welcome everyone to our Seder this year," Abba began. "We're happy to have Yossi with us for the first time. This Seder might be different from others you've experienced, but we hope you'll feel at home. Please feel free to ask questions."

"Thank you for inviting me," Yossi said. "What a beautiful table, and the aromas—"

"Yemenite food's the best," Michal said. "That's the hawaij you smell, Imma's special spice mixture, sort of like curry, that she uses for the roast meat. You're probably also smelling the ginger and cloves from the Charoset."

"As Shakespeare wrote, 'Too much of a good thing'." Steve inhaled deeply and with obvious pleasure. "Shoshanna, you're incredible."

"Mary and Joey, on your fourth Seder with us," Abba said. "we feel privileged to have you in our family. This evening, as we remember the Exodus from Egypt, we're reminded of the words in the Torah that the Lord loves the stranger because you were strangers in Egypt."

Mary beamed and rested her head on Michal's shoulder. What a turn-around, Michal remembered Imma and Abba's first reaction to Mary and Joey; but actually they were just concerned for Tamar overdoing herself. However, now these kids were family. Michal realized she'd missed them.

"Just a few points before we begin," Abba continued. "The Haggadah we use is similar to traditional ones, but you'll see how we'll be making the connection between the Old and New Covenants, and between the Passover lamb and Jesus. Most Jews, as well as Christians, don't know that Jesus was crucified on Pessach, and what is called 'The Last Supper' was Jesus eating the Passover Seder with his disciples. Like the famous picture by Leonardo da Vinci."

"Leonardo da who?" Yossi asked.

"Da Vinci," Arava said. "A famous Italian artist."

"A sculptor and architect too," Gal said.

"We didn't learn about him in yeshiva."

"Back to the Haggadah," Abba said. "Let's open to page one, and we'll go around the table taking turns reading. Arava, you can start."

Yossi leaned back, laid his arm across Michal's chair, and touched her foot under the table. Her fears of him being uncomfortable at their Seder disappeared, ungrounded as fears often were. Yossi was mister mellow himself. She had made a statement by bringing him to her parents' house, one she hadn't been ready to make before Thailand. Thankfully, everyone was being cool and not asking questions … except for Mary.

"When you get married," Mary had asked. "Can I be a bridesmaid?"

∼

Michal set her alarm clock for six the next morning. The Seder had definitely been a success, so much so that no one felt like stopping the after-dinner conversations to wash the dishes and straighten the house. Imma was the first to retire, her eyes drooping shut, exhausted from days of cleaning and cooking. The talk flowed easily from Michal's stories about her recent travels in Southeast Asia, to Steve's adventures in Kenya, and then Abba's tales of arriving for the first time in Israel totally ignorant of the culture and people. Yossi seemed content to listen.

"At first, I thought a few times that a couple of Israelis were about to get into a fistfight when I heard them yelling at each other and waving their arms around," Abba said, grinning. "It was so different from us reserved Brits. But now I understand that it's their passionate nature. And as for queuing up for buses, banks, and post offices—forget it!" Michal had tried to imagine Abba as a young volunteer waiting in line at the bus stop when now he was as pushy as the rest.

Now, having pulled herself out of bed to tackle the tall stack of dishes, and hopefully finish cleaning the floor before the rest of the family rose, Michal was surprised to see the light already on in the kitchen and Steve standing at the sink.

"You beat me."

Steve's lips curled upward. "'Great minds think alike.' In 1618, a man with the remarkable name of Dabridgcourt Belchier wrote those words in *Hans Beer-Pot*. Seriously, I'm used to getting up early for dives. Maybe you can dry the dishes and put them away."

Michal turned on the kettle for a cup of coffee and grabbed a dish towel. "I'm glad you're up, not just for the help but I've been meaning to ask your advice."

"Shoot." Steve placed the dishes in the drying rack.

"It's about my roommates. A couple of girls I work with at the Reef who started the same time as I did. We got along well in the beginning. Funny, Tamar told me right away that she didn't think they were my type, but I felt she was instructing me what to do so, as usual, I paid no attention."

"I also have a big brother," Steve said, "who was the perfect son for my parents. Already at a young age, we didn't have much in common. He sat around the house reading books and listening to music, while I was outside with my friends."

"Like me. I had to find my own path, different from Tamar, and sometimes it took me in the wrong directions." Michal was ashamed now to think of all the worrying and sleepless nights she'd caused Imma and Abba.

"I believe we can learn from those missteps. Walking in the darkness can make us appreciate the light more."

"Hard to imagine you not reading. You always have a book in your hands."

"That came later when I realized I didn't have to do the opposite of my brother. Do you remember why Tamar didn't think those girls were your type?"

"I didn't say much to her, but she picked up on it. They were staying out late, smoking dope, and changing boyfriends. I didn't follow them in everything. But I thought they were my friends. I didn't like Tamar criticizing them." She couldn't explain it, but something kept her back from their crazy parties.

"So, what's your question? How do you feel now?" Steve asked.

They had developed an easy rhythm, washing and drying dishes. Steve moved on to the pots.

"I'm getting tired of them bringing different guys home all the time, and the smell of dope filling our house. Shai and I met when we were young, and the memory of him kept me from seeking other boyfriends. And now there's Yossi."

"Sounds to me like you're growing up and don't feel the need to rebel anymore, and that you're finding yourself closer to your family's values than you once thought."

They began moving the furniture back in place, and Michal filled a bucket with water as Steve swept the floor.

"To be honest, at first I wasn't happy that Yossi was becoming interested in your faith, but I've come to understand that we all need something to believe and hope in, and *this* actually makes the most sense."

"So, what about your roommates? I think you're asking me to confirm what you already know you should do."

Michal spilled the soapy water on the tile floor, glad they didn't have carpets as she'd seen on American soap operas. They both began squeegeeing it out the front door. No system cleaned as well as the good old-fashioned Israeli one.

Michal stood still and pursed her lips. "It'll be hard to tell them I'm leaving without sounding judgmental."

"I'll pray for wisdom, and the right timing and words for you," Steve said. "I'm proud of you. Thanks for sharing with me. And by the way, you found a great guy with Yossi."

The bedroom door opened and Gal stumbled out rubbing his eyes.

A minute later, Imma appeared, smiling as her eyes scanned the room.

Steve set down his squeegee. "Just finished. Sit down, Shoshanna. I'll make you a cup of tea."

37

"I thought there was energy at the Referendum party," Tamar said to Steve. "But today—"

"What? Can't hear you. The music's—"

Tamar moved her mouth close to Steve's ear. "Today's something else! Let's get a drink and join the dancing."

To Tamar, it felt like just last week that they were here in Kibbutz Eilot to celebrate the referendum in which, to no one's surprise, ninety-nine percent of the South Sudanese voted for independence. And today, six months later, the long-awaited day had arrived. And four years had passed since she came here to return a misplaced vaccination card, having no idea how it would change her life.

The weather in Eilat had turned from needing-a-sweater-in-the-evening and wanting to be inside, to stifling hot in the day, and well into the night. With the air conditioning in the clubhouse barely cooling anything and making a racket at the same time, they set up chairs and tables in the parking lot.

Tamar made a mental note to remember the date today, July 9, 2011. For the South Sudanese, their pivotal day, like the Fourth of July for Americans, Canada Day on July 1, and Israel's Independence Day on May 14. That was harder to remember because it was celebrated according to the Hebrew calendar on Iyar 5.

She had seen old movies of Israelis dancing in the streets when independence was declared in 1948. It was a day of euphoria and festivity but also a sword hanging over their heads. The attacks by five Arab countries began the next day, but as Ben Gurion read his famous speech, people chose to forget for a moment what awaited them. For the Sudanese also, now was a time to dance and rejoice, not to think about the enormous problems in their homeland, the world's newest and one of the world's poorest countries.

"Go ahead … you dance." Steve moved away from the crowd and found a seat next to one of his Sudanese friends who also seemed content to watch.

Tamar looked for the children, Mary and Joey were leaping around and waving flags with their friends, while Arava and Gal had joined a group of Sudanese teenagers.

Joanne, Michael's wife, grabbed Tamar's hand. In the center of the wide circle, dancers in traditional African clothes pranced with intricate steps to the beat of the drummers. Her friends, wearing colorful African dresses, stepped from foot to foot making the rising and lowering shrill sound she'd learned was called ululation. She hadn't tried that yet but was happy to dance.

Eva had asked if they could come, having grown close to Mary and Joey. She had also started giving Hebrew lessons in her home to a group of Sudanese women. She had been following the news of South Sudanese's independence, and she said it reminded her of Israel's history. Now she sat here with a couple of her students and her husband, Yakov. His eyes took everything in as he sipped a drink. He often told the story about being rescued at the end of World War II by an African American tank battalion, and how it gave him a special place in his heart for black people. Getting out was good for him, and the music and atmosphere here could raise anyone's spirits.

～

Finally, the music, singing, and dancing stopped, and people began to find seats. Michael and several of the other leaders stood up to speak. By this time, Tamar understood that the refugees in Eilat came from different tribes, some of which had fiercely fought one another at home. Here, they all seemed to get along; but some experts predicted a tribal war in South Sudan now that they had finished fighting the North.

When they brought out the food, Tamar looked for Steve. He was still absorbed in a conversation with his friend.

"I will bring food to you," Joanne said and moved toward the buffet.

"Thanks. but I can help myself," Tamar said. Joanne would probably load her plate with wings and sausages. "But can we sit together, away from the music? I'd like to ask you something."

A while later, as they balanced plates of food on their laps, Joanne asked, "What you are thinking?" Her plate was filled with meat, fava bean stew, a dish made with greens, and one of the porridges.

"About what?" Tamar replied. "The party? Independence?"

"All."

"Sixty-three years ago Israel had excitement of its own ... and challenge. Many died in our War of Independence, and we had much work to do to set up a country."

"We are hoping more people will not die in Sudan. We need big help to build roads, schools, hospitals, everything."

Tamar had been reading about South Sudan lately. More girls were likely to be married by age eighteen than to have finished school. The country was a mess. She prayed the enthusiasm she was seeing would carry over into practical steps to pull them out of their hole.

"What about going back?" Tamar asked. "Have you thought about it?"

"South Sudan is our country; we want to go home when there is no war, but now not."

Mary and Joey came running up to Tamar. "It's fun here," Mary said. "Can you help me get food that's good for me?"

"I'll be right back," Tamar said to Joanne.

Tamar laid her plate on her chair and went with Mary to the food table. "The chicken's okay. And the salad. But not too much rice. I brought some of your cookies, so you don't have to take the ones on the table that have sugar in them."

Tamar returned to Joanne. Between bites she asked, "Is Israel good for you?"

"We are safe here from war, have food, and our children are in school. Most Israelis are nice, but the government is no good to us. We must renew our permits every three months."

"Hard to live like that."

"Sudan is harder. My family is scattered around the world, but I have aunt in Sudan. She says no work there. We send money when we can."

Michael and Steve pulled up chairs to join them.

"I heard what you were saying," Michael said. "We want first to see things develop in Sudan, and earn more money here, to get good start, maybe open business."

"I read that our Minister of Interior says now that you're independent, you should go back to South Sudan," Steve observed.

"I know some think we are bad for Israel, but we pray to the God that truth will win and they will allow us to go in our own time."

"We're praying too," Steve said.

Tamar bit her lip and looked down at her feet.

"Something bothering?" Joanne laid her hand on Tamar's shoulder.

"I think too much, that's all." *No one could send Mary and Joey to that nightmare of a country, could they? They needed to be here with schools, doctors, and a family who loves them.*

She would fight to the end.

38

"Each of you can have two scoops of ice cream," Estie said to Mary and Joey. "The flavors on the left are without sugar. They've got some great ones."

Mary stared through the glass at the bright colors. "I want chocolate and peach."

"I'll have bubble gum and …" Joey's eyes flitted from one container to another.

"Joeeyy, just choose!" his sister said.

"… and chocolate chips in a cone."

"And I'll have pistachio and dolce de leche in a cup like Mary," Estie said.

Estie liked to find creative things to do on the twice-monthly visits with her foster children. Out of their houses, they were often more open to talking than around family members. She tried to fit the outings to the children's interests and personalities. Some children didn't get outside much, so fresh air in a park or on the beach was a healthy option. Tamar worked hard to improve Mary and Joey's language skills, and she had thanked Estie for taking them to the library today—all the more when she heard there would be a talk by Abel Abebe, a well-known children's author of Ethiopian origin.

"Now we'll sit down and eat here before going home," Estie said, leading the children to one of the sidewalk tables. "On this hot day the ice cream should cool us off and give us energy for our walk."

"Great choices of books today," she added. "*Fabulous Five* and *Pippi Longstocking*. I'm glad you enjoy reading."

"Did you read these when you were a girl?" Mary asked.

"I liked to read a lot, but in our school, we had other books."

"Why?" Joey asked.

"My school was only for girls and the rabbis chose the books for us." Estie couldn't begin to explain the different streams of Israeli education, according to the family's religion and level of religious observance. It wasn't until she was in high school that she began to discover and read other books outside of their curriculum—like *Harry Potter*, which gave her an appetite for broader knowledge.

"I'm glad we have boys and girls in our school," Joey said, "because I like playing with Mary in our breaks."

"Now tell me about the talk you heard from Abel," Estie asked. "Who is he?"

"He was born in Ethiopia—" Mary said.

"That's next to Sudan," Joey said.

"And he writes books."

"For children."

"And he goes all over the country and even on television talking about his books."

"And one of them was made into a movie."

Estie smiled. "Wow, sounds like an interesting man. What'd he talk about?"

"How he came to Israel, walking very far and then on an airplane." Mary said, between slow, small bites of her ice cream.

"And it was hard for his family in the beginning," Joey said.

"Why was that?"

"They didn't know Hebrew, and people didn't think they were Jewish because of their dark skin," Mary said.

"Children even made fun of him." Joey stopped licking his cone for a moment and stared in the distance.

"We also have dark skin and aren't Jewish," Mary said. Estie knew that hearing Abel's talk would be good for Mary and Joey but hadn't realized exactly how fitting it would be. "Do children make fun of you too?"

"Just a few," Joey said. "Abel said sometimes he came home from school crying. But his grandfather told him that God brought them to Israel, and the color of a person's skin doesn't matter to God."

"Daddy tells us that too," Mary said. "Also, if someone is Jewish or not, God loves everyone the same. Is that what *you* think?"

Estie remembered learning the commandment in school to "love your Jewish neighbor as yourself." Gentiles were not to be treated the same as Jews, and some rabbis said that a Jew should not violate the Shabbat to save a non-Jewish life. Today, living outside her community, getting to know Tamar and Steve, and especially Jens, she didn't believe anymore that God gave laws like that.

"Yes, I agree. … I'm glad you enjoyed the library so much and the ice cream. Let's get going. I'm sure you want to tell your Mommy and Daddy about Abel."

⁓

Mary and Joey burst into their house. Estie touched the mezuzah on the doorpost, kissed her fingers, stepped inside, and greeted Tamar and Steve sitting next to each other at the computer.

"Sit down and let me get you something to drink," Tamar said as she pushed herself out of the chair. "Can you stay a few minutes?" She didn't have the usual smile and bounce to her step.

"Water will be fine. Sure, I have time."

"How was the library?" Tamar asked Mary and Joey.

"Fun! I found another *Fabulous Five* book. And Abel was talking to us," Mary said.

"Abel, the children's author?" Steve moved away from the computer and sat opposite Estie on the sofa.

"You met him too, Daddy?" Joey asked.

"Not in person like you, but I've heard about him and watched an interview on YouTube. He's a good writer and has become a spokesperson and role model for the Ethiopian community."

"He said when he was little, he already wrote stories," Mary said. "I also want to write books."

"I'm sure you'll be a great writer," Tamar said. "You have a lot to tell. I've an idea, you both go to your room and do your homework. When you finish, you can begin writing. We need to talk to Estie now ... but afterward, I'll come and help you."

"Something's bothering you," Estie said when the children left the room. "Problems with Mary and Joey? They were great today, paying attention and the first to answer Abel's questions."

"I don't know how much you've heard about the Interior Ministry's deportation order for the refugees," Steve said.

"Since I met your family, I can't help but be interested." Estie fingered her star-of-David pendant.

"So you know about the directive two months ago to expel them all back to South Sudan? And that it was delayed because of a petition from several of the human rights groups claiming their lives would be in danger?"

"It's confusing to me." Estie frowned slightly. "But I understand our government says they aren't refugees anymore because they have their own country now."

"They're supposed to have the right to apply for asylum, but Israel's ignoring them." Tamar's face was reddening. She stood up.

"Everyone in my family says they came here to work," said Estie.

"Of course they want to work when they're here," Steve said. "But you must realize they came to escape their bloody civil war with the north, and no one can be sure that it's over."

"And the money the government gives them when they leave?" Estie asked.

"Bribery," Tamar said. "How far will they get with fifteen hundred dollars?"

"The Ministry of Interior calls it 'voluntary repatriation'. But there's nothing voluntary about it," Steve added.

Tamar blinked her eyes and her voice trembled. "Tell me, what about Mary and Joey? They can't be sent back. They live with us."

Estie chose her words carefully. "I'm not an expert, but at the moment, Mary and Joey are under your custody which was granted by the court, as wards of the Ministry of Welfare."

"So, they'll stay with us even if others are deported—?"

"In the meantime, yes, with God's help. In our work, we have something called 'for the child's good', and this is our priority. We want the best for Mary and Joey, though from my experience, there can be different interpretations."

"I saw on the internet that the immigration police are rounding up Sudanese on the streets and that refugees are hiding in their homes," Steve said.

"I couldn't bear hiding Mary and Joey," Tamar said quietly.

"You don't have to," Estie assured.

"But what if the police pick up their mother? Or if she decides herself to go back?" Steve said. "They wouldn't send the children with her?"

"Things could change, but for now they're safe with you. And by the way, you have great kids, all four of them. Whatever you're doing, keep it up."

39

"It's quiet here." Steve's eyes swept around the house. "Where're all the kids?"

"Arava has a shift with Magen David," Tamar said and glanced up from the cake she was decorating. "Gal's windsurfing with Ben, and Mary and Joey are playing in the park with their friends. Gives me a chance to work on the cake I'm making for a bar mitzva."

"Got home early 'cause of an early dive to track coral growth. We're working together with a team from Jordan."

"Fabulous. There should be more of that kind of stuff, though there's probably lots we don't know about."

"Right, cooperating for the good of the Gulf's ecosystem. We can go lots further."

Steve put his arm around her. "Cake looks great, they'll love it."

"You must be ready for a nap, or d'you have time to sit for a few minutes? I could use a cup of coffee."

"Always have time for you, duck." Steve sat in his favorite chair and put his feet on the table. "Who's the cake for?"

"One of Gal's friends at the windsurfing club. Can you see the shape? Tea?"

"Now I do. Wouldn't mind mint tea from the garden. You're looking relaxed."

"I feel bad for the Sudanese but heard this morning that refugee children in foster homes won't be returned to their parents without an examination by welfare authorities, so Mary and Joey are safe."

"I heard some of our friends from the kibbutz were picked up."

"Awful. What happens to them? Jail?" Tamar sat down next to Steve.

"Not sure about those they arrest. I've been to the bus station to see off some who go voluntarily. They're put on a special bus straight to the airport, and you see them with boxes, suitcases, electrical stuff, dressed in their best clothes, girls' hair in fancy braids."

"And their moods? Happy or sad?"

"A bit of both. They're refugees and unfortunately used to being uprooted. Most try to keep positive. What else can they do?"

"Terrible." Tamar shook her head. "But at least Mary and Joey can stay, I can't see them anyplace else. The beginning wasn't easy ..." In the back of her mind, she could still see those scrawny, bedraggled children.

"They were tiny," Steve said. "Joey wouldn't take a bath, and Mary with her moods."

"You went along with my craziness."

"You weren't crazy. Once God showed me the verses about the fatherless in Deuteronomy and the stranger in Matthew, I knew what to do."

Tamar stood up. "Coffee's finished and the kids will be home soon, so I'd better get the cake out of the way before I begin lasagna for dinner."

Suddenly they heard car doors slamming outside on the street and loud voices. At the same time, Gal ran into the house.

"Daddy, come quick!"

A large white van was stopped in front of their house, all the doors open, and eight men in immigration police uniforms surrounded one Sudanese man.

Steve ran out the door. "Moses! What's going on?"

"Show us your papers," an officer said to Moses.

"Gal, fast!" Tamar said. "Run to the park and keep Mary and Joey there. Don't let them come home till I let you know it's safe." *Thank God they aren't here.*

Moses fumbled in his pockets until he found his wallet and pulled out the creased document from the Population and Immigration Authority.

"I have—" Moses said.

"Hebrew!" the officer said. "How long are you here? You don't speak Hebrew?"

Tamar couldn't stand to see a grown man nearly crying. She'd known Moses since he first arrived in Eilat. He and his family lived in the housing from the hotel where he worked, and his three children were in school.

Steve stepped up. "Give the man a chance to talk. Of course he speaks Hebrew. He works in the Club Hotel."

"You have forty-eight hours." Two officers held onto Moses's arms.

"This man isn't a criminal," Steve said. "Would you please let go of him and speak in a normal voice?"

"The next bus to the airport leaves on Sunday," the first officer said while another wrote in his notebook. "You will be on that bus with your family and the five bags you are each allowed to take. When you land in Juba, you will receive the grant given to those who return. Understand?"

"All your details are written down," the officer with the notebook said. "Don't try to escape. We'll let you go home, tell your family, and get ready to leave."

The van drove off leaving Moses and Steve on the street.

"Come inside and drink some water," Steve said. "We're here to help."

"My wife, my children ..." Moses sat on a chair with his head in his hands. "We don't know anyone in Juba, many were killed, others are in Kenya, Uganda, Australia."

Steve laid his hand on Moses' shoulders. "I'll drive you home."

Tamar walked to the park to call Gal, Mary, and Joey. Were they really as safe as she liked to think, or was she fooling herself? Better try not to think about it.

40

S wim or eat first?" Yossi sat next to Michal on a beach mat.
"I'm hungry. But better swim before it's too dark," Michal
said. With Yossi's busy schedule, they hadn't found much time to
get together lately, so she'd been looking forward to this evening,
especially since he'd mentioned he needed her advice.

"After working all day at the Reef, you still want to swim?"

"I do love the Reef, but it's my job." Michal stood up and put
her mask and snorkel on over her head. "Now I just want to relax
and look at the fish and corals. What about you?"

"I'll pass. I'm enjoying sitting and watching the sun go down."
A smile parted his lips as he saw Kinneret hurling herself into the
sea. "She didn't take any time to get in the water," he said.

"She's crazy about it. Must be her Golden Retriever side. But
will you call her? I don't want her swimming after me and scaring
away the fish."

Kinneret bounded out of the sea and shook the water off herself before settling next to Yossi on the mat.

∽

Twenty minutes later, Michal emerged from the water, dried herself off, and opened the cool box. "Now I'm really hungry. Guess
what I saw?"

"A turtle?"

"How'd you know?"

"You look happy, and they're your favorite."

"Yeah, don't see them often. He came up to breathe right next
to me, and then I followed him for a while till he took a deep dive.

He was huge." She extended her arms.

Michal began to unpack the food. "Ready for some hummus, eggplant salad, and pita? The salads are homemade, picked them up at that hummus joint."

"I've got a couple of beers and some baklava from the new Arab bakery. I know you like it."

"L'chaim!" They raised their glasses, broke off pieces of pita, and dipped them in the hummus.

"Everything tastes better when you eat outside." Michal leaned back on her elbows, enjoying the sound of the gentle waves and the feel of the breeze in her hair.

"The grandfather of a family from New York, who came on our boat, said he'd traveled to more than sixty countries, and this was his favorite sea."

"I've only been to a few…" Michal said.

"And me only to Israel."

"But I'll take his word for it. I never get tired of this view." With the setting sun, the mountain ranges became sharper and the different shades of red and brown stood out.

A sliver of moon appeared over the horizon, rising like a red ball.

"How'd you plan for a full moon?" Michal asked. This relationship was moving awfully slowly, so it was probably too much to expect that he wanted a romantic evening. She was waiting for Yossi to say something, but maybe she should ask him for clarity.

"This evening just worked out," Yossi said. "I'm busy these days with my course for the matriculation exam and all the studying I need to do for it." Even if he hadn't planned a romantic evening around the full moon, it could still turn into one.

"The moon looks huge," she said.

Silence. Kinneret put her head on Yossi's lap.

"By the way, I met Steve last week at Aroma for coffee and he told me about the Sudanese being rounded up and put on buses to the airport? Moses, a friend of Steve and Tamar's, was stopped in front of their house."

"Horrible. You get together with Steve sometimes?" Michal wasn't surprised that Steve hadn't mentioned it. He had a way of keeping things confidential.

"Talking to him helps me. He listens and asks the right questions so I can figure out what to do. And he gives me assignments to read in the Bible, and then we talk about it."

"We're proud of him," Michal said, "for rushing out of the house to stand up for Moses."

"He told them to at least treat people with respect and quoted a verse from the Torah to them about not depriving the alien of justice. He's teaching me a lot."

Michal got up and opened the back of her scooter. "I have my little gas stove. How about a cup of herb tea to round things off?"

"Perfect. You think of everything. Have some baklava."

"Delicious," Michal said. "Tamar's worried about Mary and Joey, and I'm worried about her."

"Steve told me that according to the law, they're safe for now being in a foster home."

"Tamar believes God brought them to her family and they'll never leave. I hope she's right or she'll be crushed."

Yossi and Michal lay on their backs in silence on the mat. The moon was already higher in the sky and not red anymore.

"Speaking of family. I need your advice." Yossi turned on his side to face Michal.

Michal sat up. "You told me one of your younger brothers left the yeshiva recently and wants to join the army."

"He's doing okay, in touch with an organization that helps people like us who come from an orthodox background and leave. But it's something else. My older sister called about our father."

"Your father? I thought after he walked out, he wasn't in touch with anyone." Michal poured them both a second cup of tea.

"Now he is. He got married again, divorced, and has been living in a tiny room from his small National Insurance payment. He borrows a friend's phone and calls the older brothers and sisters to ask for money."

"Crazy." Yossi didn't often talk about his family. But when he did, it reminded her of a movie, something from a different world. "So what advice do you need? He wants money from you, too?"

"Not money." Yossi paused. "My sister told me he has cancer and not long to live. He says that one of his last wishes before he leaves this world is to see me again."

"No way."

"What should I do? He was the one who was the angriest when I left and said he'd do anything to bring me back to our religion. They sometimes try to get you to meet with rabbis who are experts in de-programming. I know I'm too old for that now, but I can't get over the trauma, and the anger at how he treated my mother."

"That's a hard one. What're you thinking?" Michal touched Yossi's hand lightly and looked into his eyes.

"Not sure." He didn't pull his hand away.

"Did you talk with Steve about it?"

"Not yet, but I will. I think I know what he'll say. We've been talking a lot about forgiveness, what the Bible says and also practically."

"Steve had issues with his father, too. Not as heavy as yours, of course."

"I feel like I have to let go of my bitterness and resentment in order to go on with my life."

"I went to therapy after Shai was killed. I was angry with our government, with his murderers, and with the army. I learned that as long as I held on to those feelings, I permitted them to rule me. Maybe meeting your father will allow you to be free."

"I think that too but hope they're not trying to trap me."

41

Tamar had thought a lot about how to share her news with Steve and decided the Bird Sanctuary was the perfect place for them to spend time alone. She was surprised he hadn't suspected anything; but it was the farthest thing from his mind.

"I heard on the Eilat radio station that the fall migration has begun, and flocks are being seen in our skies," Tamar said. "What if we go check them out? We haven't been to the Bird Sanctuary for ages."

"When were you thinking of going?" Steve asked.

"Tomorrow evening." The sooner they had this conversation the better.

"Take the kids?"

"Not this time. I'll prepare dinner, they can eat by themselves. We'll take a picnic."

"Sounds good. A friend from work said he saw a Bridled Tern there last week."

∿

The scents of the Birding Center greeted Tamar as they stepped through the gate. She took a deep breath. "How would you describe the smell here?" she asked Steve. "Reminds me of the Dead Sea."

"Like salt marsh, reeds, and flowers all mixed up. Did you know they plant bushes here in order to attract the different kinds of birds as they fly between Africa, Asia, and Europe?"

Steve looked at the sky. "Do you hear the gulls? Might even be a laughing gull."

The bird calls provided melodic background music, though

unlike Steve, she couldn't distinguish one birdsong from another.

"Will you carry the cool box with our dinner?" Tamar asked.

"No problem. Let's first walk around on the path then eat on the picnic table next to the salt pan."

As she'd anticipated, the walk through the bushes and along the ponds went slowly with Steve stopping frequently to look through his binoculars at the many bird species. From one of the bird blinds along the way, she spotted a heron standing on one leg in the water, and as they watched, he gracefully lifted himself into the air, pulling his long neck in to form a bulge.

"Any chance to see a Steppe Eagle?" Tamar asked. "Those are my favorites, especially when I think of them migrating twenty-thousand kilometers from Mongolia to South Africa and back."

"What?" Steve paused and turned to her. "You've been studying about them?"

"I read the sign, and Mary came home from her class trip here last March excited to see Steppe Eagles flying over. Their guide told them that while birds have small brains, no scientist can explain how they navigate or prepare for their migration by eating extra. Mary commented, 'It's from God.'"

"Wow. What'd the guide say to that?"

"Not much. They also watched birds being ringed and released. She says she wants to volunteer here when she's older. Of course I encouraged her." Tamar grinned. "She's taking after her Daddy."

Steve stopped and raised his binoculars to his eyes. "It's not just the large birds. Look at this Reed Warbler. It doesn't look impressive, but do you know where it came from? Probably summered in Scotland and is on its way to Sub-Saharan Africa."

Although not knowledgeable like Steve, Tamar enjoyed looking at birds. Today, however, she was anxious to get to her point.

Having meandered around the curving path, they found themselves overlooking the salt pans. "We should come here more often," she said. "Must be one of the best places in Eilat to see the sunset." She gazed at the pink wisps of clouds in the west.

"What a view." Steve chose a seat on the bench. "Glad you thought of this."

Tamar spread a tablecloth on the picnic table and began unpacking the food. "Broccoli and mushroom quiche with tofu. I left the rest for the kids. Plus sliced vegetables and guacamole dip."

"Looks and smells great."

"That's the garlic and fresh basil."

Steve bowed his head and reached across the table to hold Tamar's hands.

Tamar could feel her heart pounding.

"Those dives today gave me an appetite. We were sampling corals at forty-five meters." Steve placed a large piece of the quiche on his plate.

"Isn't that awfully deep?" To be certified for one star, Tamar had to dive to twenty meters. That was enough for her.

"It's called a technical dive. You're not hungry?" Steve looked closely at her. "Feeling okay? You seem tired lately."

"Actually, that's what I wanted to talk to you about." Tamar stared past Steve towards the sun dipping behind the mountains and flaming the whole sky. She and Steve had been through a lot together. *What is my problem? There's no one as easy to speak to as Steve.*

"You noticed? … Well, I'm pregnant." She leaned back in her chair. *There, I said it.*

Steve pursed his lips in silence for a moment. Then, "Are you sure? I thought—"

"I'm already a week late. I did the test."

"I guess you understand these things. You're not too old?"

"I also couldn't believe it myself at first after all these years of trying. In a way, I was glad not to get pregnant again because I didn't want to go through another miscarriage."

"How do you know this one will stay?"

"I don't. It's hard but I just want to trust God."

"Me too. But I'll need time to process." Steve closed his eyes and took a calming breath. "A baby? How will we manage?"

"What do you mean? 'How will we manage?' We've managed with babies before."

"We were young then."

"Now we're experienced." Tamar tried to sound confident. But she was having the same thoughts and doubts. When she had seen the result of the pregnancy test, she hadn't known whether to laugh or cry.

"We're not the first couple in history who've been surprised to find they're expecting. Sarah, Hannah, Elizabeth—"

"But they had revelations from God."

"I've had cases at work of older women." Tamar poured glasses of mint tea from the thermos.

"You're feeling sick?"

"Just mornings." She handed him an almond cookie.

Steve shook his head. "I thought things were getting easier for us. True, the deportation hangs over our heads. But at home, the kids don't need as much care as little ones do, and we can go out alone like we're doing now. What will we do with a baby?"

"What do you mean, 'what will we do?'" Tamar's voice rose. "Love it, what else?"

"Even our car is too small—"

"That's what you think about when I tell you you're going to be a father? Our car?"

"My parents—"

"Here come your parents again. You're forty-three and you still let your parents run your life?"

"Not run my life, but how will I tell them?"

"That they're going to be grandparents again. They should be happy."

"Not them."

42

I can smell the *makloubeh*," Gal said. The distinctive aroma of cinnamon and allspice floated up as Tamar took the top off the pan to peer inside. "I remember when you came back from Jordan and made this for us. You told us it means 'upside down' in Arabic."

"Yes," Tamar said. "Now everyone wash your hands and come to the table."

"Before Mommy lights the candles and blesses the hallah ..." Steve cleared his throat and looked at Tamar. "We have something important to tell you."

"We'll be having a big change in our family and wanted you to know as soon as possible," Tamar began. "Maybe you've noticed I've been tired lately—"

"And running to the bathroom to throw up," Steve added.

Arava caught her breath and stared at Tamar. "You don't mean—"

"Yes. I'm pregnant."

Their usual noisy dinner table became silent. Mary was the first to react, jumping up and laughing. "I'll take care of it!"

"I like babies." Arava pursed her lips in thought. "But in another year, I'll be in the army, so I won't see it much."

"Where will it sleep?" Gal asked, practical like his father.

Joey was the hardest to read. Was he realizing he wouldn't be the youngest anymore?

"Did you tell Saba and Savta?" Arava asked.

"We wanted to tell you first," Steve said. "We'll share with them in person when they come to visit next."

Silence again. Tamar was the first to speak. "And now Daddy will turn over the *makloubeh*." Despite her nausea, she'd cooked a celebration meal.

"I'll hold the tray," Gal offered.

"Careful." Steve gripped the large pot by its two handles and quickly turned it upside down, revealing layers of rice, potatoes, cauliflower, and eggplant.

A short time later, as Steve was scooping up the last rice kernels on his plate with a piece of Tamar's whole wheat hallah, he said, "We have an interesting week coming up. Who wants to come with me to beer-on-the-pier tomorrow at my work?"

"Will there be other children there?" Mary asked. "Can I have another piece of hallah?"

"Sure, we always bring our families."

"Ugh." Joey wrinkled his nose. "I don't like beer."

Steve looked at Joey. "They bring snacks and other drinks, too. And you can jump in the water."

"Would it be okay if I stayed home this time?" Tamar sank into her chair. "I could use some quiet time." She didn't feel like socializing these days.

"And don't forget Monday is Yom Kippur," Steve added. "Whose turn to do the dishes? Mommy needs to rest. Are your bikes in order?"

Tamar loved how Steve had become like a sabra and understood that for Israeli children, Yom Kippur was about biking, so different from his Jewish community in Toronto.

Mary turned from clearing the table. "Daddy, can Joey and I bike around by ourselves this year?"

"Mommy and I talked about this already and yes, we trust you. You're big now. And with no cars on the road, it will be safe."

Tamar moved to the sofa to lie down.

Steve eased into his favorite armchair. "And who wants to ride bikes with me to the Taba border the next day?"

"Yay!" Joey ran over and gave Tamar a hug. He was ten and growing up fast, but in many ways still the little boy who jumped on her lap back in the kibbutz that first eventful day.

~

As Mary and Joey prepared to head out the front gate on their bikes, Tamar instructed them to be home by nine o'clock.

"Watch out for any cars." Occasionally people did drive, and rare accidents occurred.

"You can ask someone for the time," Steve added.

"We'll probably see you, because we'll be walking around too." Tamar had put on the traditional white blouse with her jeans. But, with Arava and Gal also out with friends, she decided to sit for another few minutes in the quiet house.

Yom Kippur in Eilat was a special atmosphere. On her kibbutz, they had tried to erase the religious significance of Yom Kippur. They didn't have a synagogue, and regular meals were served in the dining room. From what she heard at work and from neighbors, most Eilati's fasted, even the non-observant, at least for part of the day.

Steve stood up eagerly. "Ready to go?"

Tamar pulled herself out of her chair. "I'll see how far I get."

They headed to the main street and then up the hill. People of all ages were walking down the middle of the streets, many dressed in white. Some sat on curbs and others had set up plastic chairs on the sidewalks. Bicycles and scooters zoomed down the road while parents pushed their younger children on tricycles. Next to synagogues, congregants spilled out onto the sidewalks, as the sounds of mournful prayers came through the doors and windows. Thanks to her work at Tipat Halav and to parents she met from her children's classes, every few minutes they stopped to greet someone.

"Can we sit down for a few minutes?" Tamar said, and

collapsing on the grass in the middle of a traffic circle, just as Mary and Joey sped by on their bikes with a group of African children. Joey's eyes were wide open, and he had a huge smile on his face.

Tamar scratched her head. "Interesting that after five years living with us and acting like Israeli children, they still gravitate to the refugee kids. What d'you think?"

Joey screeched to a halt in front of them. "It's not nine yet, is it?"

Steve checked his watch. "You've got another hour."

Joey sped off again with his friends.

"We're not perfect," Steve said, a pensive expression on his face. "But I think we're doing our best to give them a home. What more can we do?"

Tamar could see Mary and Joey's personalities developing and their desire to venture further from the nest, but they still hadn't developed into rebellious teenagers. Watching Arava and Gal grow up, she knew what was coming, but thankfully, even they didn't test the limits much. What did she care about Gal's ponytail and Arava's nose ring? Yet, seeing Mary and Joey and their Sudanese friends, Tamar understood they faced other challenges.

God willing, they would stay forever but would they ever really feel Israeli, or would they someday have an identity crisis? Maybe that was something natural she had to accept. Expecting this new baby made Tamar think about Mary and Joey's early, formative years which she'd missed.

"We love them, don't we?" Tamar's hand moved to her belly. She usually became reflective on Yom Kippur. "And we always will."

Steve rose from the grass. "We better get home before they do."

Tamar hadn't walked so much since their outing to the Bird

Center. She was ready to go home. When they got there she collapsed on the sofa and kept checking the clock. At nine-twenty she asked. "Where are they?"

"They're having fun and forgot the time," Steve said.

"Or something happened, another bike or car crashed into them."

"You go to bed, and I'll stay up."

Was he serious?!

"Sometimes a cup of coffee helps you, shall I make you one?"

"Can't drink coffee anymore. Makes me sick. But I could use a piece of fruit. Thanks."

"I don't think we should punish them," Steve said. "Do you?"

"Let's wait and see." If they were sorry, and didn't come too late, she wanted them to have positive memories from this evening. Hopefully, it was a small slip-up and not symptomatic of a bigger problem. As parents, they needed wisdom to negotiate the coming years. She didn't even want to think about the possibilities of deportation or their mother coming back.

The door flew open. Mary and Joey bounded in, out of breath. "Are we late?"

"You did great," Steve said. "Just a few minutes. Let's get to bed."

43

Remembering her miscarriages, Tamar was trying not to become too attached to the baby. But on the other hand, she couldn't stop thinking about it especially with her tiredness and nausea. The children, living in the here and now, rarely spoke about it. And, even with Steve, she barely mentioned it—only when he brought up the subject, which wasn't often. Fathers didn't experience pregnancies the way mothers did, especially in the early stages. How could they? Although the baby was Steve's also, it was growing inside of her.

The children couldn't wait to tell Michal and Yossi the first time they came over.

"What are all the smiles I'm seeing?" Michal had asked when she walked in the door.

"Guess what?" Mary burst out.

"You have a new puppy?"

"No, a baby!" Joey said.

"No way, you're kidding," Michal said, throwing a look at Tamar, who shrugged her shoulders and showed a half smile.

"It's true," Gal said. "Mommy's tired and sick all the time."

"Because of the baby growing," Mary put her hand on Tamar's belly.

"I guess you deserve a mazal tov." Michal gave Tamar a hug.

On Michal's subsequent visits, she'd been surprisingly supportive and understanding. In the past, Tamar never knew how she'd react, but this relationship with Yossi was softening her, his kind and gentle spirit rubbing off.

"If there's anything I can do to help," Michal said. "Like if you don't feel like cooking one day, I could bring in take-away from the vegan restaurant. Even for a non-vegan, the food's awesome."

Tamar hadn't realized how soon she would take up Michal's offer.

~

Tamar went to bed even earlier than usual. She was used to being tired, and although she tried to ignore it, the nagging pain in her abdomen wasn't going away. Hopefully, she'd feel better in the morning. No need to mention it to Steve.

Apparently she dozed off. She didn't notice Steve coming to bed and lying down beside her. But the next thing she knew was a sharp stabbing pain in the right side of her belly. At the same time, she began to bleed. When she twisted in bed, the pain increased. Her mind returned to her last miscarriage when she was also seven weeks along, which also began with light bleeding. But not this shooting pain.

She prodded her husband and gasped, "Steve, it's bad!"

Steve, normally a deep sleeper, sat bolt upright.

"The hospital …" She barely managed to get the words out. "I'm bleeding."

"Like the other times?"

Tamar could feel the concern in Steve's voice. He'd also suffered with the miscarriages, though without her depressions. Joining a support group for women with miscarriages had helped pull her through.

"Call Michal to come, don't want to wake kids." Tamar tried to sit up. She knew Michal didn't turn off her phone these days, because she was waiting for a dolphin to give birth.

Steve grasped her shoulders, easing her into a sitting position.

"Ow, my shoulder hurts too." She'd never had this pain before. But from her nurse's training she recognized the sign.

"Sit on the edge of the bed for a minute while I bring you water and call Michal."

Steve went into the kitchen but kept an eye on his wife. She heard his voice, as if from far away: "Sorry, it's not the news you were expecting about a dolphin baby. I'm taking Tamar to the hospital. Bleeding and pain. ... Thanks."

"Easy does it." Steve helped her to stand. "God, have your way, and take Tamar's pain away."

"I need to change out of my pajamas." Pain or no pain, she couldn't go out dressed like this.

～

Tamar didn't know how she made it to the hospital—step by step thanks to Steve's gentle firmness. On the way, Tamar went over in her mind the symptoms and risk factors for a tubal pregnancy. The pain, especially in the shoulder, and the bleeding were warnings, but risk factors? Tamar didn't smoke, hadn't had a previous tubal pregnancy or surgery. Only her age, being over forty.

At the Women's Emergency Department Tamar was admitted immediately. The nurse took a urine test to confirm the pregnancy and asked her questions.

"Have you seen a doctor already?"

"No." Tamar knew she was like many nurses who took care of others but not themselves.

"Your history of pregnancies and births?"

"Two births, three miscarriages."

Steve helped her undress, put on the hospital gown, and lie on the bed. He held her hand while they inserted the IV, her small veins always making it a painful procedure.

"We'll be doing blood tests and a transvaginal ultrasound," the nurse said. "It's not fun, but doesn't hurt either, and will show us the exact location of your pregnancy. The blood tests show us the level of hormones so we'll know whether you are carrying a live fetus, and they'll be our baseline for your follow-up tests."

The dizziness and pain decreased as she lay down. The nurse's calm manner gave her courage. "Treatment options?" she asked.

"After we see the outcome of the blood work and ultrasound, we'll know more, and the doctor will explain options to you."

Tamar kept gripping Steve's hand as he sat next to her. While thay waited, she had time to think. Her life had taken unexpected turns. It was like hiking through a wadi with bends and boulders in the trail. Growing up in the kibbutz children's home, Tamar longed for a large family on whom she could lavish the parental love she'd missed. Although Steve hadn't always shared her desire for more than two children, he was the perfect father. And with Mary and Joey, God added to their family in an amazing way. Two months ago, she was content with their four children. Then came this miracle pregnancy. And now what?

Most of all, what was she to learn through this? Trust God more? Be ready for surprises? Be more thankful?

The kind nurse checked on her periodically. Then after two hours a solemn-faced doctor stood by her bedside. "I'm sorry to say it's a tubal pregnancy. The fertilized egg has implanted itself in the fallopian tube instead of the uterus and cannot develop. Leaving it would be life threatening. But don't worry, many women go on to have normal pregnancies."

Not me. I never want to put myself through this again.

"We'll be doing a laparoscopy operation under general anesthesia, a small cut in your tummy. We just need you to sign these papers."

Tamar looked at Steve, and her hand shook as she signed the form giving permission for the surgery, including the possible removal of the fallopian tube.

"You'll remain in the hospital overnight while we give you

medication to manage the pain," the doctor explained. "Tell your husband goodnight. Here's our anesthesiologist. You'll be asleep soon."

Steve kissed her forehead. "Love you, duck."

~

"How are you feeling?" Steve was next to her again. "You made it through the laparoscopy. The doctor says it went well."

"I'm okay, I think. A bit confused." Tamar looked around through half closed eyes. The strong pang was gone, replaced by a lighter pain from the cut.

"We'll get through this together." Steve squeezed her hand and kissed her on the cheek.

She wanted to sleep.

44

"We'll give you a week sick leave," the doctor had told Tamar when she left the hospital. "Even if you feel better sooner, your body needs time to recover."

And her soul too. She couldn't envision doing nothing for a week and figured she'd use the time to bake cakes and go for long walks, but the first days she really did need to be still. When her mind started racing around or her chest tightened, she reminded herself to trust in God's goodness. And Steve's.

"Don't worry about the house," he would say. "We've got it all under control."

It was fun to see him and the children shopping, cooking, and doing the laundry. Under Arava's guidance, Mary and Joey had outdone themselves preparing pizza with a no-knead whole-wheat crust, her frozen tomato sauce, vegan Parmesan cheese, and their favorite toppings—olives, corn, and mushrooms. She should turn the cooking over to them more often.

After a few days, Tamar found that sitting on the ground and scooting along in the garden didn't require too much effort. Steve bought some petunias and begonias for her to plant. Digging her hands in the dirt, and focusing on pulling weeds and removing dead leaves, her breathing slowed down.

As she was surveying the garden and trying to decide where to plant each flower for the best effect, Tamar's phone rang. Estie.

"Would you have time for me to come over at five after I finish work?" Was Tamar imagining it, or did Estie's voice sound strained? Her heart rate shot up.

"Everything okay?"

"I'd rather talk in person. Will Steve be home?"

Tamar barely managed to put the remaining plants into the ground before lifting herself up and going inside. Tears came to her eyes. Must be the hormones. She needed a cup of coffee.

Whatever Estie wanted to tell them couldn't be good news coming outside of her regular appointments. She remembered Estie's visit when they heard about the deportation order. She'd spoken about Mary and Joey being wards of the Welfare Department and their custody agreement. It sounded secure at the time. Or was she fooling herself? Even as they heard about Sudanese being expelled, she continued to believe in her happy illusion. How would she pass the next couple of hours until Estie arrived?

"Take it easy, duck." Steve walked in, joined his wife on the sofa, and put his arm around her. "You haven't heard anything yet, your mind is just going round and round." Tamar had called to tell him to be home before five, then she made sure the children were away.

"My hormones are a mess, but I don't have a good feeling."

"Remember your favorite verse, all things work together for good—"

A knock on the door interrupted them.

"Come in."

Estie touched the mezuza and kissed her fingers.

"Something to drink?" Steve stood up and moved toward the kitchen.

"Water's fine." Estie looked at Tamar. "Are you okay? You look pale."

"And a cup of coffee for me, thanks." Tamar spoke slowly. "I didn't tell many people, but I was seven weeks pregnant, and last week had an emergency operation for a tubal pregnancy. That means the baby wasn't growing as it should in the uterus—"

"I know, my cousin had one." Estie fidgeted with her star-of-David pendant. "I'm sorry."

"I'm feeling better slowly. But you must have come here for a reason." Tamar reached for Steve's hand.

"You know what's happening with the Sudanese refugees." Estie cleared her throat. "And the government's policy to send them all home."

"As if it's really their home." Heat flushed through her body. "Many haven't lived in South Sudan for ten or twenty years and have no home to go back to."

"But this doesn't apply to Mary and Joey, right?" Steve combed his fingers through his hair.

"Something with their mother?" Tamar asked.

"The last time we heard from her was two years ago, when she called you sounding confused." Estie looked around. "Are the children here?"

"They're at friends' houses."

"Two days ago, in one of the round-ups in south Tel Aviv, the immigration police stopped her." Estie paused then continued. "She didn't want voluntary repatriation and had managed to avoid them so far, but now she has no choice. And she wants to take the children with her."

"I don't understand." Tamar stood up, forgetting the pain from her operation. She grimaced. "I thought as foster children they were safe with us in an out-of-home placement."

"That was true when I spoke to you before, but you understand the direction the Ministry of Interior is moving." Estie looked out the window.

"So?" Tamar's voice rose.

"They took her to the detention center in Ramla, and Catherine was given a week to leave the country. When she told the immigration officer that she was taking her children, he understood the complexity of her case, and the following day they took her to the Court of Appeals for Immigration. My supervisor in Tel Aviv was there—she's the one that told me this—and also a representative from the South Sudanese government and from the Ministry of Interior."

Tamar's head was full of fog. Last week she lost their baby, and now were Mary and Joey being snatched away?

"My supervisor made the case that Catherine isn't capable of caring for these children whom she barely knows. But the embassy deputy believes all Sudanese belong in their homeland, and you know the goal of the Ministry of Interior."

"Catherine thinks she can care for them?" Steve asked. "What was the outcome?"

"She said they have an aunt in Sudan they can live with."

"An aunt?" Tamar, her hands on her belly, paced slowly around the room. "She takes them away from us to pan them off on someone they've never met?"

"I'm sorry to have to tell you this. ... But there is a little piece of good news," Estie said. "The judge scheduled a hearing next Wednesday to allow all sides time to gather information, though it's possible they'll change the date due to the overload of cases. You're invited, and the children too. They'll be asked what they want."

Mary and Joey testifying in court sounded awful, but if it would help their case ...

"What're our chances?" Steve asked. "There's no way Catherine could fly in a week from when she was picked up with this hearing coming up."

"They'll have to postpone it. But according to my supervisor, our chances aren't great. At best we might gain a few weeks. But we'll try."

"I'll have our friends praying," Steve said. "We believe in miracles."

"Me too," Estie said. "With God's help."

They heard the children's voices outside the door. "We're home!"

45

Jens's steps were confident as he and Estie walked up the stairs to the Ministry of Interior. His voice was calm as he asked, "You're not nervous, are you?"

"A little," Estie said. "I've collected all the papers they requested, so there's no reason you shouldn't get the visa, with God's help." Thanks to her job, paperwork came easy for Estie, though they asked for a lot here.

"Why the guard?" Jens asked as they stepped up to the entrance.

"He gives us our number and breaks up fights." She checked their number with the one on the screen. They'd be here a while.

"Fights?"

How could she explain the Middle Eastern mentality to a Dane? "This place often brings out the worst in people, including those who work here. The crowds, long waits, visa issues, and the clerks don't get paid well." She hadn't told Jens about Dalia and their previous run-in.

After waiting months to get an appointment, it finally came up the week of Mary and Joey's deportation. Estie didn't know why she connected these two events. As a social worker, Mary and Joey were her job, though after five years visiting them every two weeks, she naturally had become attached to them, and Tamar had become a friend. On the other hand, her whole future depended on this meeting for Jens's visa.

Finally, they were together for a longer period, not like her quick trips to Denmark and his to Eilat. Not that she didn't enjoy those vacations—long walks through Copenhagen's colorful streets and along canals, Tivoli gardens, Little Mermaid, pastries, beer, and especially getting to know Jens's family and friends.

Estie had gone through a lot to reach this point. Her parents hadn't wanted her to move to Eilat in the first place. Most of her extended family lived in Sderot and viewed Eilat as a wild and depraved city. Abba was afraid she would drift away from the values she'd been taught.

Though she'd liked Jens from the beginning and found him easy to be with, it was hard to maintain a long-distance relationship. She kept hearing the rabbi's voice inside her head: "We only marry Jews." She suggested he find someone else. Meanwhile, her sisters and cousins tried to set her up with nice local boys, but no one measured up to Jens.

She continued to see Jens's Facebook posts, they exchanged messages on birthdays and holidays, and he had another girlfriend for a short time. But neither were happy being apart. Why judge Jens by his religion? He believed in God as she did, and she'd never met anyone with a higher moral character and who shared her same ideals. Observing how he related to his mother and father told her a lot, as well as staying in the home of his married sister and talking together till late in the night.

She hadn't told her parents about Jens. Her younger sister had met him while in Eilat and liked him, so that was a start. But her sister had promised not to say anything to the rest of the family. Estie, meanwhile, had convinced herself that once they met him, they'd love Jens as she did.

They sat down to wait on metal chairs in the crowded room. "They'll probably first look at the papers," Estie said, "and then take us one at a time for questioning." She'd gone over this with Jens multiple times but couldn't help saying it again. "With God's help, the interview part shouldn't take long."

"Estie Levy." She finally heard her name called and walked

with Jens through the open door. They sat down in front of the large desk.

"I'll pray for you," Tamar had said when Estie told her about this interview. Despite recovering from the tubal pregnancy and the stress around Mary and Joey's hearing, Estie knew that Tamar cared. Even if she didn't pray to exactly the same God, it couldn't hurt.

"I see you're requesting a partner visa for Jens Christensen," Dalia observed. "You know that normally you are expected to apply while he is out of the country in case he is refused."

"A friend of mine—" Estie started.

"I'm not interested in your friends." Dalia frowned. "I'm telling you our policy."

"I didn't read anything about that on the document I picked up here with the list of documentation needed," Estie said.

"I also read the paper," Jens said. "And didn't see this law."

Dalia cleared her throat. "We don't write it because it's not an absolute requirement, but if you are refused and are already in the country, we're afraid you may not leave."

Estie's eyes met Jens's. Her friends had made this process sound simple.

"Nevertheless, since you're here, I'll continue with our appointment." She opened the binder Estie laid on the desk. "I'm checking your papers for three categories—your relationship, your information, and Jens's."

Estie reached for Jens's hand and nodded. She'd printed out their emails and Whatsapp messages, pictures of them together in Eilat and Denmark including some with his family, and receipts from their flights as had been requested. The picture of them in Copenhagen looked like an advertisement from a travel agency, and anyone could see they were in love.

Dalia scowled at Estie. "I see your rent contract, pay slip, and record of paid bills. We're looking for someone who supports themself. Umm, social worker. I believe we've met before. Aren't you handling the case of the African children?"

Estie's stomach tightened and she blinked her eyes, but Dalia didn't wait for an answer.

Dalia looked down at the file as she flipped pages. "For Jens, I have his original birth certificate and the declarations stating he isn't married and has no criminal background." Dalia still didn't smile. "Jens, can you step outside while I question Estie, and afterward I'll call you."

A colleague from work had been through this process and gave them ideas of what questions would be asked so they could coordinate their answers ahead of time. "It's nothing," she'd said. "When you have all the papers, it's a ten minute interview for each, and we heard back from them in two weeks."

Estie was prepared to answer questions about their first date, Jens's favorite color and ice cream flavor, and the names and ages of his family members. But as Dalia went on with her examination, Estie fidgeted in her chair.

"Where does Jens stay in Eilat?" Every time Dalia looked up from scribbling rapidly on her paper—apparently, she hadn't graduated to using the computer yet—she glared at Estie.

"He rents a studio apartment not far from me."

"He doesn't stay with you? It sounds like he's just a friend, that you're not a real couple if you're not living together. What kind of love is that?"

Estie hadn't expected to discuss her intimate life with the Ministry of Interior clerk and touched her star-of-David pendant. "Uh, we're waiting till after our wedding, with God's help, to move in together."

"Umm, you can go now and tell Jens to come."

While Jens was in the office, Estie worried. Wasn't Dalia overstepping her boundaries as a clerk? They only wanted Jens to be allowed to stay for longer than his three-month tourist visa, but they found themselves under cross examination.

After half an hour, Jens opened the door. "Estie, you may come in," Dalia called past him. Jens grinned at her and held himself in a relaxed posture as she joined him.

"We don't have to approve every visa request," Dalia said. "People abuse our immigration system, and our job is to determine who deserves to stay here. You see how busy our office is and know what's going on in our country. We're overwhelmed, and don't have enough room for everyone." Dalia looked straight at Estie and frowned.

Estie remembered their meeting when she applied for her passport to go to Greece and understood Dalia's not-so-subtle hint. "How soon can we expect to hear from you?"

"Your file will be sent to Jerusalem. I can't say how long."

At least someone else besides Dalia would be looking at it. Surely, a simple clerk who was opposed to refugees didn't have the power to strangle her relationship with Jens.

46

Normally, Tamar looked forward to the family going out together on Shabbat afternoon, though coordinating it with the older kids was like an army operation.

"It's important for everyone to come," she'd told them. "We're going to the Coral Beach Nature Reserve and afterward for pizza."

"Yay!" Joey said. "Last time Saba bought us ice cream from the kiosk there. Do you think we can have some today?"

"You know you're not supposed to ask," Tamar said. "But I have a feeling Daddy might buy you one." Today she'd do anything to spoil them.

She hadn't told the children why they needed to come to the beach and wasn't sure how to share the news. Everything seemed to be happening at once, beginning with losing the baby. Tamar hadn't slept much since Estie came to their house two days ago with the shocking news that Mary and Joey might leave with their mother in ten days.

How could they tell Mary and Joey they were being deported, and prepare them emotionally and mentally, when it wasn't even sure? Tamar's thoughts flew in all directions and she found herself asking people to repeat themselves. Even at work she wasn't herself and slipped up with entering data on the computer. Steve kept reminding her to take one day at a time—they weren't gone yet.

"Your job is to prepare the picnic, duck," Steve told her that morning when they spoke about their strategy and plan. "And I'll begin telling them while we eat." Steve's scientific objectivity often annoyed Tamar, but now she appreciated his ability to step back.

~

When Shabbat arrived, it was one of those lovely November days still warm enough to swim, maybe the last time they'd go to the beach before springtime.

After finding a picnic table not far from the water, Tamar began unpacking the food. "We're all hungry," she said, "so we'll eat and then snorkel. Who liked the lasagna last night?"

"Me!" Joey's eyes sparkled. "My favorite."

"I know you like it, bubi, so I made extra and hallah too, and I baked Mary's brownies." A lump formed in Tamar's throat. There was no way these kids could go to South Sudan. What would they eat?

"Who wants to pray?" Steve asked as they all sat at the table.

"Me!" Joey said. "Thank you, God, for the lasagna and brownies, and pizza later, and that we'll see nice fishes."

"I'm still hoping to see the whale shark," Gal said, gazing over the sea. "Or a spotted eagle ray."

"I'd be scared to see those." Mary shuddered. "But maybe a turtle like Aunt Michal saw."

"They're big too." Joey stretched out his arms.

"But they don't do anything to you," Mary said. "Can I have another brownie?

"Neither do whale sharks," Gal said.

"How many did you have?" Tamar looked at the nearly empty plate. Someone had eaten a lot.

"Just two." A smile tugged a corner of her mouth upward.

"Swimming will reduce the glucose," Steve said. "So you can have one more."

"Yay!"

Tamar loved how children took pleasure in simple things.

Her eyes caught Steve's, and she raised her eyebrows.

Arava took her mask and snorkel out of the beach bag and stood up. "I'm swimming out to Moses Rock. Who wants to come?"

Mary and Joey jumped up.

Steve cleared his throat. "Before we get in the water, Mommy and I have something to tell you."

"Let's sit down for a few more minutes." Tamar fiddled with a curl. She nearly jumped up but had just told the children to sit down.

"You saw Estie at our house a couple days ago," Steve began. "She didn't come this time to play with Mary and Joey, but wanted to tell us something."

Tamar put her hand on Mary's leg.

Steve paused and rubbed the back of his neck.

"Nothing is certain yet, so this might sound confusing, but we know that many Sudanese, your friends too, have left for Juba. Some chose to go and others were sent by our government."

"My friend Alice's family left last week," Mary said. "At first she didn't want to leave her friends, but her parents said they'd have a nice house there and be with all their family."

"Sudan has lots of cows, ones with big horns." Joey stretched his hands over his head in a V-shape.

"How d'you know?" Mary asked.

"You don't think I've seen pictures?" Joey said.

The houses looked like shacks from pictures Tamar had seen. And what good were cows when you didn't have running water, electricity, or schools?

"Daddy and I are happy you've been able to stay here with us and haven't had to leave." Tamar squeezed Mary's leg tighter.

"But a few days ago, the police in Tel Aviv stopped your mother and told her she has to go back to Sudan." Steve cleared his throat again.

"We haven't seen her for a long time," Mary said quietly. "Maybe when we're big, we can go visit her." Deep inside, as happy as the children were with them, they also longed for their mother.

Arava and Gal rested their arms on the picnic table and leaned forward.

Steve looked from Mary to Joey. "Your mother told the police she wants to take you with her."

There, he said it. Tamar's heart beat wildly. The children all sat up straight and were silent.

"Did the police tell her they live with us now?" Arava asked.

"Not exactly," Steve said. "The policeman, Estie's boss in Tel Aviv, and a man from the Sudanese embassy spoke to a judge, and he told them to come back in a week, and he'd make a decision about Mary and Joey."

Tamar was proud of how well Steve spoke but couldn't keep quiet anymore. "We can come to the court too. We want to tell the judge how much we love you and think you should stay here."

She hoped Mary and Joey felt treasured, but if she and Steve decided to take the children to court with them, what would they answer when asked if they preferred to stay in their familiar home or to join their mother? No child should face this dilemma, but tragically, refugees and all foster children, begin life with strikes against them. Life wasn't fair, but they had to do their best in the circumstances, and to seek truth and justice.

Steve said, "I know this is confusing—"

"You mean," said Arava, "we don't know if Mary and Joey will go with their mother or not?"

"The judge will decide," Steve said.

"Tomorrow Saba and Savta are coming to Eilat." Tamar tried to sound upbeat. She remembered how, at first, Imma and Abba didn't want them to take Mary and Joey, and now they couldn't let them leave without seeing them again. "We'll have a good-bye party, just in case, and they don't want to miss it."

Tamar had nothing else to say, and the children needed time to absorb what they heard.

She reached for her mask. "Let's all swim to Moses Rock." Swimming made everything seem better.

47

"Which table shall we use?" Michal had come early to help set up for the party. "And how many people do you expect?"

"Let's use the dining room table but put out chairs in the garden. People can eat there too since it's still warm enough." She wished it were colder and raining, but the rains were late this winter. "I didn't invite many—just our family, Eva and Yakov, one of the Sudanese families who's still here, and a couple of their best friends, maybe twenty altogether."

"Are you sure you're up to this?" Imma stepped out of Gal's room where she'd been taking a nap since arriving a couple hours ago. "You're still getting over the operation and look pale to me."

"Was there a choice?" Tamar looked around the room. "I have lots of help, and we can't let them go without doing something special."

When Imma and Abba had come down to celebrate Abba's birthday in Eilat, Tamar had told them about the pregnancy. In the children's excitement, they hadn't realized that Saba and Savta might not share their enthusiasm. In front of the children, Imma didn't say anything, but later on the phone, although she would never recommend ending the pregnancy, questioned how Tamar got herself into this predicament in the first place. Nevertheless, she wasn't as critical as she used to be, and when she heard it was a tubal pregnancy, Imma's voice cracked.

Today Imma brought a few of her special dishes like jachnun, even though it wasn't Shabbat, and malawach, her traditional pan-fried flatbread. Both were greasy and full of carbs, not good for Mary, but everyone loved them. Eva baked a Hungarian apple pie, taking care for Mary's sake to use almond and soy flours, and stevia instead of sugar.

Tamar chose some of Mary and Joey's favorites. She remembered when they had spaghetti the first time and didn't know how to eat it so picked at it with their hands. Now they wouldn't mind eating spaghetti every day.

Abba paused from helping Steve with the chairs and turned to Tamar. "Didn't you say you don't think they'll go?"

Tamar didn't know what to think, let alone explain the possibilities to Abba. The last few days were like the ride on the boardwalk where you rotate in circles high in the air in a chair, and if you dare open your eyes you can see the ground spinning beneath you. Dizzy from all the changes lately, she could barely think logically.

On the one hand, she refused to believe that after the hearing in three days, Mary and Joey could soon leave for South Sudan with a mother they didn't know. Surely the judge would see the injustice and allow them to stay with the family who'd cared for them the past five years. On the other hand, if they did have to leave, God forbid, she needed to prepare them emotionally and physically. What do you take to a country which has nothing?

"As I told you, after the hearing with the judge this Wednesday, then we'll know more." Tamar took the flourless chocolate cake out of the oven and stuck a toothpick in its center. Perfect.

"I believe justice will prevail," she said. "God brought them to us in an amazing way, and I can't believe they'll be forced to leave to a danger zone."

"I'll pray for a wise judge," Abba said. "Like Solomon in the story of the two women who claimed the baby as their own, and he was given supernatural understanding."

Imma looked over the table with her experienced eyes.

"Everything's ready. You lie down for a few minutes before we begin in half an hour. We don't want you to collapse."

Tamar went to her room and gladly put her feet up. She began rehearsing what to tell the judge. Could they reach a compromise, let the children stay until they're eighteen and complete high school? Maybe in another eight years, life would be better in South Sudan, although it didn't seem likely considering the history of inter-tribal conflicts and the rampant corruption.

The social worker would talk about "the good of the child," and explain how with foster families, the child transitions gradually to the birth family, not suddenly one day. A letter from the doctor about Mary's diabetes would help, another item for her to-do list, as well as researching diabetes in South Sudan to see if insulin was available there.

She and Steve hadn't resolved the question of taking Mary and Joey to the hearing. On first thought, it seemed too traumatic. How could children ages ten and eleven express whether they preferred living with their birth mother for whom they had a deep, inner longing, or with the family they knew and who loved them? On the other hand, Estie said it would help for the judge to see the children and the connection they have with her and Steve. Unless the hearing was postponed, they had three days to decide and get the evidence in order.

Tamar must have nodded off for a few minutes when Mary came running into her room. "Mommy, everyone's here. We're waiting for you!"

She stepped into the living room and blinked back tears as she grasped Steve's arm. The table overflowed with dishes set on a white tablecloth, and her favorite people surrounded it. Mary, who loved flowers, had picked a variety from the garden and arranged them in vases. Mary and Joey looked surprisingly calm and happy. Children lived in the present.

Steve cleared his throat. "Peter, will you pray?"

～

"Now that we finished eating," Tamar said, "let's gather in a circle in the yard." They'd save the cleaning-up till later. "Whoever wants, can bless or share a memory about Mary and Joey. Who will begin?" Even if they didn't leave, the children would be encouraged.

Steve had told her they didn't do this in Canada, but Tamar liked the Israeli tradition of a blessing circle for birthdays and other occasions.

Michal went first: "It was awesome having you come to the Reef and seeing how you became friends with the dolphins."

"Mary, you are one of the most courageous people I know," Arava said. "I've watched you grow up and have seen how you handle diabetes without complaining. I love having a little sister and hope you can stay forever."

"And a little brother for me," Gal said. "I love playing football with you and hope you can play a lot in Sudan." He paused. "If you ever have to go there."

"I'll never forget our jeep trip in Arad when you both helped me drive," Peter said. "I think there are lots of jeep tracks in Sudan."

Because they don't have paved roads, thought Tamar.

"You made pottery with me on my wheel. I've seen African baskets but I wonder if they make pottery in Sudan," Shoshanna said. "Whatever happens, I'll always be your Savta."

"You're lucky to have two mothers who love you," Eva said, her voice breaking. "I lost all my mishpocheh when I was little and was also taken to another country, from Hungary to Israel. God gave me a new start, I met Yakov, and have vonderlach children and grandchildren. I'm sure God will bless you wherever you are. Don't forget, you're special."

There was a silence as they looked around to hear if anyone else wanted to speak.

"I'm cold," Mary said. "I need my sweater." Though not the skinny, grubby girl Tamar had met on the kibbutz, Mary still didn't have a lot of meat on her bones and was always cold.

"Just a minute and we're through." Tamar motioned for Mary and Joey to sit next to her and hugged them close, as she had when she brought them home the first time. They didn't snuggle much anymore, though.

"I love you forever and ever. You're an answer to my prayers in a way I never could have imagined. I … whatever happens …" Tamar choked up.

Steve moved to stand behind Tamar and rested his hands on her shoulders.

Tamar's phone rang from the kitchen.

"I'll answer," Steve said.

"That was Estie," he said when he returned. "The hearing's postponed till next Sunday."

48

Michal thought Tamar's house seemed unusually quiet as she, Yossi, and Kinneret stepped into the open front door. "Anybody home?"

"I'm back here."

They found Tamar sitting on the ground in the garden, trays of petunias, begonias, and geraniums next to her as she patted a seedling into the ground.

Michal smiled. "Planting time again? Where's everyone? Don't the kids usually help?"

"Arava and Gal aren't around much anymore, busy with friends and activities. Mary and Joey were helping but then Mary had her gymnastics and Joey his chess club. I'm trying to keep them in their normal routine as much as possible. Steve's teaching the Coral Ecology Course to a new group of master's students."

"Looks like you're nearly finished. Ready for a coffee break? We wanted to stop by with presents for the kids."

"Five minutes," Tamar said.

"Awesome. I'll make coffee." *Tamar's magic word.*

Returning with the coffee and two cups of red tea, Michal sat next to Yossi on the garden swing.

"I love the flowers. Even the smells," said Yossi.

Tamar smiled her agreement. "Brings life and color, ... and planting calms me down."

Michal wondered how Tamar was coping. She was like some kind of split personality these days. On the one hand, she continued to maintain that Mary and Joey wouldn't be leaving with

Catherine next week to South Sudan. She would shake her head and declare, "Impossible. This is their home. The judge will understand a clear-cut case of children being abandoned by their mother and finding a new family." On the other hand, yesterday was the goodbye party, and Tamar had two large suitcases in the corner of the living room which she was slowly filling. "They shouldn't lack anything. I want them to have the best possible start," she'd say.

Now Yossi reached into his backpack and pulled out a bag. "We brought a gift."

"We wanted something practical but lightweight and small," Michal said.

"You always have music in your home," Yossi added.

"He had the perfect idea: MP3 players!" Michal grinned at Yossi.

"I downloaded songs you sing in your congregation, so Joey and Mary can keep listening to them in Juba."

Michal wasn't sure what to think about Yossi going with the family to meetings on Shabbat, though he'd obviously given it a lot of thought. He was not someone to make quick decisions. He spent hours talking to Steve.

She admired his courage and search for truth. First, when he realized he didn't believe what he was taught in the yeshiva, he left it behind and set off on his own. His younger siblings, who were following him, had it easier. And second, his openness to Jesus also set him outside the Israeli mainstream.

Michal could tell Tamar was touched by the gift. "Mary and Joey will be home soon," Tamar said, "and you can give them the MP3's personally. What a fabulous idea. They'll be thrilled."

"How are they taking it?" Michal asked. It felt comfortable to have Yossi's arm resting over her shoulders.

Tamar gave the garden a sweeping look. "Kids live for the moment. They don't understand what's happening."

How could they? Mary and Joey were born in Sudan, fled from there with many other South Sudanese, then lived in Cairo. Even now, as black-skinned refugees in a white society, they still had a strong Sudanese identity.

"We're trying to decide whether to take them to the hearing," Tamar said. "We found a lawyer through the organization that helps refugees, and she agrees with Estie, that being there would make a good impression on the judge. I don't want to put them through the trauma, though. Steve and I are trying to figure out what's best."

"And what about you?" Yossi looked into Tamar's eyes. "How are *you* doing?" Coming from Yossi, these weren't casual words.

Unlike Michal who never gave a thought about having children, Tamar had always wanted a large family, saying she wanted to give her children what she lacked growing up on the kibbutz. The more children, the more love she could share. With the disappointments of her miscarriages, her dream was shattered, and working with babies must not be easy when she wasn't having more herself.

When Mary and Joey suddenly landed in the family, though raising them was a challenge, Tamar was able to pour her love into them, fulfilling her passion for justice and helping the underdog.

Tamar took a deep breath and pursed her lips before answering Yossi's question. "I'd say confused. When we took Mary and Joey, we understood their mother abandoned them. Adoption even entered my mind. But after three years she reappeared, and now she wants to take them to Juba. It can't happen. … They'd die there, especially Mary with her diabetes."

Michal had been reading stories about families who'd been deported to South Sudan, only to have their children die from malaria and dysentery. Many didn't stay in Juba but fled again to Kenya and Uganda. Some had even gone back to Egypt where they'd been treated so badly.

"I told Steve that if they go, we go too. We have nothing to do here anymore." Tamar brushed her curls back from her face.

Michal hadn't heard Tamar say this before. Surely Steve wouldn't agree to that plan.

"How could we leave them alone there with that mother or some aunt?"

"What did Steve say?" Yossi asked quietly. He had a good rapport with Tamar.

"He said there aren't corals in Sudan ... he wouldn't have work. After they arrive, he said, we can go check on them ... but I say that's not enough. He can find something else to do, I told him."

Michal wanted to ask what Arava and Gal would do in Sudan. If it was dangerous for Mary and Joey, how did it make sense to take the whole family? But she knew Tamar's words were coming out of pain and desperation. So she kept silent.

Yossi sat up straighter. "I'm new to this and don't have experience trusting God and praying like you do. We prayed in the yeshiva, and I've always believed in God, but I don't have the relationship with God your family has."

Michal was so focused on their conversation that she didn't notice Steve coming through the house and sitting next to Tamar. He reached out and held Tamar's hand but didn't speak.

"You believe God brought Mary and Joey to you, and you thank God for them," Yossi said. "You've not only helped and changed their lives, but they've helped and changed you too. I hope to be a father someday ..." Yossi glanced briefly at Michal.

In spite of the present sadness, Michal's heart gave a joyful little leap when his eyes met hers.

Then to Tamar, Yossi continued slowly. "I see that with every child, you learn about love and surrender. Maybe now's the time for another sacrifice, trusting that God will continue working in Mary and Joey and can bring good out of even the worst situations. Does this make sense?"

Steve looked around. "I came in late. But Yossi, this makes complete sense. God loves these children more than we do."

Tamar rested her head in her hands. "I'm trying but it's not easy, I'm scared about the hearing next week."

"You're stronger than you think," Michal added. Yes, Tamar was the bravest person she knew. In nursing school, one of the professors touched her inappropriately when she stayed after class to ask questions; and at first she didn't know what to do. She'd heard rumors about him, but he was a famous doctor, and she was afraid that if she reported him, he'd take revenge and fail her. Tamar finally decided to do the right thing for the sake of other students, and later told Michal about her ordeal.

Taking foster children was super courageous also, a step few would take. Pouring out unconditional love to children whom you may lose, sets you up for pain, but Tamar excelled anyway.

"Life isn't easy, but I'm learning a lot from you two," Yossi said. "God will give you the words, and I pray for a righteous judge."

49

Tamar wasn't used to sitting alone on the beach. What should she do first—swim, read, order coffee, or nap? Michal had insisted Tamar take time off by herself and she'd cook dinner for the family. She was noticeably more kind and thoughtful lately ... thanks to Yossi's influence.

"Go out and relax," Michal had said. "You need it."

"What're you making? Shall I buy the ingredients?"

"A surprise, Mary and Joey want to help."

The Lighthouse Beach wasn't busy on a weekday afternoon in November. Tamar stretched out on a sunbed next to the water. A group of Russian tourists sat to her left, and in front of her, a French family stood in the shallow water pointing to the colorful fish swimming around their legs. They must be thrilled to relax in the sun and to swim in the middle of the winter.

First a swim and then coffee. The sun set early this time of year, and it would soon become cool, though probably not for those Russians.

Swimming always did the trick and raised her spirits, the repetitive stroking and breathing giving her time to think, revealing solutions to dilemmas, even shapes of cakes or garden designs.

She knew she couldn't solve everyone's problems; but besides the fog that enveloped her when she thought about a possible future without Mary and Joey, Eva and Yakov weighed heavy on her. She hadn't had time for them lately, and she wished she could think of a solution. How long could they continue to live on their own? Eva put on a brave face. But with Yakov frail and forgetful, she couldn't really care for him properly.

Tamar shivered as she stepped out of the water and wrapped herself in a towel. The sun touched the mountains in the west, and the clouds in the winter sky turned the heavens red and purple, and the sea too.

Now time for coffee.

"Large, with soy milk," she told the waiter who set a low table in front of her on the sand.

Sipping slowly, she tried to concentrate on enjoying the moment and began to doze off after days of not sleeping well. Steve slept like a baby and said she should stop the coffee. But when she lay down, her mind began going in all directions concerning the hearing next week, what to say to the judge, and whether to bring the children.

She couldn't stop thinking about what Yossi said two days ago ... a quiet guy like him could surprise you. His words stuck in her head: "Time for another sacrifice ... trusting God's plan for Mary and Joey ... He knows what's best for them."

She didn't like people praising her for caring for Mary and Joey, something natural that parents did for children. But this was the real sacrifice—letting go of her plans. What did it mean to trust for Mary and Joey? She'd been sure they'd live forever with her family where they had a good life, and were loved, safe, and healthy. Catherine and South Sudan were the opposite—unstable, unsafe, and unhealthy. Yet, she couldn't deny the children longed for their biological mother. And however Israeli they behaved, they still identified with their Sudanese side. Was it time for her to offer them up? Abraham was willing to sacrifice Isaac, and God gave him back again. Did things like that still happen today?

She and Steve sometimes prayed for Catherine, though Tamar wasn't sure what to pray, but she was the children's birth mother. But if Catherine did get her life together, unlikely as it seemed, they could lose Mary and Joey. Her mind couldn't grasp the implications.

Tamar put on the sweatshirt and pants she brought. The tourists were gone. Maybe they didn't realize the sunset show was about to begin. She was startled out of her thoughts when her phone rang.

"Hey, duck. Still on the beach? How're you feeling?"

"It's good for me here."

"I just finished work. Can I join you? Diving and tending the new coral reefs gave me insights about our family."

Tamar hesitated. What could she say? Steve knew she had no time for herself and had looked forward to being alone. The pressure of Mary and Joey's possible leaving and the upcoming hearing, had stressed their relationship. He didn't understand her crying bouts and kept telling her to trust God. *Easier said than done.* Was he coming now to try to convince her again to take Mary and Joey to the hearing when all she could think about was the trauma it would cause?

"Sure, come quickly. The clouds are day-glow colors, and it's such a clear evening, you can see the lights of Saudi Arabia and Egypt flickering." She couldn't refuse Steve … and she wondered what he was talking about—corals and their family?

In a few minutes Steve was dragging over a beach chair and setting it next to hers. "Shall I order coffee for you?"

"One's enough. I'm taking your advice and cutting down." She had a stubborn nature. But Steve was the best husband in the world, and she was trying to trust him more, about her coffee habit and bigger things too.

Steve reached over and held her hand. "This is a tense time, and I'm not always sensitive to your feelings. Sorry I made fun of your wish to move to Juba. But we'll go visit."

She'd spoken out of pain and thankfully Steve had set her on the right track.

"You were right."

"Here's what I was thinking," Steve said. "I was experiment-ing on the corals we grow in open aquariums, you've seen them outside. It's slow work but I love being part of the process, know-ing we're helping the planet."

Steve spoke with such passion, no wonder the director asked him to teach classes.

"Then later, I was diving. Being weightless in the water gives me time to think."

"So, what's the connection with our family?"

"Hard to explain … but at the moment, I saw this word pic-ture and wanted to share it with you."

Steve had her attention. "Has to do with corals?" she asked.

"They're living organisms that need the right conditions to grow and flourish—clean, clear water; sunlight, nutrients, and warmth. We collect samples from reefs, grow them in water tables outside—their temporary home—then move them to boxes on the bottom of the sea—their permanent home."

"I know you invest a lot in your projects, and if a storm destroys them, you're disappointed. But I still can't follow your reasoning."

Steve's eyes sparkled. "It's like this … we provide Mary and Joey everything they need to thrive—love and their physical require-ments too—while not sure whether this is their temporary or per-manent home. In the end, God gives the increase and goes with them wherever they end up, like intricate, colorful corals."

Tamar reflected on what he said. "So every stage is impor-tant and affects the next one. Collecting samples, maintaining, and growing them. I'll never doubt Mary and Joey were meant to come to us, but we don't know for how long."

She shivered and moved closer to Steve. The air turned cold after the sun went down. Steve reached out his arm, drawing her close.

"At first, I was just thinking about giving two lost children a new start. But through time my understanding has changed, and they've taught me a lot through their trust and resilience." Tamar continued haltingly: "Whatever happens …"

They sat silently for a few minutes. A wind came up and Tamar became aware of the waves splashing on the pebbles and the tension slipping out of her body. She could have stayed here longer, but her teeth were chattering.

"You're freezing," Steve said. "Better get going, I think I can smell Michal's pizza from here."

50

A small sign next to the entrance of an old building in a run-down section of Tel Aviv saying "Appeals Tribunal" alerted Tamar and Steve that they'd come to the right place, not what Tamar had expected for a courthouse. Their lawyer, Adi, with whom they'd had long phone conversations, waited for them outside for a final briefing.

"Keep calm and speak the truth," Adi said. "We have a good case ... but let's hope for the right judge."

Can some judges be the wrong ones?

∾

For Mary and Joey, driving up to Tel Aviv on Shabbat afternoon and staying with Aunt Sarah who still lived in the family house in the Yemenite Quarter, was like going on vacation.

"Estie and the lawyer both think it's important we bring the children," Steve had finally asserted. "It's time for you to ease off from being so protective."

Understanding that the lawyer and social worker had more experience than she, and that Steve also wanted the best outcome, Tamar finally came around.

A few times in the car on the way up, Tamar wanted to suggest answers to questions the children might be asked, but she restrained herself and let the kids watch cartoons on her phone.

The narrow streets, old houses, and spicy aromas wafting through open windows, reminded Tamar of visiting her grandparents as a child, leaving the kibbutz behind and driving into the metropolis. Aunt Sarah was waiting for them with her table set.

"You don't like my soup?" Aunt Sarah asked when Mary and Joey lay down their spoons. "You barely touched it."

Joey wiped his mouth. "I like it."

"Savta also makes Yemenite soup," Mary said.

"I had two bowls," Joey said. "I'm stuffed."

Aunt Sarah dipped the ladle in the pot. "Have another one."

"Daddy promised to take us for ice cream on the promenade for dessert," Mary said. "Mommy searched the internet for a place with sugarless."

A security guard inspected their bags as they entered the building. They rode the elevator to the third floor. Thankfully, when Aunt Sarah heard Tamar and Steve's disagreement about who would be present, she offered to come and wait outside with the children and even brought snacks for them to munch on.

Entering the small room, Tamar's heart pounded as they took their seats behind their lawyer and the prosecuting attorney representing the Ministry of Interior. The clerk sat behind a table on the podium with a flag next to her. Catherine, sitting alone, stared straight ahead. This woman, who wanted to take her children to Juba, didn't feel like an enemy—a position Tamar reserved for the Ministry of Interior. They were the ones with the deportation policy and who had sent police to arrest Catherine.

Catherine, who had experienced horrors during Sudan's brutal Civil War, and during her escape to Egypt and then Israel, would be a pawn of the system without a lawyer to speak for her. She was caught between the Ministry of Interior who wanted her out, never mind it meant taking two children she didn't know who'd begun a new and peaceful life, and Tamar's family who believed they should stay where they were.

Tamar reached for Steve's hand. The judge, dressed in her robe, entered through the door and seated herself behind a large desk in the center of the platform. As the two lawyers rose to their feet, Tamar quickly understood the protocol and stood also.

"The court will come to order," the judge said.

Did judges *try* to look unengaged?

"We will first hear from the Ministry of Interior represented by Attorney Moshe Tal." The judge riffled through a tall stack of papers on her desk. "We have an Arabic interpreter."

"This woman, Catherine Deng, infiltrated Israel illegally over five years ago and has been living here without a visa," declared the attorney. "She claims to be an asylum seeker, but we know that she and thousands of others came here to work, stealing jobs from needy Israelis."

As if Israelis wanted to clean streets and wash dishes.

The court recorder's fingers raced over the computer keys.

"They claimed it wasn't safe to go home. But now South Sudan has achieved independence, and she can return to her homeland. If we let Ms. Deng stay, millions of Africans will be storming our borders." The lawyer raised his voice and looked around for effect.

How many times have we heard that ridiculous argument? Tamar felt an urge to rise and open her mouth to stop his ugly talk. Steve rested his hand on her thigh to calm her.

"Objection!" Adi said. "We're talking about one woman, not all the Africans."

"Objection sustained."

"Can you tell me about the children?" the judge asked.

"They will go with her," Moshe said. "They're her children, Sudan is their country, and she wants to take them."

"Will they be safe there?"

"As safe as anyone in South Sudan." Meaning rampant malaria and dysentery, no schools, and no clean water.

"Thank you," the judge said. "Ms. Deng will now have a chance to speak."

The judge looked at Catherine. "Please stand. You are under oath to speak the truth. Do you understand?"

Catherine nodded.

"Are Mary Thon and Joey Thon your children?"

"Yes."

"When did you see them last?"

Catherine looked at her feet. "Two years ago."

"Please speak up. Where do you live?"

"Tel Aviv."

"And the children?"

"Eilat."

"Why are they not with you?"

"I go through hard time."

"And today you can care of them?" Though unfriendly looking, the judge was asking good questions.

"I have an aunt in our village who will help."

Tamar glanced at Steve.

"Thank you. At this time, we will hear from the defendant's lawyer, Attorney Adi Wolf."

Adi stood up. "I would like to tell you the truth about Ms. Deng and her children, Mary and Joey Thon."

Steve and Tamar had debated whether to engage a lawyer, but already from Adi's opening words, Tamar knew they'd made the right choice.

"Ms. Deng, like many of her countrymen, has suffered unspeakable tragedies, was forced to flee her home to save her and her children's lives, and after a long journey, ended up in Israel. I'm not going into the details of her nation's history or her life, but needless to say, this has not been a path she would have chosen."

"Objection!" the prosecutor said. "Ms. Deng chose to come and work in Israel. She and her people are infiltrators."

"I want to hear what Attorney Wolf is saying," the judge said.

"For reasons only she can explain," Adi continued, "Ms. Deng left her children on Kibbutz Eilot, and at the request of the social services, Tamar and Steve Goldman took Mary and Joey—who were sickly, undernourished, and fearful—as foster children."

A day I'll never forget. How little they knew then about the place Mary and Joey would fill in their hearts, about the welfare system, and how one day they would sit here in court.

Adi looked down at her papers. "I have submitted reports from the social worker about their successful absorption into this family and into Israeli society and have letters from their teachers. Mary was diagnosed with juvenile diabetes soon after her arrival at the Goldman's and is under a strict regimen of glucose testing multiple times a day and insulin shots to keep her alive. This treatment would not be available in South Sudan, certainly not in the aunt's village."

Adi straightened up and looked straight at the judge. "Finally, my conclusion, according to the law 'For the good of the child', Mary and Joey Thon must remain in custody with the Goldman family."

"Thank you," the judge said. "Does one of the foster parents have something to add?"

Steve had agreed that if they were asked, Tamar would speak. She now rose.

"Please state your name. Remember, you are under oath to speak the whole truth."

"Tamar Goldman."

"Tell me your relationship to Mary and Joey Thon."

"Through my work as a nurse in Tipat Halav, I met the Sudanese community in Kibbutz Eilot. While visiting, I noticed two young children, Mary and Joey, who were dirty, smelling like urine, skinny, and runny-eyed—as a nurse I notice these things. The kibbutznik in charge of the Sudanese told me their mother had disappeared. On a following visit, she said they'd be sent to an orphanage if a home wasn't found for them. She suggested my family take them in. After speaking with my husband, Steve, and our two children …" Tamar looked at Steve who nodded at her.

"We felt this was what God would have us do. In the Torah, we're commanded to care for the orphans, widows, and strangers."

"Objection," Moshe said. "We're not here for a Torah lesson. Can Ms. Goldman make her case shorter?"

"Objection overruled. This is important." The judge motioned for Tamar to continue.

"We went through the channels to be accepted as a foster family, and since then, Mary and Joey have lived with us."

Tamar watched Catherine sit upright on the bench, no emotion on her face, and wondered what she was thinking.

"Which year was this?"

"2007, over five years ago."

"I understand you do not want them going to Juba now with Ms. Deng, their mother, but what do you see as the long-term solution?"

Tamar wasn't prepared for this line of questioning.

"Do you want to adopt them?"

Tamar froze and took a deep breath. "I … I … want what's best for them." She looked at Steve and again at Catherine. "Once, I wanted to adopt Mary and Joey. But now understand they have a mother who, though having suffered appalling traumas, has maternal feelings for her children. But the children don't know her, and she isn't capable of raising them. They are living in a stable, loving environment and growing physically and emotionally." Tamar looked in Catherine's eyes and detected a faint glimmer of light. No, Catherine wasn't her enemy.

"We believe we should keep Mary and Joey with us until they're at least eighteen years old and have completed high school. Hopefully the situation in South Sudan will be more stable then. Furthermore, I would like to see Catherine continue to live in Israel, be allowed to work in a respectable manner, and reconnect with her children, if that's what she wants." Tamar hoped for no more questions … she needed to sit down.

"Objection," Moshe said. "It is not for Ms. Goldman to suggest Ms. Deng remain in Israel. The Ministry of Interior decides who is legally entitled to be here, and all the Sudanese have been ordered to leave. We can arrange for them to receive their laissez-passer travel documents within a week."

"Ms. Deng, would you agree to a solution such as suggested by Ms. Goldman?" the judge asked.

Catherine continued to stare at her feet. "I think so."

"I will now speak to Mary and Joey Thon. You can remain here or go outside while I invite them into my office." The judge stood up and walked out.

Moshe Tal hurried out of the room, probably for a smoke, leaving Tamar and Steve with their lawyer, and Catherine sitting in her place.

"What do you think?" Tamar asked Adi. "You did great." Was Adi also exhausted? Or was she used to courtroom dramas? Anyway, they weren't *her* children.

"You spoke well, too," Adi said. "But the judge will decide." Tamar tried not to think about what Mary and Joey might be telling the judge, but she knew children spoke the truth.

Tamar remembered seeing a machine selling hot drinks in the lobby. Maybe she could buy coffee for Catherine.

A few minutes later, Tamar and Catherine stood silently drinking their coffee.

"Thank you," Catherine said.

"I figured you'd also need a coffee after sitting so long."

"Not for the coffee." Catherine looked up at Tamar. "For what you said." She probably wasn't used to anyone taking her needs and desires seriously.

"I mean …" Tamar didn't know what to say. "I thought that if you stay in the country, you could move to Eilat and come visit your children."

"Come back to Eilat?" Catherine sounded surprised.

It hadn't occurred to Tamar that Catherine might not want to return to the place where she'd messed up.

The judge entered the courtroom and banged her hammer on her desk. "The court is convened."

Tamar took her seat next to Steve. The judge didn't say anything about her conversation with the children.

"My decision is to suggest a compromise. For the good of the child, Mary and Joey Thon will remain in custody with the Goldman family for one year, and then we will examine the situation again. Their mother, Catherine Deng, will receive a residence permit and begin visiting her children. I will give all sides ten minutes to think about it and accept or reject this offer."

We have to go through this again in a year?

Moshe stood up right away. "The respectable judge, I don't need time. We do not agree." Of course he wouldn't agree ... this was against everything he aimed for. "Illegal infiltrators Ms Deng and her children have their own country to go home to, and they must leave as soon as possible."

Adi turned to face Tamar and Steve. "With your permission," she said softly, "we'll accept. We can't expect better than this. Shall I give the judge our consent?"

Tamar looked at Steve.

"Go ahead," he said.

Adi stood up. "The respectable judge, we would like to give our answer."

The judge nodded.

"We agree with the compromise." Adi sat down again.

A year would go by fast, but at least Mary and Joey weren't leaving immediately. And until now their custody agreements had lasted for only three months.

"Ms. Deng, do you agree that you won't take the children with you next week to Sudan but they will remain with the Goldman family, and you will have visiting rights?"

"Yes." Catherine brushed her braids off her face.

"We will send a fax to the lawyers' offices to notify you of our verdict. The court is adjourned." After the judge stood and walked out, they all followed.

Aunt Sarah was waiting in the hallway with Mary and Joey. Never did they look so beautiful.

"Give me big hugs." Tamar held them close. "What grownup children we have."

"That woman with a coat like Batman took us to her office and gave us cookies," Joey said.

"But I told her I couldn't eat cookies, so she cut an apple for me," Mary said.

"That's all you did," Tamar said, "cookies and an apple?"

"She talked with us," Joey said.

"And asked questions and listened," Mary said. "Now I'm hungry again."

"Everyone must be ready for lunch," Aunt Sarah said. "I made a big pot of soup yesterday so we can eat the rest today. And I have some malawach prepared that I can fry up. Can Mary eat that?"

Only when they were driving off, Tamar realized she didn't see Catherine afterward. *I should have given her time to talk to her children.*

She couldn't allow herself to relax yet; they still had to hear the official verdict from the judge. But Tamar felt much better as she left the hearing than when she entered.

51

"Anyone home?" Estie called through the open door as Mary and Joey came running up to her with big hugs.

"So good to see you." Tamar hugged Estie. "You received my message?"

Tamar hadn't been sure whether Estie would ever come again to their house for her regular visit, or would it just be to say goodbye. The last time they had seen Estie was when she brought the startling news that Catherine had been picked up by the police and would fly to Juba with Mary and Joey in a week. So much had happened since then—the goodbye party, her talk with Yossi, the peace she experienced sitting on the beach, talks on the phone with their lawyer, and the blitz trip to Tel Aviv—she could barely process it.

Estie touched the mezuzah and stepped inside. "Thanks be to God. Good to see you too."

"Can you sit down, or do you have something planned?" asked Tamar.

"I've got a few minutes. How are my Mary and Joey?"

"We were in Tel Aviv," Mary answered. "Mommy, can I put fruit on the table?"

"Tel Aviv?" Estie said. "Sounds exciting."

"Put some tangerines on a plate with the oatmeal cookies you helped me bake," Tamar told her.

"We stayed with Aunt Sarah, and ate ice cream on the promenade," Mary said.

"She made soup and malawach for us," Joey said.

"And came with us to court."

Mary took a cookie and began peeling a tangerine.

"Court?" Estie wanted to find out what Mary and Joey understood.

"Our other mother wanted to go to Sudan with us," Mary said. "She was in court too."

"And you want to go?" Estie asked.

"That's what the lady who was dressed like Batman asked us … and she gave us cookies." Joey said.

"And an apple," Mary added.

"What did you tell her?"

"That I like Eilat with Mommy, Daddy, Arava, Gal, friends, dolphins—" Mary said.

"Me too," Joey added. "We don't know what's Sudan. Maybe when we're bigger, we can visit."

"I told her I didn't know who'd give me my shots in Sudan," Mary said. "Daddy always remembers and knows how much to give me even when I don't feel well. When I'm big, I can do it myself."

"What did Batman say?" Estie asked.

"She needed a few days to think about it, but she liked talking to us."

"Mary, Joey, we're going today to the street theater festival on the boardwalk," Estie said. "There's a mime performance at five that you'll like, but I want to talk to your Mommy for a few minutes first."

Tamar turned to the children. "You can watch a cartoon in your room on the tablet."

"How was it?" Estie asked when they were alone.

Tamar hadn't wanted to speak in front of the children. "We and Adi, our lawyer, requested they remain here, but the Ministry of Interior's attorney was awful, using all kinds of loaded words. Thank God, the judge wasn't moved by his poison, but instead considered 'the good of the child.'"

"What about Catherine?"

"She sat there unmoving, staring straight ahead, poor thing." Tamar was trying to sort out her mixed feelings. "Till now, I was angry with her for abandoning her children. What mother would do that? On the other hand, through her act, Mary and Joey joined our family. Seeing her caught between the forces determining her fate, I felt sorry for her and could see abuse and trauma written on her face and in her body language."

"Did the judge ask her to testify?"

"She barely said three words. After speaking to Mary and Joey privately, the judge suggested a compromise. Instead of deporting them immediately as the Ministry of Interior demanded, or allowing them to stay till they finish school as we wanted, she suggested we receive a one year custody agreement while the mother will receive visiting rights."

A lot was unclear, such as what would happen if Catherine did manage to reconnect with Mary and Joey? But Tamar was beginning to learn to let go.

"I can't imagine going through this again in a year. However, we felt this compromise was the best we could hope for," she told Estie.

"The lawyer from the Ministry of Interior accepted it?"

"Of course not. But yesterday, Adi called to tell us that she received a fax from the court saying the judge ruled in our favor and issued a verdict in accordance with the suggested compromise."

"Praise be to God. I've seen enough of these cases to know they can be tricky when the court must decide between the foster or biological family. All foster mothers are wounded, but as a refugee, Catherine adds a twist to the story."

"God is teaching me," Tamar said. "And giving me peace. The first time Catherine came to our house wanting to take the children to Tel Aviv, I hoped never to see her again. But knowing more about her and seeing the children's longing for their mother, I can picture them living with us and involved with her."

Estie looked up at the clock in the kitchen. "We have to be going to make the show.... Mary will like the gymnastics.... But there's something I want to tell you—"

"Jens?" Seeing Estie's smile, Tamar knew she wouldn't be talking about anything else.

"His partner visa was approved. He's studying Hebrew, volunteering at the kite surfing center, and next weekend we're going to Sderot to meet my family."

"You're brave, Estie."

"It's about time.... And I'm trusting God."

"Can we meet him?"

"Of course. I've told him a lot about your family. He and Steve would get along, with his way of looking at the world and explaining things."

"Come for a Shabbat dinner. Mary and Joey would love that." Tamar began mentally reviewing her schedule for the next weeks. "And from your experience, do you think Catherine will get in touch?"

"Hard to say, she's hurting and confused, but I hope so for her sake ... and that the children will know their mother, with God's help."

Tamar was beginning to think she hoped so too.

52

Bathing suit, hiking boots, binoculars. Tamar didn't want to forget anything for their second honeymoon. Since Arava's birth, she and Steve had never gone away by themselves ... not that Imma hadn't encouraged them by offering to watch the children. In the beginning, especially on their anniversaries, Steve had tried to get her to loosen her hold.

"Duck, you're like an orangutan mother."

"Orangutan?"

"The most protective animal in nature."

But after a while, Steve gave up.

Deep inside, she knew she was being unreasonable, but she couldn't bear the thought of her children searching for her in the night as she'd searched for Imma, and the rejection she experienced when they placed her in the children's house. Why hadn't they left the kibbutz earlier? Couldn't they see her suffering? No, she'd prove to be a better mother.

Yet, observing Catherine, she was learning not to judge a person by how they behave today when you don't know their history. Life takes us in unexpected ways, one decision or act at a time. For Catherine, being born a girl in war-torn South Sudan began a path to suffering.

Imma's life as a Yemenite kibbutznik was also unexpected. Coming to the kibbutz during her army service, she'd met Abba. Her dark skin and curly hair stood out among her Ashkenazi comrades. One thing led to another, and Tamar ended up in the children's house.

Tamar understood now that those times were different.

Parents didn't have the current psychological and emotional tools for raising children.

"We want to give you and Steve a weekend in the Ein Gedi Hotel for your birthday present," Imma had said recently. Ein Gedi was one of Tamar's favorite places and not a long drive.

"I ... I'm not sure." Imma's suggestion caught Tamar by surprise. "Mary and Joey—"

"We'll come down and stay with them. I know Arava and Gal are capable of doing everything, but I want to cook and spoil them." Tamar could already picture Imma standing over the pots in the kitchen.

"I'm not going to force you to do something you feel uncomfortable about, but you need a break after all you've been through, and you and Steve need time together."

Tamar couldn't argue. And it seemed to her Imma's voice was sounding kinder and less judgmental.

"I'll check my calendar."

"Steve already looked and said next weekend is fine. ... And the hotel has a vacancy."

"Are you sure it's not too much? You'll be coming two weeks later to celebrate Michal's birthday."

Imma flashed a smile. "I can never spend too much time with these four sweet children."

Since that call a week ago, Tamar kept picturing herself sitting on their balcony overlooking the Dead Sea and the mountains in Jordan. She drew inspiration from the kibbutz's botanical gardens, and Steve looked forward to birding. They'd hike up Nahal Arugot—hadn't been there for years—and float in the Dead Sea. ...

~

Imma and Abba arrived on Thursday and both Tamar and Steve managed to get home early from work in order to arrive in Ein

Gedi in time for a dip in the pool. She smelled Imma's Yemenite chicken soup from the street, stepped inside, and gave her parents hugs.

"The children like chicken," Imma said. "I asked Steve, and he said it was fine. Hope you're okay with it." She was right about the children liking meat, and somehow Tamar was able to accept this from Imma now.

"Sure, you're the best savta the children could have. I'm sorry I've been hard on you." She gave Imma another hug and placed her already packed bag next to the door. "A cup of coffee, and we're off."

"Anything we should know?" Imma asked.

"Joey has football practice at four today and Mary gymnastics at five. Both activities are close by, so they can go by themselves."

"Would it be okay if I went to watch Joey play?" asked Abba. He had played football for years, and on the kibbutz had been esteemed as the "Liverpool Torpedo."

"He'd love to have Saba watch him," Tamar said. Joey liked doing anything with Abba.

"And I'll go with Mary to gymnastics." Imma said. "I remember you dancing in the kibbutz's troupe."

"Nothing much to say. You've been here enough, and the kids can tell you everything."

"You're educating them well." Was it Tamar's imagination, or was Imma's heart also softening? Tamar rose to bring her cup to the sink. There was Eva standing at the open door.

"Can I come in for a minute?" Eva walked more slowly now since her fall a few weeks ago. She saw the suitcases. "You're going someplace?"

"My birthday present from Imma and Abba at Ein Gedi Hotel." Tamar sat down again. "But I always have time for you." Oops, maybe Imma wouldn't like how that sounded—time for

Eva who lived next door while they lived far away? "Imma and Abba are staying with the children," she added.

"What a wonderful present. You're lucky to have such parents." Eva eased herself into a chair. "I wanted to share our news."

"Yakov's okay, I hope?" In his state, she could expect anything.

"That's it. He's not getting any younger, and we knew we had to make changes but didn't know what."

Tamar had been breaking her head trying to think of something for them.

"Our children found us a lovely retirement home in Beer Sheva called Desert View House and begged us to move closer to them."

Ahh. The children were finally taking responsibility. "Sounds fabulous."

"It won't be easy, but they visited there and sent us a virtual tour. We'll be moving in two months." Eva sighed.

"Wait a minute." Imma laid her hand on Eva's. "My niece is the doctor there. I'll tell her to look out for you. And we'll visit you. You won't be far from Arad."

"Yakov has a hard time leaving his trees, the ones in memory of our families. He's so attached to them." Eva put her head in her hands.

"I'll keep an eye on them for you," Tamar said. "I'm sure when the new owners understand their meaning—"

"They're a nice young couple with small children," Eva said. "They'll be happy here, as we were."

"I have an idea," Imma said. "I can suggest to my niece to plant a memorial garden with trees like that in your new place."

Life would be different without Eva and Yakov next door. But Imma wanting to be involved with them was more than Tamar ever conceived. She pictured herself in a relay race passing the baton of her love and care for Eva and Yakov to

Imma, while they passed the care of the trees to her.

Tamar stood up and hugged Eva. "You've had a long life and experienced miracles. This too will be good. I'll come by when we get back, but now we have to get going."

Imma stood up too. "Can I walk you to the car? Just a quick question—"

Steve joined them, then, and opened the car to put their two small trolley bags in the trunk.

Imma continued, "I've got to hear about Mary and Joey's meeting with their mother last week! Can you just tell me in short?"

"Not bad, I guess, under the circumstances," Tamar began. "It's all well organized through the social services with meetings in their center. The kids were excited to meet her, of course, and Catherine brought them candy and new clothes. They liked that. Communication is challenging because they have to speak in Hebrew—the children have forgotten all their Arabic. But her Hebrew is passable."

"What happens next?" Imma asked.

"Who knows? She wants to keep meeting them, and the social workers want to give her a chance. But even if she does improve, it will be a long process."

Imma took hold of Tamar's hand. "And how do you feel?"

"Thanks for asking. ... Mixed. Trying to trust and take a day at a time as the kids do. But it feels like jumping into the unknown."

Steve was sitting in the driver's seat, ready to leave and trying not to be impatient.

She gave Imma a hug. "Sorry, really have to be going. Thanks for everything, and see you Saturday evening."

"Thanks for entrusting us with your children. We don't take it for granted."

53

Welcome to the Mermaid. On behalf of the crew, we're glad to have you aboard today. We'll have a wonderful time together for the next four hours." Yossi stood on the bow of the yacht and spoke to the family sitting on the benches around him. "In five minutes, we'll be loosening the ropes and setting sail for the Egyptian border." Tamar felt she was on a school field trip.

The children had been looking forward to sailing on the Mermaid for weeks, ever since Michal had announced that Yossi was inviting them to celebrate her birthday on the boat where he used to work. He'd come a long way since then, his first job after finishing the army. Interesting, they met Yossi when Michal invited him to celebrate his birthday at their house, and now he was inviting them to Michal's birthday party. From a guy who barely opened his mouth, he was speaking with such confidence.

"I'll give you updates as we go along, but for now, as we leave the harbor you'll see the Navy base on your right, Dekel Beach, and then the Dolphin Reef. We'll pause there to view the dolphins, though I know this won't be your first time seeing them." Yossi beamed a smile at Michal. "Michal can even tell you their names."

"Me too!" Mary jumped up, then fell back again from the motion of the boat. "Mitzi's the baby and Coco has a spot on her back."

"And she jumps the highest." Joey lifted his arms over his head.

"From there we'll pass the Coral Reef Nature Reserve, the Underwater Observatory, Marine Science Institute—"

"Where Daddy works," Joey said.

"And finally at the Princess Beach, we'll anchor, swim, and have lunch. We also have a surprise planned." Yossi put his arm around Michal sitting next to him. "Everyone ready to go?"

"Ready," Abba said. "On behalf of Shoshanna, myself, and all the family, we already want to thank you for inviting us today. You don't know how much this means to us to be together to celebrate Michal's birthday."

"It's the least I could do after the way you've welcomed me into your family and done so much for me."

"When will you tell us the surprise?" Mary asked.

"Is it something to eat?" Joey asked.

He must be in a growth spurt, thought Tamar.

Soon they were sailing southward in the crystal blue waters of the Gulf of Eilat. Not only the children, but Tamar had also looked forward to this day. If it weren't for Yossi's invitation, they would have all been at her house, and now she could sit back and enjoy the party. She had offered to make the cake, though. It was dulce de leche and chocolate layers, Michal's favorite.

Eilat appeared different from this perspective over the sea with the white buildings climbing up the hill toward the rough, brown and red mountains. What could Yossi's surprise be? He and Michal had been cozying up to each other more lately, and the way he looked at her …

"By the way," Yossi said, "help yourselves to the drinks and snacks in the galley to keep you going till lunch."

Mary and Joey rushed down the ladder, coming up a minute later, wide grins on their faces. They didn't often get soda pop to drink.

"Even a diet coke for me." Mary lifted her can in the air. "And the sugarless cookies I like." Yossi had planned to the details.

They anchored five hundred meters before the Egyptian border. "Who wants to swim while I grill the fish? We've got masks and snorkels on board for everyone," Yossi said. "Or if it's too cold for you, just relax and enjoy the view."

The end of November was sometimes cool in Eilat for those used to swimming in the heat of summer. Today, the sun kept peeking in and out of the clouds.

"I'll pass," Imma said. "Can I set the table, or cut vegetables?"

"Never too cold to swim." Steve began taking off his shirt. "As you know, the water temperature doesn't vary much in Eilat throughout the year, from twenty-eight degrees in August to twenty degrees in January. Today it's twenty-four! Who's coming with me?"

"Me!" Mary and Joey said in unison.

Yossi began to light the grill. "Lunch will be ready in an hour."

"Kinneret would love to swim," Michal said. Then she looked at Yossi. "Or do you need my help with lunch?"

"On your birthday? Enjoy. Shoshanna and I have it covered."

～

An hour and a half later, everyone was lying back on the pillows. "I couldn't eat another bite," Abba said.

"That was one of the best meals I've eaten," Steve said. "Nothing like fresh sea air and a swim to work up an appetite. The grouper was cooked to perfection."

"I hope everyone has room for birthday cake," Tamar said.

"For one of your cakes," Yossi said, "always."

"But now we want to hear your surprise," Gal said.

Yossi cleared his throat and reached for Michal's hand. "Michal and I want to announce—"

"Your engagement!" A bunch of voices chimed in at once. Yossi kissed Michal as everyone surrounded them with hugs.

"I requested Peter's permission to marry his daughter, and yesterday, on our favorite beach, I asked Michal."

All eyes turned to Abba, who was silent for a moment to pro-long the suspense before smiling. "I agreed," he said.

Yossi reached into his pocket and pulled out a small box. "For my new wife." He slipped a thin gold band with a small diamond on her finger.

Michal wiped away a tear even as she was beaming with joy. Tamar noticed Imma also sniffing and wiping her eyes.

"And we have something else to tell you," Michal said. "After our spring wedding, we'll move up north. Yossi will study Marine Biology in Tel Aviv University, and I'll look for work. His sister has a house in Ramat Gan with an extra apartment we can rent."

"Since I visited my Abba in the hospital when he was dying, walls began breaking down," Yossi said. "My sister's not so strictly religious anymore and wants her children to know their uncle and new aunt. Some of my family may even come to our wed-ding. I'd like my two families to meet."

"We'd love that," Steve said. "Whatever we can do—"

"Michal and I were wondering if you have friends like you up there who we can meet with."

"Absolutely, and we'll still have lots of time together before you leave. Hanukkah is coming soon."

54

"What an aroma." Steve sat in his chair, with a thick book in his lap, and inhaled deeply. "Nothing like the smell of latkes frying. Reminds me of my grandmother."

"What's latkes?" Mary asked.

"The fried potato pancakes Mommy's cooking. It's a Yiddish word, what we call levivot in Israel." Steve laid his book down. "And why do you think we eat latkes and jelly doughnuts at Hanukkah?"

"They're so yummy," Mary said. "Can I eat them?"

"Oil isn't the best for you," Tamar said. "But I baked some in the oven, and they're just as good." Hanukkah was a difficult holiday for Mary, being all about fried foods, carbs, and sugar.

"Of course the oil they're cooked in reminds us of the miracle of the Hanukkah oil. You must have learned about that in school," Steve said. "Come here a minute, or does Mommy still need your help?"

"Go ahead," Tamar said. "I'm nearly finished."

Mary and Joey came and sat close to Steve in his chair.

"Who knows where Hanukkah took place?"

"Jerusalem!" Mary said.

"In the Temple," Joey added.

"Who were the heroes?"

"The Maccabees," Mary said. "You're asking easy questions."

"They were fighting the Greeks, the bad guys," Joey said. "Can I try one of the levivot, to make sure they're okay?"

"Take one each," Tamar said. "You were such big helpers."

"What were the Greeks doing that was so bad?" Steve asked.

"They wouldn't let the Jews pray to God." Mary wiped her hand on her shirt.

Joey frowned. "They wanted them to pray to statues."

"Wow, you've learned a lot," Steve said. "And who won in the end?"

"The Maccabees kicked out the Greeks and then had to clean the Temple."

"So why the oil?"

"The priests had only enough oil to light the menorah for a day, but it lasted for eight days!"

Tamar loved it. Mary and Joey soaked up learning just like the latkes absorbed the oil. Sudanese kids accepting Jewish history as if it were their own.

"We have some smart kids," Tamar said. She was almost sorry to interrupt, but … "The levivot are done, Michal and Yossi should be here any minute, Gal's gone to help Eva and Yakov, and soon we'll light the candles. Today's the last night, so you can get ready by each putting eight candles in your menorah."

The door opened and Michal, Kinneret, and Yossi sailed in. "Figured we should eat doughnuts one last time." Yossi placed a box of jelly doughnuts on the table next to the plate of levivot.

Mary's eyes moved to the doughnuts, and Tamar pulled the girl close to her. "Bubi, these doughnuts are so filling, we'll split one between us. You're my hero."

Yakov in his wheelchair entered next, guided by Gal, with Eva slowly pushing her walker behind them.

"What a beautiful table," Eva said. "I could smell the latkes from my house, just like we used to eat in Hungary."

Tamar helped her take a seat.

"Where did you get those lovely menorahs?" Eva asked.

"Savta helped us make them in her pottery studio last time we were in Arad," Mary explained proudly.

Steve turned off the lights. "Welcome to the last night of

266

Hanukkah, the Feast of Lights. We'll pray, light the candles, sing Hanukkah songs, and then while we're eating the latkes and doughnuts, anyone who wants can share a Hanukkah memory or thought."

"Blessed are You, O Lord our God, King of the universe, who performed miracles for our fathers in days of old at this season." Steve recited the traditional Hanukkah prayers and then added words of his own: "Thank you for this reminder of your light, for this symbol of freedom and new beginnings. Thank you for family and friends."

Mary and Joey had placed their menorahs in the front window and focused on lighting the candles so as not to tip one over or snuff out a burning wick.

As they all belted out the Hanukkah songs they knew so well, they seemed oblivious to their identities—Sudanese, Israeli, Christian, Jewish—just happy families basking in the glow. After lighting the candles, the Mary and Joey again curled up next to Tamar.

"I'd like to start," Steve said. "Every year, every holiday, it's a privilege for me to celebrate in the land of Israel where it all took place. I'm thankful to be here and feel blessed beyond measure with my wonderful family and friends."

Yossi leaned forward on the sofa where he was sitting close to Michal. "As a child, holidays were stressful, not enough money to celebrate, us kids fighting, and our parents arguing. I didn't look forward to these times. But now I do since I found a new family." He leaned back and draped his arm over Michal's shoulder. "Thank you and thanks to God."

"Can I share a memory?" Yakov asked. "I'll never forget my Hanukkah in Auschwitz. We had nothing to eat and were freezing, but there was a rabbi who was determined to celebrate Hanukkah with us. From the little food we received, we managed to save up bits of fat and to pull threads from our torn clothes to make wicks. We shaped a menorah out of a raw potato and quietly sang the prayers and songs." Yakov's voice broke. "The Hanukkah lights gave us hope, and here I am."

Everyone became silent until Eva spoke up.

"New beginnings..." she said. "We'll be moving soon to Beer Sheva to begin a new chapter in our lives. It's not easy, and I'll miss you all terribly, but Hanukkah is about re-dedication and heroism. The Maccabees weren't afraid to take steps of faith ... and even at our age, that's what we're doing."

"We'll miss you terribly, too," Tamar said. "But you'll be near your family, and when we come to visit Imma and Abba, we can visit you too."

"I like playing the dreidel game," Mary said. "Yossi explained it to me. It can fall four different ways when you spin it, and you never know which it will be."

Mary reached for the wooden dreidel on the table with the four Hebrew letters written on its sides. "When the *gimmel* turns up, you get all the pieces on the table—"

"Like candy or coins," Joey said. "But if it's a *shin* you have to put a piece in, and the *hey* is half and *nun* is nothing."

"Yossi said it's like life," Mary continued. "What looks good, can turn around, or the opposite, things change quickly ..." She looked up at Yossi. "How's it go again?"

"It's usually a mixture of the four—getting all the pieces, half, nothing, or putting one in ... so it's not about winning or losing but about trusting and accepting." Yossi had weighed his words carefully. Now he squeezed Michal's hand.

Michal stared at the dreidel. "In the end it evens out. The fun is in playing and being together."

"As Ralph Waldo Emerson wrote, 'Happiness is a journey, not a destination,'" Steve said.

"Does that mean the same as the dreidel game?" Mary asked.

"I've never heard of Emerson, but I get it," Yossi said.

With a contented smile, Tamar pulled Mary and Joey close. "It's about enjoying the moment, being thankful, and spending time with people you love."

Tamar's dreidel had turned around a lot recently—the tubal pregnancy, Mary and Joey nearly leaving, the court hearing, and renewed contact with their mother ... but she was ready to accept where her dreidel fell, knowing that whatever happened would be okay and would work together for good.

"This is my best Hanukkah ever," Tamar said, hoping not to lose control or sound too mushy. "God led Yossi into our family, the perfect match for Michal. Eva and Yakov will remain in our hearts even when you're far away. And Arava is going next year to work in a hospital for her national service."

She looked at her grown-up daughter and blinked back a tear. "We'll miss you. Gal, you will be the big brother at home before you too fly from the nest. Mary and Joey, I have no words to thank God for how you've changed me more than you know. And Steve, my love and gift that never ends."

"Maybe we can hold hands and sing one more time, Banu hoshech l'garesh." Steve grasped Tamar's and Yakov's hands, and they joined their voices together: "We have come to banish the darkness with light and fire in our hands. Each one is a tiny light, but all of us are a mighty light. Away, blackness. Make way before the light."

Hanukkah was one of Tamar's favorite holidays, though she loved them all ... the symbolism, contrasts, and universal message. Light and darkness, freedom and oppression, hope and despair. She wouldn't mind if this evening never ended, and as she gazed around the room, the faces of her loved ones shone in the soft candlelight.

ACKNOWLEDGEMENTS

After finishing my third non-fiction book and thinking about a new project, the topic of refugees and foster families gripped my attention, and while recognizing the challenge of writing fiction, a novel seemed the best approach. We were involved at the time with the South Sudanese refugee community, and while our daughter and son-in-law fostered two South Sudanese boys, the characters in *To Belong* are in no way modeled on them or on anyone else I know; they are products of my imagination. I chose to use my hometown as the book's location to introduce people to the place I love.

First of all, I would like to thank my publisher, Catherine Lawton, for believing in me and allowing me to become a published author. With your expertise and experience, you brought my manuscript to new levels. I appreciate the ease with which we work together and the friendship we've developed.

I am grateful for my family as they continually showed interest in the progress of this novel and always gave me a listening ear.

John, I couldn't have written this book without you at my side. In fact, I can't imagine life without you. During the period I was writing, you even took over the shopping and much of the cooking, granting me undivided time to fulfill my daily word goals. And you were more than willing to make scouting trips to the sites I planned to write about.

Joshua, your experience as a lawyer working with refugees was an enormous help for all the legal scenes and those with the Ministry of Interior.

Racheli, thank you for patiently explaining CPR to me and as a midwife, describing an ectopic pregnancy in an understandable way.

Sarah, Yonatan, and Stefanie, our three social workers in the family, you give me insight and respect for your profession. And Yonatan, thanks for helping me choose some of the names.

Moriah and Tom, with your unconditional love and commitment, you are my inspiration, and I thank you for allowing me to learn from you.

Angelina, Daniel, and Sunday, you are my heroes. I feel privileged to hear the boys still call me "Savta."

An aspect of writing that I enjoy is interviewing experts in their fields and am thankful for those who helped me with technical and professional advice. I tried to be as accurate as possible, but please forgive any mistakes in the information you conveyed.

Carolyn Burns, you were the first expert I turned to as I began creating the character of Tamar. I loved hearing your experiences and stories as a Tipat Halav nurse. Rachel, you also helped when I visited your well-baby clinic and made it come alive.

Meghan Valerio, many thanks for your tour of the Institute for Marine Sciences, and when I needed more specific information, Nati Kramer, you made the effort to clarify things for me.

Ayelet Hassan, it was fun talking to you about your hobby of cake decorating.

Jamie Stark, you helped me understand the experience of having a daughter diagnosed with diabetes, and Karen Mizrachi, I appreciated how we could use your daughter's Celiac disease to add to my understanding of having a child with a chronic illness.

Advat, thanks for kindly taking a break from your work as a dolphin trainer to share with me your love for these amazing animals and the vision of the Dolphin Reef.

Noy Roth, I enjoyed sitting on the beach with you as you answered questions about ectopic pregnancies.

My beta-readers played an important role in bringing this book to print. You made me believe that this was actually a book. Jane Haigh and Amy Galblum, my two sisters, thank you for taking the time to critically read my manuscript. And Jane, I'm thankful to have a sister who's an author and that we can bounce ideas off one another. Mary Schmidt and Eileen Chee, you both read the book carefully and gave useful suggestions.

Linda Walker, I'm grateful for your experience as an editor and your willingness to work out many kinks in the manuscript.

Faith Goldberg, I'm thankful to have you as my writing friend.

Finally and most importantly, I thank God for life, love, friends, purpose, and hope.

ABOUT THE AUTHOR

Judy Pex was born in Washington, D.C. and immigrated to Israel in 1976 with her husband, John. They still live in Eilat where they raised their family. In 1984 they opened the Shelter Hostel, a guest house and community, which is open to people of all ages and backgrounds. They have hosted guests from over 110 countries who have stayed anywhere from one night to eight years. John is also the leader of the Eilat Congregation, a multinational fellowship worshipping Jesus Christ together and seeking to make a difference in our world.

John and Judy have four grown children. Their ten biological and four foster grandchildren are the joy of their lives. In her free time, Judy enjoys spending time with family and friends, hiking, traveling, swimming, running, and reading.

Find Judy online at www.JudithPex.com.